UNSCRIPTED LOVE

A STEAMY SMALL-TOWN CELEBRITY ROMANCE

ALPINE RIDGE

MELANIE A. SMITH

WICKED DREAMS PUBLISHING

Published by
WICKED DREAMS PUBLISHING
info@wickeddreamspublishing.com
Boise, ID USA

Cover design, editing, and interior formatting by Wicked Dreams Publishing

eBook ISBN: 978-1-952121-85-2
Paperback ISBN: 978-1-952121-86-9
Discreet Paperback ISBN: 978-1-952121-87-6
Hardcover ISBN: 978-1-952121-88-3

CONTENTS

CONTENT WARNING

Unscripted Love is a small-town celebrity romance novel that includes elements that might not be suitable for some readers. If you are sensitive to any of the following, please put your mental health first:

Sexual assault (brief groping)
Sexual harassment
Abusive parents (emotional/mental)
Explicit language
Graphic sexual activity
Mention of drug possession/use

CHAPTER ONE

EVAN

"Cut! For fuck's sake, just stop." John, one of the most patient directors in the movie industry, pinches the bridge of his nose and lets out a long-suffering sigh before looking up at Kaitlyn and me. "Evan. You're leaving her behind to go bust up a fucking drug cartel. A mission from which you likely won't return. And you're kissing her like I kiss my goddamn Aunt Ethel."

My brows shoot up, but I bite back a sarcastic retort. Because he's not wrong. Kaitlyn and I have practically zip in the chemistry department. Don't get me wrong, she's cute. But she's fifteen years younger than me and doesn't have much going on upstairs or great acting chops. Unfortunately, she was clearly hired to be set dressing. Trying to talk scene blocking and motivation with her has been pointless, as has attempting to drum up a nonexistent attraction. Even John McKennon, the best action director I've worked with in my sixteen-year career, isn't good enough to direct us out of this awfulness.

"Okay," I reply diplomatically instead of suggesting

we find a replacement with only two weeks left to shoot. Given that we only started shooting her scenes yesterday, I wonder if the timing wasn't intended to ensure we had no choice but to go with her. My bet's on nepotism. It wouldn't be the first time. "What would you like us to do differently?"

John blows out a breath so hard his cheeks puff up. "Give me more *passion*."

Translation: he's just as clueless as I am about how to fix this.

"So, what, like, more tongue?" Kaitlyn asks, twirling a piece of her long blond hair around her finger.

I shoot John a look that says, "You see what I'm working with?"

He waves a hand dismissively at my unspoken comment. Or maybe at Kaitlyn's question. Who knows. At least we've been nailing the rest of the non-Kaitlyn shots. But this one? This one has taken all damn day. Or it feels like it, anyway.

"Just … do something different," he grumbles. He signals to the makeup person to touch us up. A few pats and swipes later, he calls action.

I deliver my lines, which are at least convincing, and then go in for the kiss. I've tried a dozen different methods so far. Save one. As I close my eyes, I feel like Harry Potter trying to conjure my first patronus. Clearly, I will have to pull my absolute sexiest memory to make magic here. I don't like to resort to this since it usually gives me a hard-on. But desperate times and all.

So, as our lips meet, I let my mind slip back to last summer in Bali. The hottest model of the moment, naked under me in the sand, beautiful huge tits bouncing as I fucked her under the stars. The things that woman could do with her mouth. She gave the most amazing blow job ever, had this way of flicking her tongue over my nipples that could get me hard in an instant, and — most importantly for this moment — she was the *best* kisser. So, I imagine it's her as I press myself against Kaitlyn and devastate her with my mouth.

I'm so absorbed in my little fantasy that I almost don't hear John when he says, "Cut." Followed by, "That'll do, kids. And we're done for the day. *Finally*."

I pull back with a sigh of relief to find Kaitlyn looking at me like a hungry wolf.

Shit. That's the other potential negative side effect of that technique.

Kaitlyn leans close, batting her eyelashes. "That was totally hot," she breathes. "Wanna go fuck in my trailer? It's closer than yours."

I huff a short laugh under my breath. "Thanks, but I'm going to shower and head out," I reply shortly. "I've got places to be."

She reaches out and gropes my still semi-hard dick over my pants. "Really? You can't tell me *that* doesn't say you want me."

I jump back, throwing my hands up to bypass the urge to push her away. "Whoa, hey, not cool," I growl. "You wouldn't like it if someone touched your crotch, would you?"

Her smile turns feline. "You can touch me all you want. Come on, I know your rep. You don't have to play hard to get."

I step back, noting that everyone else has left the set. Great. They probably all cleared out thinking we'd be fucking right here. Awesome. Clearly, they all know my reputation, too — Evan Edwards, playboy action star extraordinaire.

"I'm not playing, and I'm not interested." I run a hand through my shaggy light brown hair, shake my head, and walk away.

"If you change your mind, you know where to find me," she calls to my retreating back.

"Not gonna happen," I mutter.

When I get to my trailer, I take the quickest shower known to man in case Kaitlyn has designs on catching me naked. It gets most of the stage makeup off, anyway. Once I'm dressed, I breathe a sigh of relief and grab my phone.

I note that I missed a call from my brother, Nate. It's been a while since we've spoken, and it's not like him to call. We usually just catch up at Mom and Dad's at the holidays, and I just saw him at Christmas a few months ago.

"Hello?" Nate answers.

"Hey, bro, what's up?"

"Evan. Wow. I wasn't expecting you to call back so fast." My big bro is usually pretty stoic, but right now, he sounds happy, which piques my interest.

"Yeah, we just wrapped up for the day, and I saw you called. You never call."

"Hey, you're not the only one keeping busy," he replies jokingly. "And obviously, I call when I have something to say. Mia and I set a date. September twenty-third. Can you make it?"

I collapse onto the overstuffed loveseat in the trailer's tiny living room. "Damn. So, this is for real. You're getting hitched." They've been engaged so long I was starting to wonder. But then again, they both own their own businesses, even if they are in a sleepy little town in Washington's Cascade Mountains. Still, I imagine they've been busy enough without wedding planning.

"It's for real," Nate confirms. "And while I know it's a long shot, I'd love to have you there."

I let out a sigh. "You know I'd love to come."

"But?"

I huff a sharp laugh. "But I don't want to take away from your big day."

Nate's quiet for a moment, presumably considering that. It wouldn't be the first time I stole his limelight.

"I really want you there, Ev, so I'll deal with whatever else comes with that," he finally says. "It's going to be a small, casual wedding anyway. Just family and a few friends."

I nod slowly. I'd love to be there. And it would be damn good to get the hell out of L.A. for a bit. "I'll check with my assistant and let you know."

"Sounds good," Nate agrees.

A soft knock comes at the rickety trailer door. "Hey, hold on just a second," I tell him.

I get up and open the door. Only to see Kaitlyn on the step. She opens a long jacket to reveal her naked body. Lithe and supple and totally inappropriate in the bright March Southern California evening, out where anyone could see.

"Shit. I gotta go, Nate. I'll call you back, okay?"

I don't even wait for his response; I hang up and reach out, wrenching Kaitlyn's jacket closed.

"Are you insane?" I ask bluntly.

She tries to push past me into the trailer, but I don't budge. "Oh, come on, Evan. You know you want it," she says coyly, opening her jacket again.

I glare down at her and shake my head firmly. "No means no, Kaitlyn. I don't sleep with costars during production. Period." That much is true anyway. Maybe the non-personal rejection will do the trick. Doubtful, but worth a shot anyway.

She angrily ties the closure of her jacket and folds her arms over her chest. "Fine. But I'm going to tell everyone I fucked you anyway, so I figured you might as well get something out of it."

Oh lord. Here we go.

Again.

I take a calm, deep breath before pointing at the camera mounted on the corner of the trailer. "You can try, but that —" I jerk my chin at the camera for emphasis "—has high-resolution video and audio. It'd be a shame for this little episode to become public knowledge. Might ruin what could be a promising start to a career." She isn't the first wanna-be starlet to try to fuck her way onto the A-list via my cock, and I'm sure she won't be the last.

Kaitlyn's eyes narrow, and her nostrils flare. I can practically hear the rusty wheels in her head turning.

"Fine," she eventually snaps. "Your loss, then." And then, thank God, she turns on her heel and leaves.

Sighing, I collect my things before heading to my car. I'll call Nate back later when I'm in a better headspace.

As I drive home, even with the top down on a beautiful evening, I feel bone-deep exhaustion. The shit that went down today with Kaitlyn today is the kind of thing that just wears on me. I've learned to fight back against the users over the years. I've had to, if for no other reason than to save what little is left of my reputation. One false accusation, one wrong decision, and I know I could become persona non grata in the industry. It's why my contract rider includes not being left alone with female costars. Something I'll have words with John about later. But mostly? I'm damn sick of having to worry about this kind of crap.

You'd think my success would've earned me more respect, more privileges, and less bullshit. And in some ways, I suppose it has. Dibs on scripts. My pick of projects. Choosing what directors I work with and, to an extent, which co-stars. But the total loss of privacy and control of my personal life … that hole just keeps getting deeper. Some days, it's worth it. When a movie gets a great response, or I really connect with the fans, or a particularly exciting script comes my way.

But some days … besides blatant sexual harassment, the industry has just changed. Appearances are *everything*. Even when I'm not on a shoot, I feel like I'm play-acting my entire life to project a certain image that keeps me hot, current, and in demand.

Or maybe I wasn't clued into this part of the gig early on. But boy, do I miss anonymity. Being able to go to the grocery store. Or out for a run without paps chasing me down. Or dating someone without internet trolls tearing apart her entire life for their own entertainment.

And there's no escaping it. I have houses in New York City, Miami, and Honolulu, but none provide anonymity. If anything, they're worse than L.A. because most people are used to seeing celebrities here. If only there were somewhere I could go that nobody cared about that shit. Somewhere where I could just be myself.

As I pull into my multi-million-dollar estate in the Hollywood Hills, I have to laugh at myself — poor rich and famous me. I know I'm an ungrateful asshole. I'm living the life everyone else wants.

So why aren't I happy?

CHAPTER TWO

CARRIE

Spring break. To anyone else, those two words conjure up images of sunny beaches, exotic locales, and wild parties. But not for me. No, instead of living it up, I'm stuck running errands for my overbearing parents, dog sitting — for free, like the chump I am — for a friend of a friend, and trying (and failing) to progress on my master's capstone project. Some break this is turning out to be.

I sigh as I clip the leash onto Rufus, a loveably energetic golden retriever. He wags his tail excitedly, his pink tongue lolling out. At least someone's happy.

"All right, buddy, let's go," I murmur, leading him out the door. The early Seattle spring air still holds a chill, and I zip my jacket up higher, burying my chin in the fleece collar.

We make it about halfway around the block when my phone buzzes in my pocket. Glancing at the screen, I see it's my older sister, Mia. A smile tugs at my lips. We haven't talked in a while, as both of us have been wrapped up in our lives.

Okay, that's not totally true. I mean, I have been wrapped up with school. But I've also been avoiding her after the epic fight with my parents that followed visiting their other, "traitorous" daughter on New Year's Eve. I shake my head, shaking off the memory, wishing everyone could just get along.

"Hey, Mia, what's up?" I answer, trying to infuse some cheer into my voice.

"Carrie! I have big news," Mia gushes, her excitement palpable even through the phone. "Nate and I finally set a date. We're getting married on September twenty-third!"

"Oh wow, Mia, that's great," I reply, genuinely happy for her. Mia deserves this after everything she's been through, especially with our parents. She may have quit her job at his law firm, but normal parents would've understood how miserable she'd been there and would be happy that she's doing so much better now. "I'm so excited for you!"

There's a beat of silence.

And I know what's coming next.

"I'd love to have you there. Do you think you can make it?" Mia asks gently, an undercurrent of tension in her voice. She knows as well as I do how complicated that request is.

I hesitate, biting my lip. I can't tell her that our parents are still furious about the New Year's Eve party and have all but said they'll disown me if I keep seeing her. That's not her fault, as much as my parents want to put the blame on her.

"I mean, I want to, of course," I hedge. "It's just, you

know, I haven't lined up a job yet after graduation, so I'm not sure where I'll be ..."

It's a flimsy excuse, and we both know it. But I can't bring myself to admit the real reason for my reluctance — that I'm terrified of upsetting our parents further. They are paying for my education, after all, which Mia knows. But she doesn't know that after months of pressure, I finally caved and agreed to work for Dad's company after graduation. How could I not? I know he'd be miserable if I didn't, even if it's not what I want to do. But who knows? Maybe I'll end up loving it. Despite my parents' temperaments, they've always made sure we wanted for nothing. Well, nothing material, at least. So, it's hard to say no to them. If only I had Mia's courage.

"Oh. I see." Mia's disappointment is evident, and my heart clenches. "Well, if you can make it, we'd love to have you there. But if you can't, I totally understand."

My eyes burn with tears at the thought of letting down my big sister. My parents are already upset with me — or *still* are, as it were, but I'm sure I can find a way to go without them knowing. Mia is my sister, and now that Gran's gone, she's the only family member left who doesn't pressure me to do things I don't want to do. My parents know I just want to make everyone happy, and they use that to their full advantage.

"No, you know what? I'll be there," I promise impulsively. "I wouldn't miss your big day for anything. I'll figure out the details later."

"Really?" Mia brightens. "Thank you, Carrie. It means so much to me. I can't imagine getting married without my little sister there."

I press my lips together and wipe away a tear as Rufus pulls me down the sidewalk. "And I can't imagine not being there. Love you, big sis."

Mia tells me what they've planned so far, and then we say our goodbyes, and I hang up. My chest is tight with excitement for my sister and dread of hiding this from my parents. It irks me that I have to. I'm twenty-six years old, for crying out loud. But this is my life.

Lost in thought, I don't notice Rufus lunging after a squirrel until it's too late. His leash flies out of my hand as he takes off, barking excitedly.

"Rufus, no! Come back!" I yell, jolting into action.

But he's already halfway down the street, his fluffy golden tail disappearing around the corner.

Panic rises in my throat as I sprint after him, my mind spiraling. I can't even handle dog sitting. How am I supposed to juggle my family drama, finish my degree, and start a job I'm not even sure I want?

Tears prick at my eyes, making it difficult to see where I'm going as I bolt after the overgrown puppy. A frustrated scream builds in my chest. Everything is spinning out of control, and I feel powerless to stop it.

Rounding the corner, I scan the street frantically for any sign of Rufus. But he's nowhere to be seen. Defeated, I slump against a lamppost, burying my face in my hands.

Some spring break this is turning out to be, indeed. I need to get my life together fast. But right now, I'll settle for finding that damn dog.

With a heavy sigh, I push off the post and trudge down the sidewalk to continue my search, the weight of my future pressing down on my shoulders with every step.

CHAPTER THREE

CARRIE

TWO MONTHS LATER

I stare at my laptop screen, the email cursor blinking mockingly. I've been agonizing over this invitation for days, but I can't put it off any longer. Graduation is only two weeks away, and I need to make a decision.

I want Mia there. No, I *need* her there. Just like she couldn't imagine getting married without me, I can't picture walking across that stage without my big sister cheering me on. She's been a constant source of support, even from afar, as I've poured my heart and soul into finishing my master's degree in political science.

But I know inviting her will cause a shit storm with our parents. Even if I ask Mia to sit separately, Mom and Dad will view it as a betrayal even if they never see each other.

I'm starting to understand why Mia didn't invite them to her wedding. The constant walking on eggshells, the fear of setting off their hair-trigger tempers — it's exhausting, even soul-crushing.

I take a deep breath, steeling myself. Despite my people-pleasing tendencies, I have to talk to my parents about this. I can't let their bitterness rob me of sharing this milestone with Mia.

Hands shaking slightly, I rise and go downstairs, where my parents are sitting, watching the nightly news as usual.

"Mom? Dad? Can I talk to you guys for a minute?" I ask meekly.

Dad looks up from his place in the armchair across the living room, a greying dark-brown lock of hair curling onto his forehead, his square-rimmed glasses framing the dark blue eyes he passed on to Mia and me. Technically, we also got his wavy hair, but ours is just dark brown. Though I may wind up with a few grey hairs after this conversation. Mom's shoulder-length, curly brown hair bobs as she swings her gaze toward me from the end of the couch closest to Dad.

"Is everything all right?" she asks with an undercurrent of suspicion. I never interrupt their evening ritual.

"Everything's fine, Mom. I just ... I need to talk to you and Dad about something. About graduation." I settle uneasily on the opposite end of the couch from my mom.

"What's this about?" Dad asks gruffly, clearly irritated at the interruption.

I swallow hard. It's now or never.

"I've been thinking a lot about graduation and how much I want my whole family there to celebrate with me. I know things are difficult between you and Mia, but —"

"Absolutely not." Dad cuts me off; his tone is as sharp

as a knife. "After what she did, abandoning her family, her responsibilities? No. She's not welcome."

"You wouldn't even have to see her," I plead, hating how small my voice sounds. "She could sit separately and —"

"And what? Pretend she's not there? Pretend she didn't choose her little bakery over her own flesh and blood?" Mom's voice is suddenly shrill, and I flinch. "Carrie, I can't believe you'd even suggest such a thing. Are you choosing her over us?"

Tears prick at my eyes, frustration and hurt welling in my chest at this old refrain. "That's not it at all! I appreciate everything you've done for me, and I'm not choosing sides. I just want my sister there for one of the biggest days of my life."

"If she goes, we won't," Dad declares flatly. "That's final."

A sob catches in my throat, and I crumple, all my carefully practiced arguments dissolving like mist. Mia will understand that I can't graduate without my parents there.

"Okay. I just thought you might understand, just this once. But I won't invite her. I'm sorry I brought it up."

"No, you know what? I don't believe you," Mom snaps. "You're just telling us what we want to hear, but you'll probably sneak behind our backs. Just like Mia."

"That's not true! I wouldn't —"

"I think," Dad cuts in, his voice cold as ice, "that if you're so eager to side with Mia, perhaps you should stay with *her*. Since you clearly don't appreciate everything *we've* provided for you."

"What?" I gasp, my stomach plummeting. "Dad, no, I —"

"As a matter of fact, you can find your own place to live *and* your own job," Dad growls. "Consider this a lesson, Carrie. Betrayal and ungratefulness will not be rewarded in this family. You can stay the night, but tomorrow, go find someone else to take for granted."

I stare at them in shock, tears streaming down my face. This can't be happening.

I rise on shaky legs, a maelstrom of emotions spinning inside me. I raise my chin. "Fine. If you don't believe me, I won't *burden* you anymore. I'll leave tonight."

I flee the room, not wanting to hear their response or see the expressions on their faces. I have no doubt it would only make me feel worse.

In a daze, I return to my room and pack my things, cramming clothes and books haphazardly into bags and suitcases. My mind races as I load up my car while my parents stare at the television, pretending I'm not even there.

Where will I go? What will I do? My whole life plan, the security of my parents' support and their love, gone in an instant.

It takes me less than an hour. One hour to erase my presence like I was never here. One hour to remove any trace of twenty-six years of life, I realize, as I make my last trek downstairs, that there isn't so much as a picture of me displayed anywhere.

Pride has always been a weapon to be wielded against us, Mia and I, never displayed freely and openly. Maybe I'm not losing out on as much as it feels like I am, after all. Unfortunately, the thought brings me little solace as I leave my key on the small table by the front door.

Still, they don't look up. I hold back another sob as the door clicks shut behind me.

I walk mechanically to my car, open the door, and slide into the driver's seat. As soon as I do, everything that just happened crashes over me like a wave, and my throat clogs with tears as I attempt to hold back the floodgates.

Knowing I can't drive like this, I let go and sob uncontrollably for a few minutes. Only the darkening sky brings me to my senses enough to think about my next steps.

I text my grad school friend group, desperately hoping for a lifeline. While I haven't told them everything, they know enough about my parents to know how they are.

> Epic fight with the parents tonight, and I'm officially homeless. Can I come crash with one of you until I figure out what I'm going to do? A day or two, maybe? I'll cook and clean!

SAVANNAH

> I'd say yes, but my roommate would never be okay with that. You know how she is!

CELESTE

> I wish I could help, but my new BF just moved in, and we really need our privacy, if you know what I mean. 😬

IMOGEN

Ugh, I'm drowning in my capstone
project. I can't handle any distractions
right now. Sorry!

Each reply twists the knife deeper. These girls, who I've poured so much time and energy into over the last two years, can't even offer me a couch to crash on? A shoulder to cry on? A single word of sympathy?

With painful clarity, I realize these friendships have been a one-way street. I've always been there for them, but they scatter like leaves in the wind when I need support.

With shaking hands, I hold back a fresh wave of tears and dial the one person I know I can always count on. Mia.

She answers immediately, concern coloring her voice as I pour out the whole awful story, hiccupping and sobbing.

"Oh, Carrie ... I'm so sorry. This is all my fault," she murmurs, and I can hear the pain in her voice.

"No, Mia, it's not. They're the ones who can't let go of their anger. You were right to get away." The realization hits me like a freight train.

"Listen, let me make a few calls. I'll get back to you in a few minutes, okay? Everything will be all right, I promise."

Even though she can't see me, I nod and whisper a thank you before hanging up.

True to her word, Mia calls back shortly. "I spoke to Joanie. She says you're welcome to stay at her condo in Fremont. She's living here with Greg now, so it's empty, though it's still furnished. The building super will meet you to give you the key."

Fresh tears spring to my eyes, this time from overwhelming gratitude. "Mia ... I don't know what to say. Thank you. And thank Joanie for me, please."

"Of course," Mia says, her voice thick with concern. "Just take care of yourself, Care-bear, okay? And call me tomorrow to let me know you're settled in."

"Will do. Thanks again, Mia. I love you."

"Love you too, kiddo."

As soon as I hang up, Mia texts me the address.

As I navigate the Seattle streets, the streetlights glinting off the windshields of passing cars, a strange sense of calm settles over me. Yes, my life has just been upended. Yes, I'm terrified of what comes next.

But I'm not alone. I have my sister and her friends. People who love and support her, and by extension, me, unconditionally. They demonstrated that on New Year's Eve, when I showed up crying, thanks to more awfulness from my parents. They reassured me, listened, and even cheered me up. And then the whole thing with that Ned creep who apparently tried to spike my drink. I didn't even know it had happened before Nate, Mia's fiancé, swooped in and handled it. And now they're making sure I'm housed and cared for. I tear up again, this time for very different reasons.

As I pull up to Joanie's building to see the super waiting with a kind smile and a shiny new key, I feel the first flicker of hope.

Maybe, just maybe, everything really will be okay.

CHAPTER FOUR

EVAN

"So, Evan, tell us about your favorite scene to film in *Rogue Agent*," the interviewer asks, her smile a bit too wide, her eyes too hungry for a scoop.

I lean back in my chair, painting on my patented charming grin. "Oh, definitely the rooftop chase scene. Lots of stunts, very physical. It was a blast to shoot."

"Any funny behind-the-scenes moments you can share?"

I chuckle and launch into a rehearsed anecdote about a prank my costar and I pulled on the director. The interviewer laughs on cue, but her eyes are glazed over. She's not interested in movie talk.

"Now, Evan," she segues, leaning forward conspiratorially, "what do you like to do when you're not busy being an action hero?"

I shrug, keeping my smile easy. "The usual. Hang out with friends, work out, catch up on sleep."

"No special someone to spend your downtime with?" She arches a perfectly plucked brow.

And there it is. The question I've been fielding for years, the one that never fails to set my teeth on edge.

"I like to keep my personal life private," I deflect, my standard response rolling off my tongue. "But I'm sure you'd rather hear about the incredible special effects in *Rogue Agent*, right?"

But she's not having it. "Come on, Evan. Inquiring minds want to know. Do you ever see yourself settling down? Leaving your playboy days behind?"

I force a laugh, even as irritation prickles under my skin. "Never say never, but I'm focused on my career right now."

The rest of the interview crawls by, a tug-of-war between her probing personal questions and my increasingly strained attempts to steer the conversation back to the movie.

It's a relief when it's over, but short-lived. I'm shuffled to the next interview, then the next, each one a carbon copy of the last: the same inane questions, the same thinly veiled obsession with my personal life.

One interview includes the whole cast, and Kaitlyn is all over me, touching my arm and laughing a bit too loudly at my jokes. She drops hints about our "connection" but never outright says we're dating. It's infuriating.

I try to physically distance myself, scooting my chair away, but she leans closer. By the end, I'm practically hugging the armrest, my jaw clenched so tight I'm surprised my teeth don't crack.

When the press junket finally wraps, I'm exhausted and irritable. I plaster on a smile for the fans outside, sign a few autographs, and then make a beeline for my car.

As I navigate the L.A. traffic, my mind drifts. There was a time when all of this — the interviews, the attention, the adoring fans — was exhilarating. A high I chased relentlessly. But now? Now, it just feels like a never-ending headache.

I realize, with startling clarity, that I need a break. A chance to breathe, to just be Evan for a while, not Evan Edwards, Movie Star.

But my promotional duties are just ramping up. *Rogue Agent* premieres in a month, and then it's off to Europe and Asia for more press tours. I won't have a moment to myself for weeks.

Except for Nate's wedding. A small smile tugs at my lips at the thought. Maybe I could extend my visit and take some real time off.

I pull into my driveway and head inside as I place the call.

"Hey, bro," he answers, sounding surprised but pleased. "What's up?"

"I was thinking about your wedding," I begin, kicking off my shoes and flopping onto the couch. "How would you feel about me sticking around for a bit? I could really use a breather from all the Hollywood insanity."

There's a pause, and I can practically hear Nate's thoughtful frown. "We'll be pretty swamped leading up to the big day," he says slowly. "Then Mia and I are taking off for a week for our honeymoon ..."

"I was hoping to stay for a few weeks total. Maybe through mid-October? I can entertain myself while you're gone, then we can catch up when you're back."

"Yeah, okay," Nate agrees, warmth seeping into his

voice. "That sounds great. It's been too long since we've had some quality brother time."

Relief washes over me. "Thanks, man. I'm really looking forward to it."

We chat for a few more minutes, then say our goodbyes. As I hang up, I feel lighter than I have in weeks. Having something to look forward to, a light at the end of the endless press tour tunnel, makes everything seem more bearable.

The feeling lasts approximately four days.

"Evan, darling," my agent greets me over the phone, his tone a mix of forced joviality and underlying tension. "A little birdie told me you're planning quite the extended vacation this fall."

I sigh, pinching the bridge of my nose. "It's not a vacation, Rick. It's my brother's wedding and some much-needed R&R."

"Right, right. But here's the thing. You haven't been getting as many scripts lately. After the *Rogue Agent* press tour wraps, I plan to line up some new genre auditions for you. Expand your audience and keep your career fresh. Can't do that if you're MIA for a month."

My stomach drops. "New genres? Like what?"

"Rom-coms, for starters. Big money right now, and you're a charming, good-looking guy, Evan. You could totally pull off the leading man in a romantic comedy."

I barely suppress a snort. "Flattery will get you nowhere, Rick. I'm not interested in rom-coms."

"Just think about it," he wheedles. "It could be great for your career."

"My career is fine," I snap, but doubt niggles at the back of my mind. Am I not getting as many offers? Have I been so wrapped up in the *Rogue Agent* hype that I haven't noticed?

"At least consider reading a few scripts when you're back," Rick presses.

"I'll think about it," I concede grudgingly. "But the break is non-negotiable. I need this, Rick."

He sighs heavily. "Okay, okay. Go, recharge. But don't stay away too long. This industry has a short memory."

We wrap up the call, but his words linger, echoing in my head long after I've hung up.

Is my career on a downswing? Will I have to start branching out, taking roles outside my wheelhouse, just to stay relevant?

The thought unsettles me more than I care to admit. I've worked hard to get where I am and make a name for myself in action films. The idea of starting over, of having to prove myself all over again ...

I shake my head, pushing the thoughts away. I can't deal with this now. All I can do is focus on the present, on getting through the next few months.

And then, finally, I can escape to Alpine Ridge. To Nate's wedding, to a semblance of normalcy, even if it's just for a little while.

But as I stare out at the glittering expanse of the L.A. skyline, I can't help but wonder if I'm running towards something better ... or just running away from a future I'm not sure I'm ready to face.

CHAPTER FIVE

CARRIE

I stand in front of the mirror, adjusting my cap and gown for the hundredth time. The black fabric feels heavy on my shoulders, weighted with the significance of the day, though the peacock blue hood gives it a pop of brightness that hints at its joy, too.

Graduation. The culmination of years of hard work, late nights, and endless cups of coffee. I should be ecstatic, and part of me is. But there's also a hollow ache in my chest, a pain I can't quite ignore.

My eyes drift to my phone, silent and dark on the dresser. There have been no calls or texts, not from my so-called friends or parents. I checked with the university this morning, and they never even picked up their tickets.

I swallow hard, blinking back the tears that threaten to spill over. I won't let them ruin this day for me. I won't.

A knock at the door startles me out of my melancholy.

"Carrie? You ready?" Mia calls, her voice warm and excited.

I take a deep breath, smoothing my gown one last time. "Yeah, I'm coming."

Mia beams at me as I step out, her eyes suspiciously shiny. "Oh, Care-bear. You look amazing. I'm so proud of you."

Her words wrap around me like a hug, and I feel some of the tightness in my chest ease. At least I have her.

We wind through the busy Seattle streets to the University of Washington's main campus, parting ways for Mia to find her seat while I get in line with the other master's graduates.

There's not much time to be nervous as they begin as I find my place in line. The ceremony passes in a blur of speeches and applause. When my name is called, I walk across the stage with my head held high, focusing on Mia's whoops and cheers, letting them drown out intrusive thoughts of the empty seats where my parents should be.

Afterward, it takes me a bit to find Mia in the sea of bodies. She pulls me into a fierce hug, her smile so wide it must hurt. "Congratulations, graduate! How does it feel?"

"Surreal," I admit, laughing a little. "Like, is this really happening? Am I actually done?"

"You're done," she confirms, grinning. "And we're going to celebrate. Dinner, my treat."

She takes me to Rossi's, a nice Italian place, and as we sip wine and twirl pasta, she asks the question I've been dreading.

"So, what's next for you? I'm sure you've got job offers lined up around the block."

I bite my lip, suddenly fascinated by the remnants of

my carbonara. "Actually ... I don't have anything lined up. Not really."

Mia's brow furrows. "What? But you're brilliant, and you've worked so hard. I thought —"

"I was able to snag some last-minute research work for a local election campaign," I interrupt, forcing a smile. "It's just part-time, but it's something."

Mia sets down her fork, her gaze sharpening like her inner lawyer just sniffed out a lie on the witness stand. She may own a bakery now but clearly hasn't lost her edge. "Carrie. What's going on? You know you can tell me anything."

I sigh, the words I've held back for weeks rising in my throat. "It's Mom and Dad," I confess, my voice barely above a whisper. "I … kind of agreed to work for Dad after graduation. At least, that was the plan. But when they kicked me out —"

"They took back the job offer," Mia finishes, realization dawning on her face. "Oh, Carrie. I'm so sorry."

"No, *I'm* sorry. I should have told you sooner," I mumble, shame burning my cheeks. "I just ... I didn't want to admit how bad it was or that I'd let him talk me into it even after everything you went through with them."

Mia reaches across the table, gripping my hand tightly. "You have nothing to be sorry for. They're the ones who should be ashamed, not you."

Her fierce protectiveness and the anger simmering beneath her words hit me hard. Tears sting my eyes, and I let them fall, too tired to hold them back.

Mia moves to my side of the booth, wrapping her arm

around me as I cry. She doesn't say anything, just holds me, letting me purge the pain and disappointment.

When my sobs finally subside, she hands me a napkin, her own eyes red-rimmed. "Okay," she says, her voice steady and determined. "Here's what we're going to do. That research position, can you do it remotely?"

I nod, wiping my nose. "I think so. Why?"

"Because I want you to stay with me and Nate in Alpine Ridge. Honestly, we could really use your help with the town elections, but I didn't ask before because I figured you'd be on to bigger and better things. While we have a few volunteers, none really knows the process's ins and outs. Not like you do."

I stare at her, hope blooming in my chest. "Really? You'd want me to do that?"

"Of course!" Mia exclaims. "It would be perfect. You could use your skills, build your resume, and have a place to stay while you figure out your next move. And the town wins, too. Plus," she adds, smiling softly, "I'd get to have my little sister around for a while."

I throw my arms around her, fresh tears falling, but this time from relief and gratitude. "Thank you," I whisper. "Thank you so much."

"Is that a yes?" she teases.

I smile through the tears and nod. She hugs me back tightly. "Good. And you're welcome. Because that's what family is for," she murmurs. "*Real* family, anyway."

We finish our meal, and the conversation turns to lighter things — Mia's wedding plans, funny stories from my grad school days, fond memories from our childhood.

But in the back of my mind, I'm already thinking ahead to Alpine Ridge, to the opportunity waiting for me there.

It's not the path I'd planned, not by a long shot. But maybe, just maybe, it's the path I'm meant to be on. A chance to start fresh, to prove to myself and everyone else what I'm capable of, away from the unreasonable demands of so-called family and fake friends.

As we leave the restaurant, Mia's arm linked through mine, I feel excitement amid the uncertainty. I don't know what the future holds, but for the first time in a long time, I'm eager to find out.

CHAPTER SIX

CARRIE

THREE MONTHS LATER

Who knew so much could change in a few short months? I was skeptical it would work out when Mia asked me to move in with her and Nate. Yet, here I am, still in Alpine Ridge. Though I'd visited here so often as a child, it's long since felt like a second home. But when Gran died, I'll admit I avoided it for a long time. Or maybe that had to do with Gran's passing coinciding with Mia's change in direction and the subsequent fallout with our parents. That sure didn't help.

Fortunately, I've finally re-found the peace I once had here. Something about the fresh mountain air and beautiful surroundings makes it impossible to hold onto a past that doesn't want to hold on to you anymore. I see why Mia and the rest of our found family decided to make Alpine Ridge their refuge. Mia's soon-to-be-husband Nate, their friend Greg, heck, even Mia's sassy, cynical best friend from law school, Joanie, seems happy here. And I'm starting to be too.

I at least have a purpose now and people who don't demand things from me but give me room to be myself. It's allowed me to shed the sheltered, spoiled version of me that was a result of being raised by shitty parents. I'm happy with myself in a way I've never been before. Though right now, that might be because I'm sitting in Greg and Joanie's living room, surrounded by friends and painting my toenails a bride-approved shade of hot pink.

In fact, the smell of nail polish fills the air as we all lounge around the living room, our hands and feet in various drying stages. It's the night before Mia's wedding, and we decided a little pampering was in order. Mia, Joanie, Rae, who works at the bakery with Mia, and even their bakery assistant, Penny. Just us girls.

"All right," Joanie announces, hobbling in from the kitchen with champagne flutes on a tray. "Time for a toast." She hands us each a glass in turn.

"God, Joanie, be careful you don't trip," Mia says anxiously.

Joanie shoots her a look. "Mia. You know my five-foot-nothing self is used to litigating in sky-high heels. I think I can handle doling out a few drinks while heel walking so I don't smudge Rae's beautiful work."

Rae chuckles and accepts her flute. "I'll go first," she says, diverting the attention back to why we're here. She lifts her glass. "To Mia and Nate, who I watched fall in love. And tomorrow, I'll get to watch them become husband and wife. Here's to watching them make some beautiful babies next." She winks, and Mia good-naturedly rolls her eyes.

"Ooh, yes, make pretty babies I can spoil!" Joanie agrees, raising her flute. "Oh, and to the bride and groom, of course. Here's to hopefully never leaving your hotel room in Hawaii." She winks suggestively at Mia. Mia rolls her eyes for real this time, but she laughs at her audacious best friend.

"To my big sister," I offer, raising my glass. "Who taught me about boys, driving stick, and how to sneak out of my bedroom window —"

"Bet those all came in handy on the same night," Joanie murmurs, and we all laugh.

I shake my head, having lost my train of thought but not minding. "Anyway … to Mia. You deserve all the happiness in the world, and I'm so glad you've found someone like Nate."

Joanie purses her lips and nods emphatically. "Have you seen him with his shirt off? She's a *very* lucky woman."

Penny, who has said very little this whole time, turns bright red. Mia gestures toward her while glaring at Joanie. "You're scaring Penny, Jo."

Penny blushes harder and shakes her head. "He is pretty hot," she offers in a small voice. Joanie sits up with a triumphant grin.

Mia bursts out laughing. "Can we not talk about how hot my fiancé is? In fact, no more wedding talk. Let's just have fun, okay?"

"Oh, come on," Joanie protests. "I haven't even inspected your honeymoon lingerie. Surely —"

"So, I can't believe the vote to make Alpine Ridge an official town is finally happening in November," Rae says in an obvious bid to change the subject while admiring her freshly painted toes.

Mia gives her a grateful look, which Rae responds to with a smile. "Right? It seems like it's all happened so fast," Mia agrees. "I hope it goes through."

"It will," I assure her, reaching over and squeezing her hand. "I've been talking to people around town. Almost everyone is on board and looking forward to all the benefits of the incorporation. It's a foregone conclusion in everyone's minds at this point."

"And my work here is done." Joanie dusts off her shoulders jokingly. She's not wrong, though. She was the one who listened to everyone's wish for it and made it happen.

Mia smiles tolerantly at her. "Yes, thank you, Joanie, master of the universe and all things lawyerly," she teases. "Seriously, though, it's exactly what I'd hoped for. And the bakery is already getting busier. I had to hire more help, especially since I'll be gone for a week." She grins, clearly giddy at the thought of her impending honeymoon.

"And we're all ready to chip in, so you don't have to worry about a thing," Rae assures her. "Penny, Riley, and I will hold down the fort while you're gone. So, you just focus on enjoying yourself."

Joanie opens her mouth, and Mia holds up a hand and says, "Nope, I'm not going there."

We all laugh.

"Oh please, that was too easy anyway. I was going to say that since we're off wedding topics … I've been talking to some law firms in Ellensburg," she shares. "Seeing if they'd be interested in having an Alpine Ridge-based partner to expand their client base. Now that my part in the incorporation is done, I've got time on my hands. I could help with their cases in my areas of expertise, and they could help with mine. I've got some promising leads."

"That's great, Joanie," I gush. I've known Joanie for years through Mia, and I've never seen her at anything but full tilt. She's clearly happy here with Greg but I'm glad to hear she's still pursuing her own passions too. "So, I guess Greg's going to have to get used to flying solo at the community center again, huh?"

Joanie smirks. "Yes, well, I suspect he'll be fine. I'm not sure he's noticed all the organizing I've been doing, though it's kept me busy enough."

Mia lays a hand on Joanie's arm. "He notices more than you think. The other day, he told Nate that you discovered a stash of tools and equipment he'd forgotten about that allowed him to fix up a few of the broken machines. Some of which Nate can use at the wellness center, too."

"Oh good, because lord knows they don't have enough exercise equipment already," Joanie jokes drily.

Rae smirks at the pair of them, then turns to Penny. "How about you, sugar? What's new in your life these days?" It's just like Rae to pull everyone into the conversation. She's such a sweetheart.

Penny blushes. "I'm thinking of transferring to the University of Washington once I finish my lower division classes at Yakima Valley College," she replies bashfully. "But I'm not sure. It's a big change."

"Oh, you should. U-dub is a great school," Mia says warmly. "Carrie, Joanie, and I all loved it there. You should go for it."

"I want to. It's just … it's so *big*," she explains. "I'm afraid I'd be overwhelmed by it all."

"Well, you know yourself best," I offer. "But they have a couple of smaller campuses in Tacoma and Bothell. Both are great and could offer you a more low-key experience."

Penny brightens visibly. "I hadn't thought of that. Thanks."

I smile warmly at her, remembering how overwhelming it was for me, even having lived in Seattle my whole life. I feel a sudden swell of affection for Penny and all these women as we listen to and encourage each other.

"What about you, Carrie?" Joanie asks. "How's the election prep going?"

I sit up a little straighter, excitement bubbling in my chest. "It's going well. I've been doing a lot of research, preparing to guide the candidates through the mayoral and town council elections. And like I mentioned, I've even started talking to people, just listening to their hopes and dreams for Alpine Ridge. It's been eye-opening."

"I bet," Mia says, pride in her eyes. "You're going to rock this."

I duck my head, feeling a blush creep up my neck. "Thanks, Mia. I'm just so excited to get started."

"And how's living with Rae?" Joanie asks, a teasing glint in her eye.

I laugh. "It's been great. It was kind of a goal for me to live apart from my family. Not that I don't love you, Mia, and while I wanted to give you and Nate space once you were married, honestly, I mostly just wanted to start living my own life. And Rae's a great roommate. I mean, she always brings home extra goodies from the bakery," I joke to take the focus off the seriousness of my confession. I didn't mention that my part-time research job doesn't cover the rent, so the inheritance Gran left me has been a safety net and a godsend. I hope overseeing the town's elections will give me the experience to land a full-time job after this.

Rae laughs, bringing me back to the conversation. "What can I say? Leftovers are one of my favorite perks of the job."

We all giggle, the champagne and good company making us loose and happy.

Suddenly, Mia clears her throat, her expression turning serious. "Hey, there's something you all need to know. About the wedding."

We sober up, leaning in.

"One of Nate's brothers ... well, he's kind of famous." She cringes a little. "Actually, like, really famous."

My eyebrows shoot up. "What?! Why haven't you mentioned this before? Who is he?"

Mia takes a deep breath. "Sorry, it was need-to-know only. He doesn't want to disrupt the wedding, so Nate and I thought it would be best if you knew beforehand." She pauses. "Nate's youngest brother is Evan Edwards."

There's a beat of silence, then the room erupts.

"Evan Edwards? *The* Evan Edwards?" Penny squeals,

waving her hands for emphasis. I've never seen her so animated.

"Holy shit, Mia!" Joanie exclaims. *Joanie*, who is impressed by practically nothing, is clearly just as surprised and interested as the rest of us.

I'm certainly stunned, anyway. So much that I sit there, shocked into silence.

Evan Edwards. The man whose movies I've watched a hundred times. Whose posters graced my college dorm room walls. Nate's *brother?* I did not see that coming.

But now that she's said it … actually, I can see it. They have the same tall, broad-shouldered build. The same artfully messy light brown hair and hazel eyes. Though from what I've seen in his movies, Evan's physique leans more like a swimmer — all lean, long muscle. Nothing like Nate's bulky bodybuilder frame.

"I need you all to be cool about it," Mia says, her tone pleading. "Please don't make a big deal. He's just Nate's brother, okay?"

We all nod, murmuring our assent.

But inside, I'm fangirling so hard I can barely breathe.

As the others start chatting again, Mia pulls me aside. "One more thing. Evan will stay at our place while we're on our honeymoon. And for a couple weeks after, too."

My heart stops. "Okay," I manage to squeak out.

"I was hoping you could make sure to include him in things. You know, so he doesn't feel lonely or left out."

I nod, not trusting myself to speak. Me? Hang out with Evan Edwards? For weeks? Why is she asking me to do this like it's a chore? I want to squeal as loud as Penny did and start jumping up and down. But Mia

37

asked us to play it cool. I can go nuts later when I'm alone.

"Of course," I finally say, my voice miraculously steady. "I'd be happy to."

Mia hugs me, clearly relieved. "Thank you, Carrie. You're the best."

I hug her back, my mind reeling. As we settle back into our spots, the conversation flowing around me, I'm only half-listening.

The other half of my brain is spinning, imagining all the ways I could potentially embarrass myself in front of Evan freaking Edwards.

But beneath the nerves, there's a thrill of excitement. This is a chance to get to know the man behind the movies. To maybe, just maybe, become friends with someone I've admired from afar for so long.

Suddenly, I'm looking forward to Mia's wedding for a new reason. As I sip my wine, grinning at a joke Rae just told, I can't help but feel like my life in Alpine Ridge is about to get a whole lot more interesting.

CHAPTER SEVEN

EVAN

The sun is just beginning to set as I drive into Alpine Ridge, painting the sky in stunning shades of orange and pink. I'm immediately struck by the town's beauty, nestled among the towering evergreens and rugged mountains. It's like something out of a postcard.

My awe grows as I wind my way up to Nate's house. The modern, glass-walled structure seems to blend seamlessly with the surrounding forest, making you feel fully immersed in nature. I can imagine how peaceful it must be to live here, far from the chaos of Los Angeles. I'm starting to understand why my big brother left and never looked back.

I park my rental car and head to the front door. I knock, but there's no answer. After a minute, I decide, fuck it, this is my brother's house, and he's expecting me, so I try the door handle. Not unsurprisingly, it's unlocked. Why bother locking your door this far from civilization?

I head inside, following the sound of animated voices around the corner to a large living room where I find

Nate's "bachelor party" in full swing. And by that, I mean Nate, our other brother Dylan, and a third guy, and they look like they've just been lounging around, drinking beer, and chatting. Not that I blame them. The large, tan leather couches and crackling fire look mighty appealing, especially after half a day of traveling.

"Hey," I greet them. All three look my way. Nate hops up. "Sorry, I'm late. My flight was delayed." I hold up a bottle of expensive scotch. "But I come bearing gifts."

Nate grins, pulling me into a bear hug. "No worries, man. I'm just glad you made it."

When he releases me, Dylan steps up and slaps me on the back. "Good to see you, Ev."

"The Edwards brothers, together again," I proclaim. "So, what kind of trouble are we getting into tonight?" I shake the bottle of booze for effect.

Nate smirks. "Unless you want to go find a bear to fight or something there isn't any trouble to be had here. One of the things I like best about this town." He gestures to the other guy. "This is my friend, Greg. Greg, this is my brother Evan."

Greg rises and steps forward to shake my hand. "Nice to meet you," he says casually. No fawning. No questions or comments. I like this guy already.

"You too," I reply. "You like scotch?"

Greg laughs and nods, so Nate takes the bottle and pours glasses for us all. We sit down and I listen as they pick the conversation back up. I don't even engage at first, happy to sip my scotch and mellow out for a bit. As I observe them, I'm struck by how relaxed and happy Nate seems. He's always been laid-back, but there's a new light in his eyes as he talks about Mia and the wedding. I've never seen him this excited, and it warms my heart.

It's great to see Dylan, too. As a cellist with a touring philharmonic orchestra, we usually only catch him around the holidays, and even then, it's hit or miss. But he's here now, regaling us with tales from the road and gushing about the woman in his life.

"I'm planning to take a break from touring," he admits, a soft smile on his face. "Spend more time with her, you know?"

Nate voices his approval, and I nod, understanding the pull of a genuine connection all too well. It's a rare thing.

As the night wears on, the conversation turns to me. Greg, who runs the community and fitness center here and apparently shares my passion for high-intensity interval training, asks how things are going in my world.

I hesitate, the weight of my career worries suddenly heavy again on my shoulders. I hadn't missed the burden. "Honestly? I've been struggling a bit," I confess, the words tumbling out before I can stop them. "Feeling stuck, like I need a change."

To my surprise, there's no judgment in their eyes, only understanding and support.

"Yeah? Is that what this break is about?" Nate asks.

I sigh and nod. "Pretty much. Though I'm not expecting to have an epiphany or anything. I just needed to get away from all the pressure."

Dylan raises a brow. "Pressure to do what?"

I smirk at him. Dylan's always been perceptive. "Rom-coms," I admit. All three men groan in sympathy, and I can't help but laugh. "Yeah, that's pretty much how I reacted, too."

"That may be a far cry from what you're used to, but if anyone can make that work, you can," Nate assures me. "But if you don't want to, that's okay too. You've got to do what's right for you."

Dylan nods his agreement. "You've been doing this a long time, Ev, and killing it. If you want to pivot, great, but it's okay to just take a step back and live your life for once."

Greg snorts, and we all look at him. "Sorry. I just … it's weird hearing them give you advice because I doubt any of us know what it's like to be a movie star," he says, giving an apologetic look toward Nate and Dylan. Then, turning back toward me, he adds, "But I do know what it's like to resist the pressure to do things you don't want to do. It all comes down to what kind of man you want to be. That's hard to remember when someone's breathing down your neck."

My chest constricts at his words. Damn, if he didn't just hit me right in the gut with that one. I nod slowly. "Fuck," I breathe out. "That's exactly what I'm going through. Thanks for that." I clap him on the back.

"Anytime." He holds up his glass. "To being the kind of man you want to be."

"Hear, hear," Nate says. And we all clink glasses and down the rest of our drinks.

I swallow hard, forcing the liquor past the emotion thickening my throat. A rush of gratitude flows through me for my brothers and this newfound friend. In the cutthroat world of Hollywood, it's rare to find people who don't pressure you to be someone you're not. But here, with these guys, I feel like I can breathe again.

We talk and drink late into the night, the worries of the outside world fading away under the camaraderie and laughter.

The next morning, I wake in the guest room to the gentle rustling of leaves and the soft chirping of birds. As I blink away the remnants of sleep, I'm struck again by the serenity of Nate's house. The bedroom's glass walls, which I hadn't noticed in the dark of night, offer a stunning view of the sun-dappled forest. With every passing moment, I gain a deeper understanding of Nate's decision to leave behind his high-powered plastic surgery career in L.A. for this peaceful mountain haven. Maybe I've been buying vacation houses in all the wrong places. Because this is what a vacation should feel like.

Unfortunately, now isn't the time for languishing in self-reflection. Today, my big brother is getting married.

With a smile, I hop out of bed and shower quickly before getting dressed and heading downstairs to help Nate with any last-minute wedding preparations. But it seems like his fiancée set everything out before heading to her own pre-wedding celebration yesterday. So, before I know it, we're driving down to the community center, where the reception will be held, apparently, to meet up with the bridal party.

In the light of day, as we drive into the town proper, it's lost none of its charm. Even the dated-looking wooden buildings are a nostalgic throwback to simpler, more peaceful times. When the world moved more slowly, and family was at the core of everything. It makes me realize how much I've missed mine.

"You all right, Ev?" Dylan murmurs from the passenger side of the backseat.

"I'm great, thanks. It's just so good to be here with you guys."

Dylan gives me an appraising look. "You seem different."

I take a deep breath. "I'm ... I don't know what I am. I've had this feeling for a while. Like I know something has to change. I just didn't think it would mean doing less of what I got into the biz for." I shrug, not sure how to explain it. Not sure I even *understand* it.

"Change is hard," he replies thoughtfully. "I never thought I'd be stepping back from the philharmonic. Yet here we are."

"But you're happy?" I ask, tilting my head.

Dylan, the most reserved Evans brother, *grins*. "Ecstatic, actually. Denise is ..." He sighs wistfully. "I love her so much," he admits. "But that doesn't mean it's not hard to step back from what I was doing."

I give him a reassuring pat on the knee. "I'm happy for you, though. And I have no doubt you'll find a similar opportunity locally. Surely, there's a musical outfit in the Portland area that would love to have you."

"Actually, before I even knew Denise was it for me, I'd started looking for something near Mom and Dad. They're getting on in age, so I figured I should be ready to move there if they needed me. Turns out there are several great ensembles that were eager to have me. It took having those options to admit that I wasn't enjoying what I was doing even before Denise was in the picture. Not like I did when I started, anyway."

"Really?" I ask incredulously. "How come you never told me?" Dylan and I were close growing up despite being four-and-a-half years apart, and we still talk often, considering our demanding work schedules.

Dylan huffs. "Because I couldn't admit it to myself. It had become so much a part of who I was I couldn't wrap my head around it not being a good fit anymore. But at the end of the day, I'm not a kid anymore. The on-the-go life was fun for a while, but at some point, I realized I wanted to settle down and plant roots. I just needed a good enough reason to make that leap."

"Denise?"

He nods. "Denise. But you're so much more decisive than me, Ev. You've never needed an excuse or a reason to be who you are and do exactly what you want."

I smile. "So, you're telling me to get in touch with my inner desires and set them free?" I joke.

Dylan lifts a shoulder. "I'm not telling you to do anything, man. Do what you want. When have you not, though?"

I pause, thinking about what he's said. I *haven't* been doing what I want, settling for scripts that came to me, bowing to my manager's "career advice." Maybe that's why this all feels like a slog lately.

I realize suddenly that the car's become awfully quiet. And that we've stopped at what is presumably the community center.

I look up to see Nate gazing back at me from the front passenger seat. He doesn't say a word. He doesn't have to. Being nearly a decade older than me, I've always looked to Nate for his opinion and, to an extent, his approval. So, I know his expressions well. And the look on his face tells me he heard what Dylan said and concurs. All the feelings I've been suppressing for months surge in my chest. I take a deep breath and shove them back down.

"I appreciate the support, guys. But right now, what I want the most is to see my big brother get married." I clap Nate on the shoulder.

Nate grins in response. "Hell, yeah."

A sharp rapping knock sounds on Nate's window. We turn to see our parents outside, and all of us, except Greg, jump out of the car like we're kids again and rush into a family embrace. As my parents' arms wrap around me, another rush of emotion swells, stronger this time, bringing tears to my eyes. I blink them back.

I tell myself it's just being on the receiving end of my brothers' love and support, seeing my parents for the first time in months, and being here for such an emotionally charged occasion. That's all. I'm most certainly not on the verge of an emotional breakdown.

Probably not.

Maybe.

Or … Am I?

Shit. I think I am.

CHAPTER EIGHT

CARRIE

"There," I say, stepping back to admire my handiwork. "You look perfect."

Mia turns to the mirror, her eyes widening as she takes in the delicate crown of white asters nestled in her long, dark waves. "Carrie, it's beautiful. Thank you."

I smile, blinking back the sudden sting of tears. "I just wanted today to be extra special for you. You deserve it, Mia. You and Nate both."

She turns, pulling me into a tight hug. "I love you, sis. I'm so glad you're here with me."

"I wouldn't be anywhere else," I murmur, holding her close.

Another pair of arms wrap around us, and we laugh. "What? You're both too cute not to hug," Joanie says affectionately.

A knock at the door breaks the moment. Rae pokes her head in, her face split in a wide grin. "It's time, ladies. Everyone's here."

Mia takes a deep breath, smoothing her hands over her

flowy lace and tulle dress. I likewise adjust my burgundy strapless cocktail dress, and then Joanie and I flank Mia, ready to walk with her toward her future.

As we step out into the main room, I see Nate standing with what is unmistakably his family: four tall men, including Nate, with light brown hair and huge smiles, one of them considerably older and standing next to a small, older blond woman.

Nate's eyes find Mia, and the look on his face steals my breath. It's pure, unadulterated love and awe, tears glistening in his eyes as he takes her in. Mia beams back at him, and for a moment, it's like they're the only two people in the world.

And then my gaze slides to the man standing beside Nate, and my heart stutters in my chest.

Evan Edwards.

He's even more devastatingly handsome in person. His navy suit and white button-front shirt are well-tailored and hug his lean, muscled frame, and his light brown hair is artfully tousled. When his hazel eyes meet mine, I feel a jolt of electricity down my spine.

"Mia's already met my family, but Rae, Joanie, Penny, Carrie, this is my dad, Steven, my mom, Diane, and my brothers Dylan and Evan," Nate says, introducing everyone with gestures.

"So nice to meet you all," Diane gushes with a smile. The warmth in her voice makes me think of hugs and family holidays full of joy. I hope Mia gets both and more with Nate's family because goodness knows we've never had either.

"Now, I've heard talk of Rae before from Nate, but

how do the rest of you lovely ladies fit into the picture?" Steven asks with his own gentle smile.

"Penny works with Rae and me at the bakery," Mia offers. "Joanie has been my best friend since law school and is our newest Alpine Ridge townie —"

Joanie scoffs. "Townie? I'm not ... okay, actually, fair," she accedes. We all laugh, and Joanie shrugs. "I'm a Seattleite originally. I guess I'm still getting used to it."

"And Carrie —" Mia pulls me close "— is my sister. Since she just got her master's in political science, she's here helping us with the town incorporation elections."

"And they're not twins," Joanie adds. Because we look so much alike, we often get asked if we are. I forget that these days since we went years without spending much time together. Though at just over five foot six, I'm almost two inches shorter than Mia and have our dad's chin.

A wave of sorrow washes over me at the thought of our father. Our parents. As much as I miss them in some ways, it's best they're not here.

"Well, I hate to rush this party, but there will be plenty of time at the reception to get to know each other, and we have some folks waiting for us outside," Rae points out.

"Oh! Of course," Mia agrees, moving forward. She gets as far as where Nate stands by the door before she stops and looks up at him. "Hey," she says softly.

He looks down at her, his eyes sparkling. "Hey." He kisses her lips softly, and Penny and I sigh in unison.

Greg smirks and leads Joanie past them. I feel a hand on my back, and suddenly, Rae propels Penny and me forward.

We step outside to a small crowd of the half-dozen

townsfolk Mia and Nate were close enough with to invite to the celebration. I recognize Meg, a sweet blond woman who works at the coffee stand, and I wave hello.

There isn't much time for talking, though, as Greg and Nate lead the way to the field of wildflowers where the ceremony will be held. It's not far, just a few minutes' walk up the path behind the community center.

When we're almost there, Evan falls into step beside me. His presence is both thrilling and unnerving.

"For the record, I think it's obvious you aren't twins," he opens. Hearing his familiar, deep voice sends a wave of goosebumps over my skin. It's really him. Evan Edwards. Here in Alpine Ridge.

Stay cool, Carrie.

"Oh? Why's that?" I ask, looking ahead toward the mass of wildflowers now peaking over the horizon.

"She's taller. You have a heart-shaped face. But mostly, while she's beautiful, you're absolutely stunning," he remarks, his voice low and warm.

My eyes jump to his face to find him watching Nate and Dylan come to a stop in the sea of white, yellow, and purple flowers framed by trees filled with leaves in blazing autumn reds, oranges, and golds.

I feel a flush creeping up my neck from Evan's unexpected compliment.

Stay. Cool.

I let out a flippant laugh. "I'm sure you say that to all the single women at weddings," I tease.

A smile tugs at his lips as he turns his gaze to mine. "I speak only the truth."

"Mhm," I murmur, unconvinced. But even if he's

totally just laying on the charm, I can't help the flip-flop of my stomach at the fact that Evan Edwards said I'm stunning. Me.

"So, who's older?" he asks.

I raise a brow. Given that Mia is more than five years older than me, I wonder if that's a compliment to her or an insult to me. "She is," I reply drily. "I'm twenty-six — well, twenty-seven in a couple of months. She's thirty-two."

"That's about how far apart Dylan and I are. Except, I'm thirty-five, and he's thirty-nine, almost forty."

"Are you all close?"

He nods. "Dylan and I especially, since we're closer in age. What about you and Mia?'

I shrug. "She's pretty much my best friend. We've been through a lot together."

His expression softens. "That's special. Family is everything."

I nod, a lump rising in my throat. "It is. Even when it's complicated."

Something in my tone must give me away because Evan leans in close. His smell almost overwhelms me — an intoxicating blend of the ocean and evergreens. "Complicated can be good, though. Means you care enough to work through the tough stuff."

I glance up at him, surprised by his insight. But before I can respond, Dylan calls everyone to order, and the ceremony begins.

I try to focus on the love and joy emanating from Mia and Nate, the beautiful vows they speak, and the tears and love they share. And I do, mostly, though my gaze keeps straying to Evan, to the strong line of his jaw, the way the sun gilds his hair.

I'm starstruck, I realize. Completely and utterly captivated by this man who, until today, existed only on a screen. But I shut it out as much as possible and focus on my sister and Nate.

So, I'm fully in the moment as Dylan declares, "I now pronounce you husband and wife!"

I watch, misty-eyed, as Nate and Mia share their first kiss as a married couple. When they break apart and turn toward us, I don't hesitate, rushing in to hug them both, my heart full to bursting.

After the happy couple has been passed around for hugs, Rae leads us all back to the community center for the reception. I'm suddenly glad as I realize I'm ravenous. I'd been so excited for Mia this morning that I forgot to eat.

Meg finds me for the walk back, linking her arm with mine.

"Is that really Evan Edwards?" she whispers.

I grin and nod enthusiastically. "Yes, he's Nate's brother." We share a look … and then an excited giggle.

"He's so handsome. Even more than on screen," she gushes. "What's he like?"

I shrug. "I don't really know him, honestly. We just met this morning. I only learned they were brothers last night."

Meg throws a hand to her forehead and feigns swooning. "Ugh. You're just so lucky to be related to him now. I'd just *die*. How long will he be here for, do you know?"

Something in her tone rubs me the wrong way. "I'm not sure," I lie, deciding Evan probably wouldn't want us telling everyone he'll be here for a few weeks.

"Well, maybe I can catch his eye at the reception. I wouldn't say no to a fling with a movie star. And lord knows there aren't many eligible men in Alpine Ridge. If he —"

"Speaking of, I'd love to sit down with you soon and talk about the kinds of businesses you'd like to see come to town first. Maybe some that would attract young, single men? More restaurants? Maybe even a mall?" I'm reaching, but hearing her talk about seducing Evan is going to turn me into the green-eyed monster.

"A mall? In Alpine Ridge?" Meg laughs. "That'll be the day. But I wouldn't say no to more restaurants. I'm a hopeless cook, and the tavern's fare barely counts as food, if you know what I mean."

I give her a vague smile. "I know what you mean. Is there even any chicken in the chicken strips?"

"Right? Knowing Jerry, it's probably some low-cost chicken substitute or something. Cheap bastard. Did you know he's thinking of running for mayor?"

I had heard that from Jerry himself, but I lead her down that conversation path as we head into the community center, load up plates, and sit down to eat. Rae and Penny join us not long after, and the distraction is complete.

Except, I'm continually distracted, too, by Evan. I can't help sneaking peeks at him as he mingles with Mia, his parents, and the other guests. I can't hear what's being said, but it's clear he's charming the pants off everyone. Hopefully, not literally.

I'd ask myself why I care, but if I'm being honest, I know why. I would never tell Mia — or anyone — this in a million years, especially not now, but Evan Edwards is a frequent lead in my personal fantasies. Yes, *those* kinds of personal fantasies. I know he's a famous movie star and a supposed playboy. He probably sleeps with tons of gorgeous women. Hell, he likely has one in every town he passes through.

But the idea of him being with someone in Alpine Ridge makes me feel all sorts of things I've never felt — jealousy, for starters. I mean, I've dated. I've had a few boyfriends, including a couple of serious ones. But I've never worried or thought about other women's interest in them. So, I don't know why it bothers me this time because, on the surface, it makes perfect sense that every woman in town has probably seen his movies and would find him just as attractive as I do. And, apparently, as Meg does.

It also makes me feel an intense longing like I've never felt. For excitement and passion. How could being with someone like him be anything but? I've had "nice." I've even had moments of passion. But I know anything I'd experience with him would blow all that out of the water. And my life could use a good dose of that right about now.

I sigh heavily as we all finish our meals but am saved from my own thoughts when Nate stands up to give a speech.

"Thanks everyone for coming," he says. "Obviously,

this is a casual affair, so I'll keep this short. But I just wanted to say how much Mia and I appreciate every one of you. We're so lucky to be surrounded by our amazing friends and family as we take this step together. We wouldn't be here without all of you, and we're so grateful." Nate turns to Mia. "And I'm also grateful for this amazing woman, who is now my wife." He clears his throat, clearly fighting tears. I blink against my own. "It took a little tough love from another amazing woman, Mia's grandmother, Dorothy — God rest her soul —but we found each other at just the right time. I love you so much, Mia, and I'm honored to be your husband."

And I can't help it; tears stream down my face as my sister embraces her new husband. As they kiss, their lips once again seal their promise to love and be there for each other no matter what life brings. It makes me feel so many things, and my heart swells to near bursting.

Mia pulls Nate toward the dance floor, where they share their first dance as husband and wife. I'm still crying like a baby when Nate's parents join in, followed by Joanie and Greg. It's only when Dylan asks Rae to dance that it occurs to me that Meg probably hasn't forgotten her quest to seduce Evan. My heart stutters anxiously as my eyes search the room for him. When I can't find him, my breath catches in my throat. Combined with having just finished crying, a little choked sound escapes me.

A handkerchief materializes in my peripheral vision. I look up to find Evan standing beside me. "You look like you could use this," he offers.

I smile gratefully and accept the proffered hanky. "Thank you," I say softly, dabbing at my eyes.

Evan crouches down. "It's my pleasure." He pauses as if hesitating. "Are you okay?"

I sniff deeply and smile. "I'm great. Just so happy for those two," I assure him. It's mostly true, anyway.

He looks over at Nate and Mia, dancing with Mia's head resting on Nate's chest. "Me too," he murmurs. Then he looks back at me and rises, offering his hand. "Dance with me?"

This time, my breath catches for a different reason, and I lose my words. So, I simply nod and take his hand. He tugs me to my feet and leads me to where everyone is dancing. He slips a hand around my waist, drawing me gently against him. My knees nearly buckle being so close to him. I think he knows because he pulls me in tighter, and I have to focus hard on breathing.

"So, Nate says you're going to be my babysitter?" Evan says in a low voice.

I can't help but snicker. "That's one way to put it."

He cocks an eyebrow, and the look is so sexy it makes my heart race. "Is there another way to put it?" he asks with a note of mischief in his tone.

I bite into my bottom lip to master myself. "Mia said I should make sure you don't get lonely," I reply in a husky tenor I don't recognize.

Now, both of Evan's brows raise. "Is that so?" One corner of his lips curls up, and my whole body flushes with heat. "And how would *you* put it?"

My eyelashes flutter of their own accord. Not flirtatiously, just because that's apparently what Evan Edwards does to me. God, I hope I don't faint.

I breathe steadily for a few heartbeats before looking

up into his eyes. "I assume you're here to get away and relax. So, I'd put it as I'm here to help make that happen. If there's anything I can do, just let me know. Even if that's staying out of your hair and making sure other people do too," I reply, blushing under his gaze and looking away.

"That's incredibly kind of you, thank you." His tone is different … raw, and honest, and I look back up at him. This time, he has no sexy smirk or tantalizing raised brow.

I shrug, equally uncomfortable with this more real, down-to-earth version of Evan. He's just as unnervingly charismatic.

I open my mouth to respond when I hear Mia say it's time to cut the cake. Everyone rushes excitedly toward the small but gorgeous confection and watches the couple gently feed each other the decadent Chantilly crème chiffon cake.

"What, she's not going to smash it in his face?" Evan remarks from just behind me.

I turn and give him a look. "You don't actually like that awful tradition, do you?"

Evan gives me a mischievous grin. "Only if it's my brother getting messy."

I chuckle and shake my head. "I am not sad I never had any brothers."

Evan slings his arm over my shoulder, and I'm so shocked by the sudden intimacy that I stare up at him open-mouthed.

"Oh, come on, it's all in good fun," he says, winking at me. "But he's probably too old for that anyway."

Rae starts cutting the rest of the cake and handing out

pieces. Evan drops his arm and heads to get one. Meg slinks up next to me.

"He was touching you," she says with wide eyes.

I can't help but let out an off-kilter laugh. Because here I thought that must have been my overactive imagination trying to make my fantasies come to life. "He was, wasn't he?"

"And he looked pretty into you on that dance floor." Meg looks at me meaningfully.

I wave her off. "He's just a flirt."

Meg snaps her fingers in front of my face so abruptly that I flinch. "Wake up, Carrie, the man is *interested*. Don't let that opportunity pass you by because if you don't take it, I will." She gives me an "I dare you" look that still somehow conveys she doesn't really mean it. She's just trying to get me to hook up with Evan.

"If he's interested, he'll say he is. But I'm not about to throw myself at him," I whisper.

Meg rolls her eyes and shakes her head. "Fine, play it safe."

I purse my lips. That's not the first time I've been accused of being too cautious. But I can't help it; it's just how I am. Always afraid of saying or doing the wrong thing and upsetting somebody. And since he's Nate's brother, I don't want to do anything to upset their family by misinterpreting his attention and making a move on him only to be rejected. How awkward would that make holidays for Mia? *I'm sorry my sister shamelessly threw herself at you, but thanks for the scarf.* I shake my head, determined not to mess anything up for my big sister.

But Meg is gone before I can respond, and Evan is

back with two slices of cake. He hands me one. "Mia brought this cake to my parents' house at Christmas, and I've been dreaming about it ever since," he admits, taking a huge bite. He jokingly rolls his eyes back in his head and moans deep in his throat.

The sound ripples through me like a physical touch, skating down my throat, over my chest and belly, and settling between my thighs.

I take a subtle, deep breath to fight off the wave of lust. And then I take a bite of cake. "It's good," I admit. "But you haven't lived until you've had her hot cocoa cake. Three words: homemade marshmallow filling."

Evan's eyes widen. "You're joking."

I chuckle and take another bite of cake. "I'm Mia's sister. I don't joke about cake."

"Damn," he swears. "Please tell me you don't bake, too."

My brows bunch together. "I'm more of a cook than a baker. But … why?"

He sets his now-empty plate down on the table next to us. "Because you're already a little too irresistible."

My mouth dries up, which is fine as I've just finished my slice of cake, so I set the plate down and sip my water. Evan looks at me like he knows.

"Feel like another dance?" he asks in a low voice.

I nod mutely and let him lead me back to the dance floor, where we're now the only couple. It doesn't deter Evan, though, as he hauls me against him and leads me to the music.

One of his hands rests on the small of my back,

spreading heat up my spine. The other holds my hand in his against his chest.

"I think I'd like it very much if you *didn't* stay out of my hair while I'm here," he murmurs as we sway to the music.

I swallow hard, my brain short-circuiting from his touch and proximity. "I'd like that too."

He rubs his thumb over my palm and pulls me close. As the song switches to a slow ballad, other couples join in. I settle my head on his chest, and he puts his chin on my head. I close my eyes and listen to the steady beat of his heart. I lose myself in it so completely that I don't notice time passing until Rae announces that Mia and Nate are leaving to catch their flight to Hawaii.

As loathe as I am to leave Evan's embrace, I extricate myself, and we follow everyone out. I slip to the front of the crowd to get to Mia. She's removed the outer skirt from her gown, revealing that the top was one-half of a wedding romper. It's so adorably Mia.

I pull her in tight for a hug. "Enjoy the crap out of yourself," I tell her.

She squeezes me back just as hard. "You too," she replies, pulling back and winking at me. I give her a confused look, and she jerks her chin over my shoulder. I turn to see Evan watching us.

"Ah. I will," I reply with a grin.

I don't even have time to hug Nate before they pack into his truck and start the nearly two-hour drive to SeaTac airport.

Once they've departed, so too do all the townies. Nate's family helps Rae, Greg, Joanie, Penny, and I clean up. It doesn't take long with so many of us. Greg and Joanie head out as soon as we're done, followed by Penny.

Steven and Diane turn to their sons. "How about we go for dinner at the tavern?" Steven suggests.

"Rae, Carrie, you're welcome to join us," Diane offers warmly.

Rae smiles. "I need to drop off these leftovers at home first, but I'll meet you there."

Steven nods. "Sounds good." He turns to the rest of us as Rae takes the first load to her Bronco. "We only have room for four. How about we take Dylan with us, if you don't mind giving Carrie a ride?" he asks Evan.

My heart leaps into my throat as Evan grins. "Sure thing." The glee in his tone does funny things to me, and a sort of giddiness settles over me.

The drive to the tavern is charged with a new kind of energy, anticipation thrumming through my veins. Thankfully, it's only a few minutes, as neither of us seems willing to voice what we're thinking.

Dinner is a boisterous affair, especially once Rae joins us. It's filled with laughter, stories about all the boys, especially Nate, as kids, and perhaps a few too many drinks. As the night winds down, Evan leans close, his breath warm on my cheek.

"I think I've had a bit too much to drink to drive back to the house," he admits.

"I can drive you back in your rental," I assure him, my pulse quickening. He gives me a skeptical look, and I realize the potential implications. The really forward ones. "I'll stay in Nate and Mia's room, and you can take me home tomorrow morning." Separate rooms aside, my cheeks heat at the idea of spending the night in the same house as him. But there certainly isn't room for him at Rae's, and the B&B is full.

He nods slowly without breaking eye contact before turning back to his parents. "Thanks for dinner, Mom and Dad. I'll see you tomorrow before you head home?"

"Of course, dear," Diane assures him. She glances between Evan and me knowingly. "Drive safe."

I smile innocently at her. "Will do, Mrs. Edwards. Thank you so much for dinner," I reply.

Rae gives me a look and leans around the table. "Text me if you need a ride back tonight. Or anything else," she murmurs low enough so only I can hear. I raise a curious brow. Rae's eyes dart briefly to Evan. "I know it's silly, but he's got a reputation, and I'm protective of you. Sue me."

I huff a laugh and wrap my arms around her. "Thanks, Rae. I'll be fine, though, I promise."

She winks at me, and Evan and I leave as the rest of our party wraps up their business. Evan leads me back to the car, seemingly steady.

The drive to Nate and Mia's is quiet but charged, the air heavy with unspoken desires, at least for my part. And unless everything he said to me tonight was just how he is, I'm hoping for his part, too.

When we arrive, neither of us moves to get out, to break the spell.

"You don't have to stay. You can drive my car back down if you want to go home. I'm sure I can arrange something for tomorrow," Evan suggests. "Though if you do, I promise I'll be a perfect gentleman.

I nod, not voicing that I'd prefer he weren't. "Like I said, I'll stay. It's easiest," I say instead.

I follow him into the house, where he heads straight for the living room. He settles onto one of the behemoth leather couches and pats the cushion next to him.

"Come tell me how a woman like you ended up in a place like this," he says teasingly.

I smile and settle beside him, folding my legs under me. "I'm not sure you had enough beer tonight to handle that story."

I expect him to be flippant, but he reaches out and runs a hand over my knee. "It's okay if you don't want to tell me. I just want to know more about you."

The unexpected tenderness undoes me just a little bit more. I'm not sure I can handle this swoony, sexy movie star also being sweet.

But I also can't resist him.

So, I tell him. Or, at least, as much of the story as it relates to his actual question. That's enough to imply the rest, which is to say a financially secure yet emotionally garbage childhood that's left me terrified to upset anyone ever. Halfway through, Mia's cat, Simba, jumps into my lap. Evan and I lavish him with attention until he's a furry, purring ball between us.

"Wow, your parents are probably the biggest assholes I've ever heard of. And I say this as someone who is an expert in assholes," he says when I'm done.

I can't help bursting out laughing. When he realizes exactly how that sounded, he bursts out laughing too. Our laughter scares Simba, and he darts off the couch.

"Okay, I didn't mean I'm into … *that*," he clarifies,

wiping away tears of laughter. "I meant Hollywood is filled with Grade-A assholes, whom I deal with on a daily basis. So your parents are like … Grade AA."

I bite into my lip. I'm not outspoken with people I don't know well. I'm too terrified to offend them. But part of me wants to tell him I'd be okay if he were into *that*.

His eyebrows pinch together at my expression. "What's that face?" he asks.

I shake my head, my cheeks flaming. "Your turn. What brings a man like *you* to a place like this?"

Evan stiffens. "I'll tell you, but first, you have to tell me what you mean by 'a man like you.'"

My chest tightens, and I reach out and touch his hand. "I'm so sorry. I didn't mean to imply anything bad by that at all," I rush to reassure him, kicking myself for upsetting him. "I meant someone as charming, successful, and well-traveled as you. That's all. I know you came for Nate's wedding. I guess I just don't get what else there would be here for you."

The tightness in his posture eases a bit. "Why does anyone come here?" he responds with a shrug. "I needed to get away from it all for a while."

And that's all he says. I can't help but feel like he'd been about to say more but stopped himself for some reason.

Me. I'm that reason: me and my big mouth.

I open said big mouth to apologize again, but he beats me to the line. "Tell me more about this town incorporation thing. I've never even heard of anything like that."

"Oh," I say, surprised. "Um … okay. Well, Alpine

Ridge isn't officially a town. It's an unincorporated area of Kittitas County. But that'll all change on election day." I proceed to tell him about all the work Joanie and the others did to file the paperwork, get signatures, and push through the bureaucracy required to set up that all-important vote to officially make Alpine Ridge a town and all the benefits that will bring to the people who live here. Then I explain the part I'll play in the next steps to elect its new mayor and town council and how that plays into my degree and planned career.

He listens intently and asks intelligent questions, but again, I can't help but feel that he's avoiding talking about himself.

Eventually, a yawn escapes me, and Evan glances at the clock. "I should let you get some sleep," he says softly. "I can drive you home if you'd like. I'm sober now."

I shake my head. "It's late, and you're probably tired too. I'll just crash in Mia and Nate's room. You can take me home when it's light out in the morning."

He nods and rises, holding out his hand. I take it and allow him to help me to my feet. My hand lingers in his momentarily as he looks deep into my eyes.

After a few tense moments, he leads me down the hall and up the stairs, his fingers still entwined with mine.

He stops at the threshold of the guest room, and I turn to face him, my heart in my throat.

His eyes darken, his gaze dropping to my lips. "Carrie ..." My name is a plea on his lips.

"Evan," I whisper back, his name a prayer on mine.

He steps closer, raising his hand to brush the hair back from my face.

I draw my lips into my mouth, wetting them almost unconsciously.

His mouth pulls up into a small smile, and he leans in.

His nose touches against mine lightly, and my body sways into his.

His hot breath fans over my face, and it's all I can do not to push into him, to give myself over completely. I want him to take it, so I know it's what he wanted.

But God, I want him so badly.

Like slow torture, he draws in a breath as if trying to inhale my desire. A small whimper escapes my lips.

And then his mouth is on mine, his kiss searing, branding, setting me ablaze.

As tentative as he was, he's just as demanding now as he pulls me roughly against him.

I melt into him without thought, my hands fisting in his hair, pulling him closer. He bites into my bottom lip, then soothes the sting with his tongue. The swipe drives me so wild that I grind against him.

This kiss is everything I've imagined and then some. Heat and passion that makes me ache for more.

But before I can deepen the kiss, Evan pulls back abruptly, his breath ragged. "Goodnight, Carrie," he murmurs, his thumb brushing my cheek.

And then he's stepping into the guest room, the door closing softly behind him.

I stand there for a long moment, my fingers pressed to my tingling lips. Then, on shaky legs, I go up to the third floor to Mia and Nate's room. Mechanically, I change into a set of Mia's pajamas and rinse my face and mouth with water. It'll do for now.

I climb onto their crazy comfortable bed and use a throw blanket to cover myself. My mind races as I lie in the dark, staring up at the star-strewn sky through the glass ceiling. Did I do something wrong? Misread the signals? I'd been so sure he wanted me, too. And he's certainly got a reputation that suggests he'd have taken what I was so clearly offering if he'd wanted it.

But then, as much as he's every inch the heartthrob I'd always fantasized about from afar, up close and personal, he's ... more. So maybe he's more than his reputation, too. More than the tabloids and gossip sites make him out to be.

With startling clarity, it hits me that that's probably what made him withdraw earlier ... the idea that I might think "a man like him" meant he was a sure thing. That I'd reduced him to a conquest that I could brag about to my friends later.

I cover my face with my hands, feeling like an idiot. Of course, that's what he was worried about. And I did nothing to reassure him with how I reacted to his kiss. I practically mauled him for crying out loud.

Still, I realize there's hope. Because he wanted to hear about me. Wants to spend time with me. *Kissed* me.

Maybe, just maybe, he feels this connection between us, this pull that's both thrilling and terrifying. All I can do is hope that he does and do everything in my power to let him know that I want to get to know him, too.

I don't want to be another person that reduces him to his fame. He came here to disconnect from all of that. To just be. And he wants to just be with me these next few weeks. It's the perfect opportunity to get to know the real

Evan. Just Evan. Not Evan Edwards, the action movie heartthrob. Because from what he's shown me so far, Just Evan is a great, down-to-earth guy. Someone worth getting to know. Someone I could see myself falling for.

With my racing thoughts, sleep is a long time coming. But when it does, my dreams are filled with searing kisses, strong arms, and the promise of something real.

Something worth waiting for.

CHAPTER NINE

EVAN

The aroma of sizzling bacon rouses me from sleep, and I smile before my eyes even open. Carrie. She not only stayed the night but now she's making breakfast. This woman is something else.

As I lie in bed looking out at the sunlit forest, memories of last night flood my mind. Her openness, her intelligence, her undeniable sexiness. That she didn't push me to talk more about myself, something I'm thoroughly sick of, and is a huge red flag for me with a woman because it usually means they're only interested in my celebrity lifestyle and status.

But Carrie is different. She's warm and caring and achingly beautiful. It took every ounce of my self-control not to take her to bed after that kiss. But I want to do this right. I have a few weeks here, and I don't want to rush whatever this is between us.

But damn, if she's out there cooking me breakfast, my resolve might not last much longer.

I dress quickly in jeans and a black henley and head

downstairs, my stomach rumbling in anticipation. And there she is, standing at the stove, a vision in the morning light. Her long, dark hair is pulled back in a low ponytail, and her pink sweatpants and white tee must be Mia's. Either way, she looks fantastic. And she's adding hot, fresh pancakes to plates stacked with bacon and eggs. I can't even remember the last time someone made me breakfast. Well, someone I wasn't paying to do it anyway.

"Morning," I say softly, not wanting to startle her.

She turns, and though her dark blue eyes light up, there's a shyness in her smile that wasn't there last night. "Good morning. I hope you're hungry."

"Starving," I assure her, but I'm not just talking about the food. Best to keep those thoughts to myself, though.

We settle at the table, and as we eat, the air is filled with a strange tension.

"Did you sleep well?" Carrie asks, pouring syrup over her pancakes. There's a formality to her tone that has me worried. Is she having second thoughts about last night?

"Fantastic. You?"

She takes a prim bite and nods. "I slept well, thanks."

We sit in awkward silence as we eat for a minute.

"This is delicious," I finally say, breaking the silence. "Thank you."

Carrie shrugs, her cheeks pinkening. "It's nothing."

God, I just want to reach out and run my thumb over that blush on her face. But I resist.

"Clearly, you've never seen me attempt to make breakfast."

That gets a small smile out of her, and I grin back.

As I finish eating, I decide I'll push just a little. I'm only here for a few weeks. What do I have to lose?

When I'm done, Carrie is staring out the dining room window at the trees. I rise and get her attention with a hand on her shoulder. She looks up at me with big blue eyes, and something lurches inside me.

"I'll just … clean this up and then take you home, okay?"

She chews on her bottom lip for a moment before nodding. It reminds me of biting that lip last night and how it made her press against me. I retreat to the sink so she doesn't see the effect the memory has on me.

After I'm done, I drive her home, and we don't speak but for Carrie to direct me to the house she's apparently sharing with Rae on the other side of downtown Alpine Ridge. I turn to her when we've stopped in front of the cute one-story rancher.

"I really enjoyed spending time with you last night."

Her brows raise. "I enjoyed it too."

I give her a skeptical look. "But?"

Carrie's nose wrinkles, and I think she's … self-conscious?

"No 'but.' I just feel like I may have offended you. I didn't mean to."

My brows draw together. "Offended me? How?"

"By making it sound like I assumed you were a certain type of man. Because while you're everything I expected you to be, you're also different. Good different. And I know you're more than the face you show the world." She reaches out and places her hand on mine. "I should've said that last night instead of rambling about myself the whole time."

I huff a laugh and shake my head, turning my hand over and intertwining my fingers with hers. "You have no idea how much that means to me," I murmur, lifting her hand to my mouth and kissing it. "But you didn't offend me in the least, and I loved hearing about you. It's just … difficult to talk about myself. I have to do it so much. I guess I get a little defensive at times."

Carrie lets out a sigh of clear relief. "I … was about to say I understand, but I probably don't. I'm just glad I didn't upset you." She beams at me, and it's like the clouds parting to reveal the sun.

"Quite the opposite." My eyes flick down to her lips, but I don't want to start something I can't finish right now. "I should let you get home, and I have some errands to run to get settled here. I'll call you later, okay?"

She squeezes my hand and withdraws. "Okay. Bye, Evan."

And I can't help it. I lean forward and capture her lips with mine. Ever so briefly. She sighs contentedly against my lips, and I smile. "Bye, Carrie."

And then she's gone, and I'm relieved that I hadn't pushed too far, too fast.

Feeling good, I head to the grocery store. I'm browsing the produce section when a familiar voice calls out.

"Evan! Hey, man."

I turn to see Greg, a huge grin on his face, his dark hair curly and messed like he just rolled out of bed. "Hey, Greg. You look like you had a good night," I tease.

His grin somehow widens. "I proposed to Joanie. She said yes."

"Congrats, man! That's amazing." I clap him on the back, genuinely happy for him even though it feels like everyone is dropping the settling-down bombs this weekend.

"Thanks. I didn't expect to see you. Sticking around for a bit?"

I nod. "I'm taking some much-needed time off, but don't get too used to me being here. I'll only be staying for a few weeks."

"Hey, I'll take the company any which way I can get it. And since you'll be around for a bit, I'm down a workout partner. Are you up for it, or is this a vacation from everything?"

I smirk. "Oh, I'm up for it."

"Good. I don't have any clients until eight-thirty on weekdays. I usually start my workout at seven. You're welcome to join whenever."

"Seven it is. Thanks, man. It'll be great to have some semblance of a routine," I reply. "And hey, while I've got you here. I was thinking of exploring the area a bit. Any suggestions?"

"Sure, of course. There's always Leavenworth. It's a kitschy Bavarian-style tourist trap, but it's a lot of fun. It's about forty-five minutes north. And if you're headed that way, Lake Wenatchee is another half hour past that. Fantastic hiking and water sports, though it's probably still pretty busy since the summer weather seems to be sticking around." He shrugs. "Oh, and there's always Ellensburg, the closest actual city. It's still small but it's

73

got all the hallmarks of civilization. Shopping, entertainment, restaurants, and a few fantastic breweries."

"Those sound great, thanks. I'll probably try them all at some point. Though today, I hoped to go somewhere nearby to enjoy the scenery."

"Ah. Well, in that case, there are some great trails behind the community center," he tells me. "Past the wildflower field where the wedding was. Lots of good hiking up there."

"Perfect. Thanks, man."

We part ways, and I finish shopping, my mind already on the trails. Hiking has always been a great way to clear my mind and put my life back into perspective. And fuck knows I need a heavy dose of that right about now.

I set out a couple of hours later, following the path Greg described. It's not all easy strolls through fields of wildflowers. It's nearly vertical at several points, but the burn in my legs and the warm air tinged with the scents of fall are invigorating. As I approach a ridge and the peaks of the Cascades begin to unfurl around me, I decide the views are worth it.

When I round the bend and reach the ridge, I spot an old lookout post at the peak. After a few more minutes hike, I climb the stairs to the doorless, sturdy structure. As I look out of the large opening facing the valley beyond, the vistas seem to stretch forever. Clearly, there's still plenty of water here because the bases of the mountains are green and lush, though their peaks are rocky and bare.

White, puffy clouds drift across the blazing warm sun, and birdsong fills the air. It's paradise, really.

I can't remember the last time I felt so peaceful. Out here, I can hear myself think.

I use the opportunity to mull over the discontent I feel in the city — well, with my whole life, really. It's been a couple of years since I was really excited about a project. Since I felt like a part was a good fit, something I could be proud of.

Despite what Rick, my agent, seems to think, it doesn't seem to be for lack of opportunities. There's always someone shoving a script my way or requesting that I audition for a part. So, it feels like there are always options, even if none seem all that appealing.

Which makes me wonder … maybe it's me. Maybe I'm just not that excited about all of this anymore.

There's something to that, I decide. At this point in my career, it's starting to feel like I'm playing the same part over and over.

Holy shit. It *is* me. I'm what's different.

I'm tired of the same old roles, the same interviews, and the same off-camera persona I have to uphold to project the same old image.

Maybe Rick has a point, and it's time to try something new. But … rom-coms?

I shake my head, unsure I want to go there yet unwilling to dismiss anything at this point. If I'm going to try something new, I know I'll need to keep an open mind.

Rick will be thrilled with this sudden willingness to accept a new group of scripts.

I chuckle as I track a hawk's progress over the valley. I

watch until the sun starts to sink toward the horizon, faint oranges and pinks starting to mellow the sky.

My chest aches a little, and it takes me a minute to realize … it's because I'm alone. This is the kind of sight you share with somebody. Somebody special.

Someone like Carrie.

I smile to myself at the thought of her. There's something so pure and kind about her. I wasn't just trying to pick her up at the wedding; the moment I saw her, I was stunned by her beauty. Only as I get to know her do I realize it's more than the kind that's skin-deep.

I'm attracted to her in a way I haven't been to anyone in a long time. Because she's not like anyone I've been around in a long time. Being immersed in the movie business doesn't put you in contact with many genuine people. And Carrie is nothing if not genuine.

I don't know where this thing between us will go. Or where it can go, given that she's here and I'm based in L.A. But I'm also not giving up on it just because of geography.

I once believed that what was meant to be will be. It was how I handled the initial rejection and climb to the top. Well, that and a shit load of hard work. But if that isn't a good parallel to finding love, I don't know what is.

So, as soon as I make the descent and find my way back to Nate's, I call her.

"You called!"

I chuckle. "That's quite the opener," I tease.

"Sorry. It's just … 'I'll call you later' is classic guy speak for 'you'll never see me naked,'" she jokes. And then she gasps. "Oh my god, that was so inappropriate. I didn't mean —"

And now I'm really laughing. "Carrie. Stop. It's fine, really."

"Oh, good. Still … sorry," she says in a small voice.

"Do you always apologize this much?"

Carrie is silent for a moment. "Yeah, I guess I do," she finally admits. "I'm a recovering people-pleaser; it goes with the territory."

Well, I didn't expect that. "I know a little about that," I admit. "But hey, I'm calling because I found something I want to show you tomorrow. Can you meet me at the community center around eight-thirty?"

"In the morning?" she asks.

"Later is fine," I allow.

"No, that's okay, I was just making sure. Yes, of course. I'm curious now. Are we talking like … a dead body or a really cool tree or something?"

I let out a sharp laugh. "Or something," I respond mysteriously.

After an invigoratingly grueling session with Greg the next morning, I'm using the stretching bars alongside the center when Carrie walks up. She's wearing sleek black leggings and a light blue fitted sporty top, with her long hair tied in a high ponytail.

Bright-cheeked and smiling, she looks ready to go.

"Ready for an adventure?" I ask, offering my hand.

She takes it without hesitation. "Always."

I grin, and we walk hand-in-hand up the path.

"So where are we going?" she presses.

I laugh and shake my head. "You just can't handle surprises, can you?"

She bounces a little on the balls of her feet. "Nope," she agrees. "But I get the sense you enjoy taunting me with it, so I'm going to stop asking."

I grin so wide I'm sure my dimples are showing. "I promise you'll like it. No dead bodies," I swear.

She smirks and allows me to lead her onward. As we hike, we talk about everything and nothing, including our likes and dislikes. She loves kayaking; I prefer running. She's an avid reader; I can't remember the last time I had a hobby outside of work and exercise.

"Okay, favorite book. Go," I prompt.

She laughs. "I could never choose."

"Come on, you have to pick one."

She thinks for a moment. "Fine. I'll go with *Pride and Prejudice*."

I nod approvingly. Even I've read that one. Didn't hate it. "Classic. Okay, your turn. Ask me something."

"Favorite movie — one you're not in," she adds quickly with a smile.

I groan. "You're killing me. I refuse to choose."

"Hey, you made me pick. Now it's your turn, mister."

I sigh dramatically. "Have a point then. If I had to pick just one … it'd be *From Russia with Love*."

Her eyebrows lift. "A Bond fan, huh?"

"Only if it's Connery," I reply with a grin as we step around the bend that allows a full view of the ridge. And the lookout.

Carrie looks up. "Is that a lookout post?"

I nod. "I think so." I lead her the last few hundred feet and propel her up the stairs before me to take in the view.

Her breath catches. "Evan, this is ... wow."

"Right?" I agree softly, stepping up behind her and wrapping my arms around her. "I had to share it with you." My eyes travel over the sunlit trees, and I see a small river winding through the valley I hadn't noticed before. The sun glints off its rippling surface, even from this distance. The view is every bit as beautiful as yesterday. Even more so with Carrie in my arms, warm against my chest, my nose buried in her coconut-scented hair.

She looks back and up at me, her eyes soft. I lean in and gently kiss her. She lets out a breathy sigh that makes me smile. A feeling of rightness settles deep in my chest.

She tips her head back to look at the horizon. "I can't believe I never knew about this place," she murmurs.

I squeeze her gently. "You've only been here, what, a few months? I'm sure you would've found it eventually."

She shakes her head and turns to me with tear-filled eyes. I turn her face me, cupping her cheek in my hand. "What's wrong?'

She's quiet for a moment. "I used to come to Alpine Ridge often as a kid to visit my Gran. She and my Gramps lived here for years. But as I got older and got busy with my life ... I visited less and less. Then, she got sick, and Mia came to take care of her. But Mia and my parents were fighting, and I didn't want to get in the middle of it, so I figured I'd visit again when everything settled down. Except, before I even knew how sick she was ... Gran was gone. And I regret not coming more.

Not spending more time in this place, with her, while I could."

I pull her into my arms, holding her close as silent tears stream down her face. We stay like that for a long time, just holding each other, the world falling away.

Eventually, she pulls back, wiping at her eyes. "Sorry. I didn't mean to turn this into a therapy session."

"Don't apologize," I murmur, brushing a strand of hair from her face. "I'm glad you shared that with me." It just underscores what a big heart she has, and I find myself drawn to her even more.

She smiles softly. "Thank you for listening. And for bringing me here. It's perfect."

She goes up on her toes to kiss me. But this time, it's different. I don't know if it's her confession or the connection it made me feel to her, but we come together with an intensity that knocks the air out of my lungs. Until her lips moving with mine is my oxygen. Her hands skating up my arms and twining around my neck is all I can feel. Until my hands sliding over her lithe body is the resurrection I didn't know I needed.

I back her against the wall as our kiss turns desperate. My mouth trails down her neck as her hands fist in my hair. The slightly painful tug turns me on even more, and I suck the spot where her neck meets her shoulder hard.

In seeming response, she wraps her legs around me, and I groan into her chest, reaching up to palm her breast as I return my mouth to hers.

Another few minutes of fevered kisses has me hard and wanting. But I know I need to stop. She's so willing and ready for me, but I can't take her here. Hell, I *shouldn't*. Not this soon. Not like this.

So I slowly trail off, easing her legs back down to the ground as I catch my breath.

"You're incredible," I whisper in her ear. She shudders against me, and I bite back another groan.

She rests her head on my chest, and I wrap my arms around her. Seconds later, the moment is broken by an outrageous rumble from my stomach.

"Sorry. Breakfast was a while ago," I say sheepishly.

Carrie laughs. "Let's head back and hit the tavern for lunch," she suggests.

A smile tugs at my lips. "I think that'd be a good idea," I agree.

We walk back down the trail, and Carrie doesn't let go of my hand once.

Not long later, we sit at the tavern, chatting while consuming some well-earned bar food and beer.

But as we're eating, the inevitable happens. A group of people approach our table, eyes wide with recognition.

"Oh my god, are you Evan Edwards?" a small, older blonde asks.

I plaster on my best movie star smile. "Guilty as charged."

The next few minutes are a blur of autographs and selfies, me slipping into the well-worn role of charming celebrity. But the whole time, I'm acutely aware of Carrie watching, of the discomfort on her face.

As soon as the last fan walks away, I lean in close. "Can we get out of here?"

She nods, relief evident in her eyes.

We escape, and Carrie suggests heading to the bakery. Though I'm wary of being noticed again, I agree.

And I'm damn glad I did. As soon as I bite into the slice of huckleberry pie Rae brought out for us to share, I sigh contentedly. In equal parts because it's freaking amazing and because we're the only people here. Well, besides Rae and Penny, of course.

"This was a fantastic idea," I mumble around a mouthful of whipped cream-laden heaven.

Carrie snorts and swallows her own bite. "I figured you could use a pick-me-up after that ambush," she replies wryly.

I sigh and set my fork down. "I'm sorry about that. I thought maybe it wouldn't be an issue here," I say quietly. "The whole celebrity thing can be a lot."

She studies me for a moment. "Is it always like that? The persona, the forced charm?"

I shrug. "Kind of comes with the job. Acting doesn't just happen on screen."

She nods, understanding flickering in her eyes. But I know it doesn't sit well with her because she demolishes the rest of the pie. Even I know what it means when a woman drowns herself in sugar.

So, once I've driven her back to her car at the community center, I take a chance to try to push past this with her.

"Carrie, will you go out with me? On a real date?"

She tilts her head, confusion clouding her features. "I thought this was a date."

"It was. Is. I just ... I want to do this right. Take you out, someplace nice."

Her smile is blinding. "I'd love that."

A weight lifts from my shoulders, knowing she's still up to see where this goes.

So, we make plans for Wednesday, after her video call with the campaign manager she's researching for. Watching her drive away, I'm already counting the hours.

Wednesday arrives, and I pick Carrie up, my nerves buzzing with anticipation. I've chosen Ellensburg, hoping the distance from Alpine Ridge will give us space to be together without thinking about anything else.

We walk through a riverfront park, the conversation flowing easily. Then we catch a movie, some big-budget sci-fi blockbuster, our hands intertwined in the dark. Next, we head to the Whipsaw Brewery for dinner, per Greg's recommendation.

Holding her hand as we walk up, everything feels right. Being with Carrie is the easiest thing in the world, and I'm happier than I can remember being in a long time.

Until we walk in the door.

And that's when the illusion shatters.

Immediately, the whispers start, and the surreptitious phone cameras start coming out. I do my best to ignore them and focus on Carrie, but it's impossible.

Finally, I excuse myself and spend the next half hour smiling for pictures, signing autographs, and talking with star-struck fans.

"Who's the girl?" one woman asks, eyeing Carrie speculatively.

"A friend," I say smoothly, the lie tasting bitter.

When I finally return to the table, Carrie is sipping a beer, her expression unreadable.

"I'm so sorry," I say, reaching for her hand. "I know this is one of the least fun parts of dating a celebrity."

She looks up at me, her eyes searching mine. "Are we dating? I heard what you said to that woman. You called me your friend. So, is that what we are? Friends?"

I sigh. "You know it's not. At least, not just that. But if I said you were my date, the attention on you would be a hundred times worse. Paparazzi, tabloids, social media. I didn't want to subject you to that."

She nods slowly, still seeming down. "I guess I hadn't really thought about what dating you would mean. The scrutiny, the lack of privacy."

My heart sinks. This is it. The moment she realizes I'm not worth the hassle, the headache.

But then she surprises me, her hand tightening around mine. "It's okay. I can't say I love it, but I'm not going anywhere."

Relief crashes over me in a wave, followed closely by a swell of emotion for this incredible woman.

We go ahead and order food, and the rest of our time there is blessedly uninterrupted. I suspect the staff is largely to thank for that, and I make a mental note to tip handsomely. But Carrie is reluctant to talk, and conversation is stilted, trailing to nonexistent.

Even the drive back to Alpine Ridge is quiet. Both of us seem lost in thought. When I pull up to her house, I turn to her, ready to apologize again.

"If you'd rather, we don't have to go out in public again. I know it's a lot to deal with."

She tries to smile, but I can tell her heart isn't in it. "It is weird and definitely not something I'm used to. I think I just need some time to acclimate. How about we stay in tomorrow, though? I can make dinner, and we can just ... be."

"That sounds perfect," I murmur, leaning in to kiss her.

The press of her lips against mine is electric, and it takes every ounce of willpower I possess to keep it chaste, to pull away before I can't.

I get out of the car and round the front to open the door for her, then walk her to her front door.

"Goodnight, Carrie," I whisper, resting my forehead against hers.

She leans up and gives me a gentle kiss. It soothes the anxiety swirling inside me over subjecting her to what my life is like so soon. I'd hoped for more anonymity on this trip, but obviously, that won't happen in this lifetime. At least there haven't been any paparazzi. Yet.

"See you tomorrow, Evan."

Watching her walk inside, I know with bone-deep certainty that I'm falling for this woman. I have to shake off the unease that comes with that because I can't say dating a non-celebrity has ever worked out well for me. I snort at my own thoughts as I get back in the car. Even dating celebrities hasn't worked out all that well but for different reasons. Normal women usually hate the attention I get. Famous women usually live for it. Neither bodes well for a stable relationship.

It would take one hell of a woman to handle the insanity that is my life. But just as I know I'm falling for Carrie, I know she's that and so much more.

CHAPTER TEN

CARRIE

I push my cart through the grocery store, my mind whirling with recipe ideas. Tonight's dinner with Evan needs to be perfect, a balm after the awkwardness of our public date. I want to show him that staying in can be just as special. Just as romantic. Maybe even more so.

As I stroll through the produce, I spot a beautiful mound of eggplants and settle on a menu—eggplant parmesan and maple-roasted carrots served with fresh rolls from the bakery. For dessert, pistachio cannoli. Also from the bakery. Mia's taught me well: Always play to your strengths in the kitchen. For me, that's definitely cooking, not baking. Though, really, it's thanks to her that I've discovered my talent for it.

After finishing at the grocery store, I quickly stop at the bakery and head up to Nate and Mia's house. As I drive, I hum happily to myself, noting Evan's car in the driveway as I pull up.

Arms laden with bags, I let myself in. Simba greets me by bumping up against my leg, but there's no sign of Evan.

I head into the kitchen, which is a dream, all gleaming countertops and high-end appliances. I set to work, losing myself in the familiar rituals of chopping, sautéing, and seasoning.

I'm so focused that I don't hear Evan approach until his arms are around my waist, his lips on my neck.

"I didn't hear you come in. Smells amazing," he murmurs, his breath tickling my skin.

I lean back into him, savoring the moment. "It'll taste even better. But only if you let me finish cooking."

He spins me around, capturing my lips in a searing kiss. It takes every ounce of willpower I possess to pull away. And the fitted acid-washed jeans and white V-neck T-shirt he's wearing that show off his amazing body aren't helping me resist him either.

"Evan," I warn, my voice husky. "Behave, or no cannoli for you."

He grins, holding up his hands in surrender. "Okay, okay. I'll be good. For now."

With Herculean effort, I turn back to the stove, determined not to let his distractions derail dinner.

We're seated at the table an hour later, with the fruits of my labor spread before us. Evan takes a bite of the eggplant parmesan and lets out a moan that should be illegal.

"Carrie, this is incredible," he says, his eyes closing in bliss.

Pride swells in my chest. "Thanks. I wanted tonight to be special. To make up for ... well, you know."

He reaches across the table, taking my hand. "You

don't have to make up for anything. But I appreciate this more than you know."

We eat in comfortable silence, punctuated by appreciative murmurs and contented sighs. When the cannoli emerge, Evan's eyes light up like a kid on Christmas.

"Have I told you yet that staying in was a brilliant idea?" he asks, biting into the crisp shell.

I laugh at how excited he seems by a simple dessert. "No, but I'm glad you're enjoying yourself."

He grins around the half-cannoli in his mouth and I shake my head, smiling, as I nibble at my own.

Once we're done, we clean up together, hips bumping and hands brushing as we rinse the dishes and load the dishwasher. It's domestic and intimate, and I can't remember the last time I felt this at peace.

"So, what's next on the agenda?" Evan asks, hanging the dish towel.

I shrug. "I thought maybe a movie?"

He shakes his head. "I'd rather not."

"Fair," I admit. Then, an idea strikes me. "Nate and Mia have a ton of board games. You up for it, or are you afraid to get your butt kicked by a girl?"

His eyes sparkle with mischief. "Pfff. You wish. Prepare to lose, Anderson."

We start with Clue. Evan, of course, wins handily, his actor's instincts giving him an edge.

"Best two out of three?" I challenge.

He smirks. "You're on."

Next up is Cascadia, a strategy game set in the Pacific Northwest. As we place our tiles and build out habitats, I can't help but appreciate how into this Evan is. Who knew the famous movie star was giddy over board games?

Still, I beat him soundly. It feels pretty good after my Clue loss. I'm not gonna lie.

"Shall we pick another, or are you ready to admit defeat?" I tease.

Evan sighs dramatically and leans back into the couch. "I know when I'm beaten," he replies resignedly. Then he smiles and gestures for me to join him. "Get your gorgeous ass over here and comfort me in my loss, will you?"

I laugh but crawl over the couch and settle next to him. "So, is this what movie stars really do to let loose? Play board games? Ooh, I bet you all love playing Scene It."

"Hardy har," Evan deadpans, wrapping his arms around me. "Being a movie star is definitely not all fun and games."

I trace a finger up his chest. "Tell me about it," I urge gently.

He looks down at me, his hazel eyes swirling with warmth and affection. "I don't want to bring down the mood."

I shake my head lightly. "You couldn't if you tried. I want to know what your life is like, Evan. I get the sense that you're avoiding something by being here. Am I crazy?"

He lets out a long sigh. "No. You're right on the money." He rests his head on his fist, his elbow on the arm of the couch. "I came here to escape the fact that I've been miserable, and apparently, according to my manager, my career is flagging."

My mouth drops open. I suspected he was having something of an existential crisis based on the few comments he'd made, but I didn't expect that.

"How is that possible? You're hot. Hotter than hot. Everybody loves you."

Evan snorts. "I wish. But even if they do, I don't love me. Or action-star me, anyway. I haven't done anything I've been really proud of in *years*. It's just been the same stuff over and over. It doesn't help that there's a lot of game-playing — not the good kind — backstabbing and politicking in Hollywood. It's gotten tiresome."

"And the fact that you can't go anywhere without being recognized," I add quietly.

Evan smiles bitterly. "Can't forget that." He sighs. "Until recently, I didn't want to admit that I'm ready to move on to something else."

I scooch up to a sitting position and look at him incredulously. "What do you mean by 'something else'? You're not quitting acting, are you?"

He reaches out and runs a hand down my arm. "No. Not yet, anyway. My agent has been pushing me to branch out. And, like I said, I'm tired of playing the same mediocre roles. So, I think my agent might be right. A change of pace could be good for me. He wants me to read some rom-com scripts."

"I think you'd be amazing in any genre. You have so much range, so much talent."

He gives me a skeptical look. "Even rom-coms?"

I grin. "Especially rom-coms. You'd be the perfect romantic lead. Charming, handsome, with a hidden depth just waiting to be uncovered."

"You're just saying that because you like me," he teases.

I roll my eyes. "Every woman in America with eyeballs likes you if you hadn't noticed."

"Mmm," he murmurs noncommittally. "Unfortunately for them, I only have eyes for you."

My cheeks heat. "See? That's the kind of thing a romantic lead would say," I deflect.

His eyes darken, his voice dropping to a whisper. "Yeah? Maybe I should practice some of my *other* romantic lead skills on you."

Heat floods my cheeks. "Oh, really?" I aim for nonchalance, but my voice comes out breathy.

Evan stands, taking my hand and pulling me to my feet and into his arms.

"Carrie," he murmurs, his hand cupping my cheek. "From the moment I saw you, I knew you were special. Your beauty, your kindness, your spirit ... you've captivated me, body and soul."

I melt into him, my hands fisting in his shirt. "Evan ..."

"I'm falling for you, Carrie Anderson. Harder and faster than I ever thought possible."

I can't help the whimper that slips out of me. "I'd give you an Oscar for that performance," I say, fighting the shaking in my knees.

"Who says I'm performing?" he asks huskily, lowering his face to mine.

My eyes close at his words, a tremor of emotion rippling through me.

But before I can gather my wits, his lips are on mine,

and I'm lost. Lost in the taste of him, the feel of his body against mine.

When he pulls back, I have to blink hard several times before the fog of lust clears. "Seriously. Rom-coms. Do it."

He smiles at me and strokes a hand down my back. "I'll think about it. But also, I meant everything I said just now."

My breath catches in my throat as I absorb that. "Really?" I whisper.

He dips his chin. "Really. I haven't ever opened up to a woman like that." He reaches up and strokes a thumb over my cheek.

My eyes search his, but all I see is truth and vulnerability. "Why me?" I didn't mean to ask out loud, but now there's no taking it back.

"Weren't you listening?" he teases. "Maybe I need to demonstrate what you do to me, Carrie." He guides my hand to the hard length between his legs, and I suck in a sharp breath.

Heat spreads outward from my center, and I arch against him. This gorgeous, amazing man, who millions of women would die to sleep with, wants *me*. I can't wrap my head around it. But mostly, I can't believe he finally opened up to me. I knew he'd been holding back something.

Hearing his doubts, fears, and concerns … I know this is real. He trusts me. Wants me. And God, do I want him. So badly.

"Too much?" he asks when I don't respond.

I blink, pulling myself back out of my head. "No. Not

enough," I respond. Feeling emboldened, I unbutton my jeans and slide his hand down my panties. "Feel what *you* do to *me*, Evan."

Evan's pupils dilate, and he groans, slipping his hand further down to my core, his fingers lightly tracing over my very slick center. He sucks in a sharp breath at what he finds.

"Fuck, Carrie," he breathes. And then his mouth is devouring mine. His fingers slip deep inside me, causing me to cry out. I cling to him as my knees shake against the onslaught of his now-pumping hand. His thumb flicks against my clit, and I moan.

"Take me to bed, Evan. Now," I say, uncharacteristically direct.

He withdraws his hand and lifts me up. I wrap my legs around him and cling to him as he carries me up the stairs, into his room, and sets me gently down at the head of the bed.

His initial urgency gives way to a slower, more deliberate pace as he methodically removes his shirt and then his jeans. Revealing the fact that he wasn't wearing any underwear. I bite my lip hard as his perfect cock slaps against the flat plane of his stomach. At the lean, strong muscles of his chest, arms, and legs. I remove my own shirt and toss it at him. With a predatory grin, he takes the challenge, slowly approaching and crawling over me.

As I lay under a very naked Evan Edwards, I can't even imagine how this is real. But I'm not going to waste a moment. I run my hands down the hard muscles of his chest as he stares deeply into my eyes.

He leans down and kisses my neck. Then down my

chest. He uses his teeth to pull back the cups of my bra, my breasts spilling out. He sucks each nipple for a moment before groaning his approval as he continues to move down my body, placing light kisses as he goes. I watch in fascination as his large, warm hands pull at my unbuttoned jeans and panties, working them down my legs until I'm almost as naked as he is. I prop myself up on my elbows, pop the clasp to my bra, and then toss it away.

Evan sits back on his haunches at the end of the bed.

"You're beautiful," he murmurs, his eyes drinking me in.

"I'm yours," I breathe.

A soft smile graces Evan's lips. He rises and retrieves a condom from a bag that sits on the chair in the corner of the room. I watch with hooded eyes as he rolls it on. I lick my lips in anticipation as he returns to me. Settles over me. Looks at me like I'm the sun and stars in his sky.

"And I'm yours." He reaches down and seats himself at my entrance, pausing for my approval.

I bite into my lip and give the softest of nods. And then he's sliding in, stretching me, filling me. He returns his mouth to mine, the warmth of his body cocooning me. I wrap my arms around him as he hits home, fully seated inside me. I squeeze his hips with my legs, wanting more.

Of his body, yes. But also of his words. His adoration. Just … him. Just Evan. As much as he'll give me.

"Mine," I whisper back, tilting my hips.

He nods and starts to move.

"God, yes," he breathes.

He buries his face in my neck as he takes me. I wrap myself around him, my whole body lit up by the joining of our bodies and hearts. It's almost more than I can bear as he takes his pleasure. I lose myself to our rhythm until I hear his breaths coming faster, and it sends bolts of desire rippling through my whole being. His pace increases, and it pushes me to the edge of bliss.

"More," I beg. "Please, Evan."

His lips find mine as he crashes home over and over. Because that's what this feels like. Home. Who knew that the place I felt most at home wasn't a place at all but in his arms?

It's the last thought I have before I tip over the edge into mind-numbing pleasure as Evan finds his alongside me, as I'm ruined completely by what I feel for this man.

After, as we lie tangled together, Evan's heartbeat is steady beneath my ear. As he strokes a hand up and down my arm, it hits me like a freight train.

I'm falling so hard for this man.

The thought should terrify me. We've known each other for such a short time, and our worlds are so different. He doesn't even live here. But then again, I only intended Alpine Ridge to be a temporary stopover, albeit longer than his. I have no idea how long I'll be here or where I'll end up after this.

But as I gaze up at him, I feel a sense of rightness. Of inevitability. Home. The word chants in my mind to Evan's heartbeat.

Still, ever the worrier, doubts pull at me. Maybe he doesn't feel the same way. Maybe he'll go back to L.A. and forget all about me. Maybe someone better will capture his interest and his heart. Maybe I'm not enough.

"Carrie?" Evan's voice cuts through the darkening room and through my troubled thoughts.

"Yeah?"

He slides closer, pulling me against him. "That was incredible." His lips meet mine briefly, gently.

I allow myself a small smile. "It was," I agree. I put my hand on his cheek. "You're incredible."

He squeezes me closer. "Stay with me?" The tenderness of his plea cuts straight to my heart.

I resist saying what I really want to — always. I'll always stay with him if that's what he wants. This all feels too fast, too unreal. Like I'll wake up in the morning, and it'll all have been a dream. But if it is, I'll dream it a little longer.

"Of course," I murmur.

He leans in and kisses me, soft and unhurried, before pulling the blanket over us. He falls asleep before I do, his deep, even breaths soothing the pounding of my heart.

I breathe in his ocean and evergreen scent and settle my ear over his heart, drifting off to its beat. I have two more weeks to soak up as much of him as possible. Instead of focusing on the fact that he'll eventually leave, I decide to make the most of my time with him.

With a smile on my lips, I fall asleep in his arms.

CHAPTER ELEVEN

EVAN

The first rays of dawn are just beginning to filter through the curtains when I wake, Carrie still sleeping peacefully beside me. I prop myself up on one elbow, watching the gentle rise and fall of her chest, the way her dark lashes fan out against her cheeks.

Last night was a big deal, I realize. Not just the incredible sex but the connection and the vulnerability we shared. I'm falling for this woman, hard and fast. The thought of leaving her in two weeks, of returning to my life in L.A. while she stays here, leaves a hollow ache in my chest.

But that's a problem for later, I decide. We'll figure it out. Together.

The idea of being part of a "we" and having someone to navigate life's challenges with ... well, it brings a smile to my face. I reach out, brushing a strand of hair from Carrie's forehead, marveling at the softness of her skin.

The buzzing of my phone shatters the quiet moment. I

glance at the screen, noting two things: first, it's barely after five a.m., and second, it's Rick, my agent.

I contemplate letting it go to voicemail, but I know that will only make things worse later. With a sigh, I slip out of bed, padding quietly into the hall so as not to wake Carrie.

"Rick, it's five in the fucking morning," I greet him, my voice rough with sleep.

"Evan, you need to get your ass back to L.A.," he says without preamble. "I've got the audition of a lifetime for you. They're looking for a new James Bond. And they want you to come in and read for them. Today. Two p.m."

I'm glad I'm leaning against the wall because my knees go weak. James Bond. The franchise I grew up idolizing. The reason I got into action movies in the first place. I never dreamed I'd be considered for such an iconic role.

"James Bond? Are you serious?" I manage to croak out.

"As a heart attack. This is huge, Evan. Career-changing. You can't pass this up."

He's right. As much as I'm falling for Carrie, as much as I want to explore what we have ... this is why I became an actor. To have opportunities like this. To bring to life the characters I've admired since I was a kid.

I close my eyes, a war raging in my heart. But in the end, there's only one choice I can make.

"Okay. Book the flight. I'll be there."

"Already done," Rick says, and I can hear the grin in his voice. "You're on a ten a.m. out of SeaTac. So get your ass in gear and get to the airport."

I let out a slow breath. I have just under an hour to get ready and head out to make it through security in time.

"I'm on my way," I tell him, then hang up.

For a long moment, I stand there, the phone clutched in my hand, my heart pounding. I'm thrilled about the audition, but the thought of leaving Carrie, of walking away from what we've just started ...

I contemplate not waking her and just leaving a note. But I can't do that to her. It would make me the world's biggest asshole. She deserves better.

Squaring my shoulders, I head back into the bedroom ... and find Carrie awake, sitting in bed, the sheet clutched to her chest, her face pinched with unhappiness.

"I heard," she says softly, her eyes meeting mine. "You have to leave."

I nod, swallowing hard. "Carrie, I'm so sorry. It's this audition, it's —"

She holds up a hand, stopping me. "It's James Bond. I get it. You have to go."

The understanding in her voice and her willingness to put my dreams before her own desires make me fall for her more.

I cross the room in two strides, taking her face in my hands. "We'll make this work," I promise. "We can talk every day. I'll come back as soon as I can. And you can visit me in L.A. anytime you want."

She nods, but I can see the doubt in her eyes. The fear that this is it, that what we have won't survive the distance.

"Carrie, I ..." The words stick in my throat. I want to tell her how I feel, to make her understand that I don't want this to be the end of us. But the clock is ticking, and I know I need to move.

"It's okay," she whispers, pressing a finger to my lips. "Go. Be amazing. I'll be here when you get back."

I kiss her, pouring everything I'm feeling into the press of my lips against hers. Then, reluctantly, I pull away.

I jump in the shower, somehow feeling nervous excitement and devastating loss all at the same time.

Carrie is gone when I get out of the shower, and my heart sinks. But after I've packed, I head downstairs to find her in the kitchen, a travel mug of coffee and a bagel wrapped in foil waiting for me.

"For the road," she says, her smile not quite reaching her eyes.

I pull her into my arms, holding her tight. "Thank you. For everything."

She nods against my chest, and I feel her take a shuddering breath. "Go kick some ass, okay?"

"I will. I'll call you when I'm out of the audition."

One more kiss, one more moment of holding her, breathing her in. And then I'm out the door, my heart heavy even as my mind races with possibilities.

As I pull out of the driveway, I glance back at the house, at the window where I know Carrie is standing, watching me go.

I'm leaving behind something amazing, something real. And given how new it is, how fragile ... I know the odds of us making it work long-distance aren't great.

But I have to try. Because Carrie ... she's worth fighting for. Worth rearranging my life for. And if I get this role, if my career takes off in a new direction ... I'll find a way to make room for her. For us.

With a newfound determination, I point my car towards Seattle and the future that awaits. It's a future full of uncertainties, but one thing I know for sure.

Carrie will be a part of it. Somehow, some way ... we'll find our way back to each other. Back to this moment, this feeling.

Back to the start of something incredible.

CHAPTER TWELVE

CARRIE

The house feels emptier than it should, given that I've only known Evan for a short time. But as I move through the rooms, tidying up for Mia and Nate's return tomorrow, his absence is a palpable ache in my chest.

I pause in the kitchen, my hands gripping the edge of the counter as I try to steady my emotions. I'm happy for him, truly. The chance to play such an iconic role is a dream come true, and he deserves it. But I can't shake the feeling that this is the beginning of the end for us.

We hadn't been together long enough to develop a bond that could withstand a separation. I know that, logically. But my heart hasn't quite caught up to that reality.

Simba winds around my ankles, meowing for attention. I scoop him up, burying my face in his soft fur. "At least you're not going anywhere," I murmur.

As the day wears on, I keep glancing at my phone, hoping to see Evan's name light up the screen. But it remains stubbornly silent. By the time I crawl into bed that night, the pit in my stomach has grown. He said he'd call after the audition. The fact that he hasn't ... well, it speaks volumes.

The next evening, I'm in the kitchen making tea when I hear the front door open.

"Hello?" Mia's voice calls out. "We're home!"

I plaster on a smile and go to greet them. Mia and Nate look tan, happy, and more in love than ever. It's beautiful to see, even as it makes my own heartache more acute.

"Welcome back!" I say, hugging them both. "How was the honeymoon?"

Mia's eyes light up. "Oh, Carrie, it was amazing. The beaches, the food, the sunsets ..."

As she launches into a detailed account of their trip, I notice Nate glancing around, puzzled.

"Hey, where's Evan?" he asks, interrupting Mia's story about their snorkeling adventure.

My stomach drops. Evan didn't even tell his own brother he was leaving. "Oh, um, he had to go back to L.A. yesterday," I say, trying to keep my voice light. "There was an important audition. So, I came up and stayed to look after Simba for you."

Nate's brow furrows. "He didn't mention anything about an audition before we left."

I shrug, aiming for nonchalance. "It was kind of last minute. You know how these things can be."

Mia looks at me intently, and I can tell she's not

buying my casual act. But I don't have the energy to get into it right now.

"Well, I should get going. Let you two settle back in," I say, grabbing my bag. "We'll catch up soon, okay?"

I make my escape before Mia can corner me with questions I'm not ready to answer.

It's not until Sunday that Evan finally calls. My heart leaps when I see his name on my screen, but I temper my excitement.

"Hey," I answer, trying to sound casual.

"Carrie, hi," he says, his voice warm but distracted. "I'm sorry I didn't call sooner. It's been crazy here."

He launches into an explanation about being wined and dined by studio execs after the audition. Then, yesterday, he spent time with his agent, going over paperwork and the next steps.

"It's not official yet," he says excitedly, "but it's looking really good. I've still got more work to do to lock it down, though, so I probably won't be able to call every day."

"That's okay," I say, even as my heart sinks at my fears coming to fruition. "I understand."

We chat for a few more minutes before he has to go. As I hang up, a feeling of dread settles over me. And so, it begins.

The next few weeks prove my fears right. Evan calls maybe once a week, if that. He talks my ear off about the part, the director, and everything related to his new adventure. To his credit, he asks how I'm doing, but it's not like I have much to report besides missing him. I text occasionally when something reminds me of him, but his replies, when they come, are brief and infrequent.

Then, at the end of the month, he calls with news.

"It's still a secret," he says, his voice barely containing his excitement, "but I've officially got the part. They need me to start filming as soon as possible. I'll be in remote locations for the next two months, but I'll try to call when I can."

"That's wonderful, Evan," I say, genuinely happy for him even as my heart breaks. "Congratulations. You're going to be amazing."

We talk for a few more minutes, but it feels like we're speaking across a vast distance, and it's not just the miles between us.

When we hang up, I know, with a certainty that settles in my bones, that he won't call again.

And he doesn't.

As the days turn into weeks, I throw myself into my work. I focus on the upcoming elections and on helping Alpine Ridge become the town it deserves to be.

The November election proves my hunch, and Alpine Ridge is officially voted into townhood. We all take a break to celebrate, including a small party for my birthday, but then it's back to the daily grind.

I spend time with Mia, Nate, Rae, and the others. I find myself building a life here, piece by piece.

But sometimes, in quiet moments when I'm alone, I think of Evan. Of what might have been. Of the whirlwind romance that felt like the beginning of something extraordinary.

And I wonder if, somewhere out there, as he films his dream role, he ever thinks of me, too.

CHAPTER THIRTEEN

EVAN

The scorching Abu Dhabi sun beats down on me as I crouch behind a sand dune, prop gun in hand. Sweat trickles down my back, and my muscles ache from holding the position. But I push the discomfort aside, sinking deep into the role of an international spy.

"Action!" the director calls, and I spring into motion, rolling out from my hiding spot and firing a series of shots. The stunt coordinator had drilled this sequence into me for hours, and I nail it perfectly.

"Cut! That's a wrap for today," the director announces, and I let out a relieved breath.

As the crew starts to pack up, I glance at my watch. It's Thanksgiving back home, I remember, with a pang. The thought of my family gathering around the table without me, of Carrie celebrating with my brother, her sister, and their friends in Alpine Ridge, hits me harder than I expected.

I trudge back to my trailer, peeling off the sweat-soaked costume. My body feels like one giant bruise from weeks of grueling physical training and stunt work. The producers want me to do as many of my own stunts as possible, which means every spare moment is filled with martial arts lessons, fight choreography, and endless repetitions of complex action sequences. It's the kind of training I'm used to, just not on such an intense, accelerated schedule. But then, they didn't expect to have to switch Bonds right before production started, and I'm not the only one scrambling to adjust.

As I step into the shower, letting the cool water soothe my overheated skin, I can't help but marvel at how different my life is now compared to just a few months ago. The role of James Bond is everything I ever dreamed of and more. It's challenging and exciting, and it will undoubtedly catapult my career to new heights.

But it's also all-consuming. The filming schedule is relentless, with early mornings and late nights blurring together. We're constantly on the move, jetting from one exotic location to another. It's exhilarating but also exhausting.

And in the quiet moments, in those precious few seconds before sleep claims me each night, my thoughts inevitably turn to Carrie.

I miss her. It's strange, considering we only spent a week together, but the ache in my chest when I think of her is undeniable. I miss her laugh, her subtle wit, and the way she saw past my Hollywood persona to the real me.

As I towel off and collapse onto my bed, I can't help but feel a wave of guilt wash over me. I've essentially ghosted her, letting the demands of the role push her to the periphery of my life. It wasn't intentional, but the result is the same.

I reach for my phone, thinking maybe I should call her. But what would I say? I'm sorry for disappearing? That I think about her constantly, even as I'm living out my dream? That I hope she'll still be there when this whirlwind finally slows down?

My thumb hovers over her name in my contacts, but I can't bring myself to place the call. It's the middle of the night in Washington, and besides, a phone call feels inadequate after so much silence. It's the same battle I fight with myself every time, and I always lose.

I set the phone aside with a sigh, staring up at the ceiling. I won't make it home for Christmas either. The shooting schedule is too tight, the locations too remote. Another holiday away from family and friends. And the first in a very long time that there's a special someone I want to spend it with. Carrie.

She said she'd be there when I got back, but I know that's not a promise she can keep forever. Life goes on, and people move on. And I've given her every reason to do just that.

But still, I hope. I hope that when this is all over, when I can finally catch my breath and return to some semblance of normalcy, she'll still be willing to give us a chance. I hope I haven't irreparably damaged what we started to build in those few precious days in Alpine Ridge.

As sleep begins to claim me, my last conscious thought is of Carrie. Of her smile, her touch, the way she made me feel more like myself than I had in years.

I'll make it up to her, I vow silently. Somehow, some way, I'll bridge the distance I've created between us. To show her that what we had — what we could have — is worth it.

With that promise echoing in my mind, I drift off into an exhausted sleep, dreams of snowy mountains and a dark-haired beauty waiting for me on the other side.

CHAPTER FOURTEEN

CARRIE

The crisp winter air nips at my cheeks as I make my way down Main Street, my boots crunching on the light dusting of snow. Alpine Ridge has transformed in the past few months, both literally and figuratively. The newly revamped grocery store, courtesy of Greg's cousin Sera, is a testament to the changes sweeping through our little town. That particular change was made possible by Greg's aunt and uncle fleeing from the fallout of their creeper son Ned's misdeeds against certain town residents and subsequent imprisonment. I say good riddance on all fronts, especially when the place, nay the whole town, is now leaps and bounds better for it.

I pause to admire the sleek facade, remembering the dingy, outdated building it once was. Sera has worked miracles, turning it into a modern, inviting space that wouldn't look out of place in a much larger city. Yet, by strategically leaving some of its original embellishments, she's managed to maintain that small-town charm that

UNSCRIPTED LOVE

makes Alpine Ridge special. Who knew wagon wheel décor could look chic?

I chuckle as I push through the doors. The warm air envelops me, carrying the scent of fresh bread and coffee. The aisles are stocked with an impressive array of products, from organic produce to gourmet international foods. It's a far cry from the limited selection we used to have, and thankfully, the prices lean more Trader Joe's than Whole Foods.

"Carrie!" Meg calls out, waving from behind the customer service desk. Her bright smile is infectious, and I can't help but grin back. I can see how happy she is to have moved on from the coffee stand.

"Hey, Meg. Gosh, the place looks great," I say, approaching her.

She beams. "Doesn't it? I can't believe what the new owner has done with it. And you know, I heard she owns a bunch of other land in Alpine Ridge that she's planning to develop come spring. I can't wait to see what else she'll build."

I nod, genuinely excited to see what Sera will do next. "Me neither. In fact, the whole town is buzzing about it."

She gives me a friendly smile as I move along. While I gather my groceries, my mind wanders to the upcoming elections. The incorporation of Alpine Ridge has set off a whirlwind of political activity, and as the person overseeing the process, I'm right in the middle of it all. It's hard to shut out, even when I'm technically off the clock, so to speak.

But I can't shut it out for long anyway, as later that afternoon, I find myself in the community center,

113

surrounded by a sea of campaign posters and eager candidates. The air is thick with anticipation and the faint smell of coffee from the machine in the corner.

"All right, everyone," I call out, my voice cutting through the chatter. "Let's go over the debate format one more time."

As I explain the rules and time limits, my eyes scan the room. Jerry, the crusty old tavern owner, looks smug in his ill-fitting suit. He's running for mayor, to absolutely no one's surprise. After all, he'd claimed to be running the town once before — well, with the help of some of his friends — so I'm not the least bit shocked that he's throwing his hat in the ring to *actually* run it. I suppress a sigh, reminding myself to remain impartial. But secretly hoping he doesn't make the cut for candidates after the first vote in just over a month.

My gaze lands next on a familiar face, and my spirits lift. Brandon Thompson, my childhood friend, is leaning against the wall, listening intently. His blond hair is just as unruly as ever, throwing me back to his teen self, but his jaw is covered with a layer of golden stubble, and he seems taller and broader. He caught me off guard when he showed up a few weeks ago, announcing his candidacy for town council.

I remember the summers we spent together when I was an awkward preteen and how he always looked out for me like a big brother. Now, he's all grown up, and his boyish features have matured into a rugged handsomeness that speaks of his years traveling the world as a photographer and aid worker. We haven't had much time to talk, but I've meant to catch up with him.

Thankfully, after the meeting, Brandon approaches me, his easy smile bringing back a flood of memories.

"Hey, campaign manager," he teases, bumping my shoulder with his.

I roll my eyes good-naturedly. "I'm not anyone's campaign manager, Thompson. I'm just here to make sure everyone plays fair."

He chuckles. "Always the diplomat. Some things never change."

We fall into step together as we leave the community center, the cold air a shock after the stuffy interior.

"So, international aid worker to small-town council member," I muse. "That's quite a career change."

Brandon shrugs, his breath forming small clouds in the frosty air. "I've seen a lot of the world, Carrie. Done what I could to help. But I realized I wanted to make a difference closer to home. This town ... it's special. I want to be part of shaping its future."

His words resonate with me, echoing my own feelings about Alpine Ridge. "I get that," I say softly. "It's why I'm doing this, too."

We walk in comfortable silence for a moment, and I'm struck by how easily we fall back into our old friendship despite the years and miles that have separated us.

"Hey," Brandon says suddenly, turning to face me. "Want to grab a coffee? Catch up properly?"

I hesitate for a moment, my mind, for some reason, flashing unbidden to Evan, like having coffee with another man is a betrayal of our relationship that couldn't be. But I quickly push the thought aside. Evan made his choice, and I need to move on. And Brandon's just a friend anyway.

"Sure," I reply, smiling. "I'd like that."

Since it's closest, we head towards the coffee stand, and I feel lighter. The past few months have been a whirlwind of activity, barely giving me time to breathe, let alone dwell on my heartache. Between advising candidates, compiling data on the town's needs and desires, and getting to know the residents, I've found a sense of purpose I never knew I was missing.

Brandon and I swap stories over steaming mugs of coffee, sitting in the little heated cubby on the side of the stand. He tells me about his travels, the people he's met, and the challenges he's faced. In turn, I share my experiences in Alpine Ridge, and the ups and downs of the past year. I skate over the mess with my parents, not wanting to wade too far into that swamp. Not when there's so much to be excited about with everything happening here.

"Sounds like you've found your calling," Brandon observes, his eyes warm.

I nod. I hadn't thought of it that way before, but … he's right. "I have. This is what I've always wanted to do, you know? Help shape government structure and make sure people's voices are heard. My dad wanted me to focus on public policy to support his law practice. But this feels right."

Brandon reaches across the table, giving my hand a gentle squeeze. "I'm happy for you, Carrie. You deserve this."

As I look into his kind eyes, I feel seen. It's nice to have him as a friend again.

But I should've known our chat wouldn't go unnoticed

in this small, hungry-for-gossip town. Later that night, as I crawl into bed, my phone buzzes with a text from Mia.

> **MIA**
> Saw you with Brandon today. Spill the tea, sis!

I shake my head but resist teasing Mia about making assumptions. I know she means well. But I also can't betray what Brandon shared with me all those years ago. It's probably no longer a secret, but I'm not about to make assumptions of my own and share that Brandon and I will never be more than friends because I have a vagina.

> Just catching up with an old friend.
> Nothing to spill.

But as I set my phone aside, I can't help but wonder when there *will* be something to spill about someone special. Because truly, I know I need to move on and date someone else. Alas, there aren't many someone elses to date in this town.

At least I have plenty to focus on for now.

For the first time in a long time, I drift off to sleep without thoughts of Evan haunting my dreams. Instead, my mind is filled with campaign strategies, debate formats, and the warm brown eyes of a childhood friend.

The next evening, I find myself at Greg and Joanie's place for our weekly game night. The living room is warm and cozy, a stark contrast to the frigid air outside. Mia and

Nate are cuddled up on the loveseat while Rae sprawls comfortably in an armchair. Greg and Joanie are busy in the kitchen, the clinking of glasses and the aroma of freshly popped popcorn filling the air.

Joanie's voice carries from the kitchen as we wait for her and Greg to join us. "Greg, have you given any more thought to running for town council?"

I perk up, remembering our earlier conversations on the subject. Greg emerges from the kitchen, a bowl of popcorn in his hands, his expression thoughtful.

"I have, actually," he says, setting the bowl on the coffee table. "And I think I'm going to do it."

A cheer goes up from our little group, and I can't help but feel a surge of excitement. Greg would make an excellent council member, with his deep ties to the community and genuine desire to help people. He also owns a fair amount of land here, so it feels right that he should have a say in town matters.

"What about you, Nate?" I ask, turning to my brother-in-law. "Have you reconsidered running?"

Nate shakes his head, his arm tightening around Mia. "I appreciate the thought, but I have to pass. It's our first year of marriage, and I want to focus on that." He pauses, a smile playing on his lips. "Plus, I've been considering getting re-licensed to practice medicine."

"Really?" Mia asks, surprise evident in her voice.

Nate nods. "Yeah, I think I want to go ahead and add a walk-in medical clinic to the wellness center. It's something the town could really use." Mia gives Nate a loving look that makes my chest ache.

I clear my throat. "That's fantastic, Nate," I say,

genuinely impressed. "I know you've been concerned about helping the large elderly population here. The town would definitely benefit from that."

"What about you, Mia?" Rae pipes up. "Are you thinking of throwing your hat in the ring?"

Mia laughs, shaking her head. "No way. You know the bakery keeps me busy enough as it is. I'll leave the politicking to the rest of you."

"And don't even think about asking me again," Rae adds with a grin. "I'd bet dollars to donuts Jerry carries the vote for mayor, and there's no way I'm working with that blowhard ever again."

Greg snorts, and Joanie smirks.

As we settle into our game night routine, the conversation naturally flows to the upcoming elections. The energy in the room is palpable. Everyone is excited about the changes happening in Alpine Ridge.

"I can't believe how much is going on," Joanie remarks, shuffling a deck of cards. "Between the elections, Sera's development plans, and now Nate's clinic idea ... this town is really coming alive."

I nod in agreement, feeling a warmth spread through my chest. "It's amazing, isn't it? There's so much potential here."

As I look around at my friends — my found family, besides my sister, who is actually family — I'm struck by how content I feel. The pain of my parents' rejection has faded to a dull ache, and thoughts of Evan, once so consuming, have become less frequent. Instead, I'm filled with a sense of purpose and excited about my role in shaping Alpine Ridge's future.

"You know," Mia says, catching my eye as if she can read my thoughts, "I'm really proud of you, Carrie. You've thrown yourself into this election stuff, and you're doing an amazing job."

I feel my cheeks warm at her praise. "Thanks, Mia. It feels good to be doing something I'm passionate about."

"And it shows," Greg adds. "The candidates all respect you, and the townspeople trust you to keep things fair. You've found your niche here."

I blush, brushing them off and refocusing on the game. As we get absorbed in it, the room is filled with laughter and playful competition, and I can't help but feel grateful. Alpine Ridge has given me more than just a place to stay — it's given me a home, a purpose, and a chance to be the person I've always wanted to be — something I hadn't even dared to dream about not that long ago.

The elections might keep me busy, but moments like these, surrounded by people who care about me and filled with a sense of belonging, remind me that there's so much more to life in Alpine Ridge than just politics.

Alpine Ridge's future is bright and full of possibility. And maybe so is mine.

CHAPTER FIFTEEN

EVAN

The roar of the jet engines fades as we touch down at SeaTac Airport, and I let out a long breath. After months of non-stop filming, reshoots, and living and breathing James Bond, I'm finally free. Well, as free as I can be before the publicity storm hits.

I check my phone and see a text from my manager.

RICK

Announcement set for Monday. Lay low this weekend.

A grin spreads across my face. Lay low? That's the plan. Just not in L.A. — but I didn't bother telling Rick about the detour on my way home for fear he'd try to talk me out of it.

After I collect my luggage, I secure a rental. Climbing into the driver's seat, my heart races as I punch the familiar route to Alpine Ridge into the GPS. I'm going to see Carrie. Finally.

The drive passes in a blur of anticipation and nervous

energy. What if she's moved on? What if she doesn't want to see me? I push the doubts aside, knowing torturing myself over it won't change anything, and focus on the road ahead.

It's late when I make it to Alpine Ridge. The January evening is every bit the frigid, snow-filled landscape I expected it to be. But at least the main roads are plowed, and Carrie's place is just off Main Street. As I pull up, I see lights glowing warmly in the windows, so someone is still up. Hopefully, it's Carrie because I'm not sure if Rae knows about us, and if she doesn't, I'm not sure this is how Carrie would want her to find out. There are so many things that could go wrong here.

I take a deep breath before approaching the door. And I knock, my stomach in knots.

The door swings open, and there she is. Carrie. Her eyes widen in shock, her mouth forming a perfect 'O'.

"Evan?" she breathes like she can't believe I'm real.

"Hi, Carrie," I say, drinking in the sight of her. She's even more beautiful than I remembered, her dark hair loose around her shoulders, her blue eyes bright in the porch light. She's wearing the most adorable pink and blue waffle pajama top and matching long johns.

She blinks, seeming to come back to herself. "What are you doing here?"

"I ... Can I come in?" I ask, suddenly aware that we're standing in her doorway and my wardrobe choices were based on a much warmer climate. These jeans, tee, and light jacket aren't doing anything to keep me warm.

She hesitates, then nods, stepping back to let me in.

"Sure. Rae's out anyway." Well, that's a relief. One thing that could go wrong off the plate. On to the next.

When I've barely stepped inside, the words tumble out of me. "I'm so sorry, Carrie. These past couple of months have been insane. The filming schedule was brutal, and then there were reshoots, and I was jumping from one location to another ..." I run a hand through my hair, frustrated with my own excuses. "I know I should have tried harder to call. But for what it's worth, I couldn't stop thinking about you. I flew straight here from our last reshoot in Australia."

Carrie sinks down on the couch, her expression guarded. "Evan, I …" She trails off, seemingly at a loss for words. Or perhaps she has so many she can't decide which to say first.

Hesitantly, I sit carefully beside her, unable to resist the pull between us. "I missed you," I murmur, reaching out to touch her cheek.

She leans into my touch, almost unconsciously, and that's all the encouragement I need. I close the distance between us, capturing her lips with mine.

For a moment, she's still. Then, like a switch has been flipped, she's kissing me back with a fervor that matches my own. Her hands fist in my shirt, pulling me closer.

We break apart, both breathing heavily. "I missed you too," she admits. "But Evan …" She trails off again, shaking her head — definitely too many words.

"I know," I assure her, stroking her cheek. "I know I messed up. I know we can't magically pick up where we left off. But fuck, Carrie. I thought I missed you before we kissed. Now?" I draw in a shaky breath, willing myself not to rip her clothes off right this second. I run my thumb slowly down her neck. "I didn't realize how much I *need* you."

She takes my meaning instantly and lets out a small moan. She closes her eyes. "This doesn't change anything."

I lean and kiss her, saying softly against her lips, "I know."

She rises, pulling me by the hand down the hall and into a small bedroom. Her messy queen-sized bed takes up most of the space, with barely room for a nightstand and dresser. She closes the door behind us.

"Show me how much you missed me, Evan," she breathes. Despite her bold words, she looks as nervous as I felt coming here.

Despite my near-animalistic need for her, I approach slowly, stopping so there's barely a breath's distance between us. I look down into her big blue eyes and cup her cheek before meeting her lips with mine.

I go slow, waiting for her to respond. She wraps her arms around my neck, and I pull her close, breathing in her sweet coconut scent. I deepen the kiss, pushing into her mouth with my tongue. She opens to me with another tiny groan that has me aching for her.

As I explore her mouth with mine and her body with my hands, I slide them under her and lift her gently against me. Her legs wrapped around me is like coming home. I carry her to the bed, laying her down softly under me without breaking our kiss.

Just being here with her like this is already driving me crazy. And I can't help myself anymore; I grind into her soft center. She gasps, her head tilting back with pleasure. I use the opportunity to kiss down her neck as I run my hands under her top. Only to find she's not wearing a bra.

"Fucking hell, Carrie," I groan, lifting her shirt to reveal her perfect tits. I can't help myself; I lean in and suck a nipple into my mouth. She arches against me. And I lose it. I rip the top off her, then shuck my jacket and shirt. I climb off her and kick off my shoes, then rip off my pants and boxers. I was going to do Carrie's next, but she's already there, tossing her own over the side of the bed.

And it's at that moment I realize she's completely, gloriously naked and laying there looking at me with lust-filled eyes.

And it's the next moment when I realize … I don't have a goddamn condom.

"Shit," I curse. "Do you have any protection?' She rolls over, opens the nightstand drawer, and then holds up a foil packet. Relief rolls through me. "Thank fucking God." I snatch it from her and roll it on in a blink.

"Hurry," Carrie says desperately.

A shiver of anticipation rolls down my spine, and my balls tighten. I climb between her legs, running the tip of my cock through her wet folds. She whimpers, and I can't take it. I slam into her. She gasps in surprise. I look up at her, and she nods, so I unleash.

It's been a long time since I was so turned on. Since I let go so completely. I grasp Carrie's hips as her warm, slick grip sends electricity gliding along my skin, coiling behind my cock. I'm not going to last long.

"Fuck, Carrie, I missed you so damn much," I groan. I rub my thumb in circles over her clit as I take her, pushing her toward orgasm. She cries out and tilts into me. My cock thickens as she works her hips with mine. It's too much, and I collapse on top of her, meeting her mouth with mine as I continue to pump in and out. Her lips feast on mine greedily as her nails scrape down my back. The pleasurable pain sends me ricocheting over the edge, groaning my release into her neck.

Unfortunately, I know she hasn't come yet, but thankfully I'm still hard. So, I pump faster. It doesn't take long before she's clinging harder to me, and her walls clamp down on my cock, her moans now muffled against my neck.

I finally slow to a stop and then roll off her. Our bodies are sticky with sweat, and the scent of her coconut mixed with *her* has me taking deep breaths, desperate to remember this moment forever. That was by far the most intense sex I've ever had.

Still ... I roll back toward her and trace a finger down her shoulder. "I'm not sure I did how much I missed you justice."

Carrie shoots me a wry look. "I think you did pretty well."

My lips tip up in a half-hearted smile because I can feel the skepticism radiating off of her, even now.

"Carrie ... I won't make promises I can't keep this time," I say. "But I hope you believe that I never stopped thinking about you. You were the first thing on my mind when I woke up and my last thought before I went to sleep at night. Unfortunately, almost every moment between, I had to focus on everything that was being thrown at me. I know any relationship I have isn't going to be conventional, but I hope that once things settle down, we can find a way to make this work."

"But do they ever settle down?" she asks wistfully.

My stomach sinks because it's not a question with a good answer.

"This shoot was particularly intense because of the last-minute change and everything I, and the rest of the crew, had to do to make up for that. But … no, my life while filming isn't conducive to maintaining a relationship. Still, that's only a few times a year for a month or two."

Carrie turns to me with a raised brow. "*Only*? So, for a quarter to half of the year, you're filming. And the rest? What about promoting? Don't you go on a tour of sorts for every movie?"

I press my lips together. She's not wrong.

"I do," I admit. "It would be a challenge, I know." I sigh in frustration and roll onto my back.

Carrie scoots in, molding her body to mine and laying her hand on my chest. "Just … stay and hold me. I wasn't expecting you to show up, but now that you're here, we might as well make the most of it."

I fold my fingers over hers and squeeze. I'd expected the worst, and this is far from it, so I'll take it. In any case, I'm too exhausted to do anything else as the jetlag catches up with me, and I fall asleep with Carrie in my arms.

The next morning, we agree to keep things under wraps for now because, as I suspected, she didn't tell anyone what had happened between us the last time I was here. Thankfully, I manage to sneak out without Rae catching me. I head into Ellensburg to have breakfast and pick up some more seasonally appropriate clothing, and then I text Nate to let him know I'm headed his way for a surprise visit on my way back to L.A.

He suggests we meet at the bakery, so I start the trek back.

When I get there, I enter to find Nate, Carrie, and Joanie sipping coffee at a table while Mia and Rae are working the counter.

"Evan!" Mia exclaims, rushing out from behind the counter to hug me. "This is a wonderful surprise. What are you doing here?"

I grin, hugging her back and, in turn, accepting hugs and handshakes from the others. "Just wanted to see my favorite people before things get crazy with work again."

We spend the day catching up, with Greg joining us once he's done at the community center. Through an afternoon of pastries, hearing about the happenings around town, and the general camaraderie, I'm struck by how much I've missed this group. How much I've missed feeling like just Evan, not James Bond or Hollywood star Evan Edwards.

Even though they ask about the shoot and how I'm feeling about my new venture, it's all coming from a place of interest and caring for me. It's a nice change. They're even super supportive and understanding when I admit that as excited as I am for the upcoming announcement, I'm terrified at the thought of filling such big shoes. Even if people have loved me as an action star, there's just no knowing how the public will react to my taking such a monumental role. But even just saying it out loud makes me feel better, and the conversation moves swiftly along.

That evening, we all head to Nate and Mia's for dinner. Throughout the night, I catch Carrie's eye across the room, the air between us charged with our secret. It's thrilling and maddening all at once. Eventually, the others take their leave, and it's just Nate, Mia, Carrie, and me.

Just being around Carrie today, watching her listen intently to her friends and be her sweet, supportive self, has me right back where I was when I left. Totally smitten.

Watching her laugh at something Mia says, I let out a small, happy sigh. Carrie's eyes shift to meet mine. I smile. She smiles back. And there must be something of how I'm feeling in my gaze because she blushes. Suddenly, the image of her post-orgasm-flushed face flashes through my mind, and my thoughts drift in that direction.

I meet her gaze again and flick my eyes up the stairs in invitation. She blushes harder but gives me a subtle nod.

When Mia yawns a few minutes later, Carrie seizes the opportunity. "Well, that's my cue that you guys want me to get the heck out of here," she says with a chuckle.

"Oh no, you don't have to," Mia protests. "Though I guess I should get to bed." She gives Nate a meaningful look. Carrie smirks at her sister and rises to give her a hug.

"I'll see you guys later," she says to Mia and Nate. "It was nice to see you again, Evan. Hope you have a good trip back home."

"Thanks, good seeing you too, Carrie," I reply casually. With a small wave, she's gone. Thank God for my acting skills because it was all I could do just then not to give into my caveman instincts and drag Carrie up the stairs by her hair.

"I won't be around when you leave, but I agree, it was so good to see you, Evan. I hope you come back soon," Mia says warmly, suppressing another yawn.

I rise and hug her. "Thanks, Mia. Me too."

Nate slaps me on the back. "See you in the morning, bro."

I nod and follow them upstairs, slipping into the guestroom as they continue upward. I pull out my phone to find a text from Carrie.

CARRIE

Are they upstairs yet?

With a grin, I reply.

Just. Get your gorgeous ass in here.

I grab a condom from the box I purchased this morning, and then I strip and lay on top of the comforter in the center of the bed, completely naked. It's only a couple of minutes before she slinks in the door. Her eyes widen as she sees me.

Without looking away, she kicks off her shoes. "And here I thought we were just going to talk," she says quietly with a smirk. And then she rips off her sweater and bra in one motion, followed by a similar trick with her pants and underwear. She saunters over to the bed and climbs onto the end, prowling toward me, her hair and breasts swinging. My semi goes to a full-on in an instant. She eyes it with interest.

And before I can speak, she takes me in her mouth. "Oh fuck," I whisper.

She gives one more deep suck before pulling away. "Okay," she says, uncharacteristically boldly. She takes the condom and rolls it down my length, then climbs over me, lowering herself slowly onto my dick. Every inch that slides into her tight pussy makes me harder and harder. Finally unable to take it anymore, I grab her hips and thrust up, burying myself completely inside her. The look on her face as I sink in to the hilt is pure bliss.

But despite my initial eagerness, our lovemaking is slower and more deliberate after that. She's clearly enjoying using my body to pleasure herself, and I'm happy to watch. It's more than pleasurable for me, too. Watching her ride my cock is next level.

Still, I try to pour everything I'm feeling into every touch, every kiss as our bodies work together, and we both gasp and pant quietly in pleasure. I want her to understand how much she means to me, even if I can't find the right words to fix what I've broken.

Her pace starts to stutter, the tilt of her hips becomes more erratic, and I know she's close. I hold onto her and pick up where she left off. Her gaze meets mine, and I nod.

"I've got you, baby," I assure her softly.

An almost pained look of pleasure crosses her face as she puts her hands on my chest and leans forward. I use the slight change in position to piston my hips under her. She nods her encouragement, so I continue until she shatters. Until she's strangling my cock with her pussy. Until she's biting back screams before slumping down onto my chest.

I stroke my hands up her sides and hold her against me, rolling us both over. I reposition her legs so I can keep taking her. I go slow, though, as she's still coming down from her orgasm, waiting until the slickness between her legs builds once more. Until she's writhing again under me.

The sight of her undone, with my cock sliding in and out of her … it does things to me. My chest aches with how much I want to please her. I test different depths and speeds until I find a stroke that has her gripping the bedspread and biting her lip so hard I'm afraid she'll draw blood. Her walls start to flutter around me, and the low ache behind my cock swells.

"Come for me again, Carrie," I whisper, reaching down to stroke her clit as my base need overrides my slow pace, as I start to fuck her hard and fast, chasing my own orgasm.

She whimpers and nods, her eyes rolling back in her head, lowly moaning, "Oh god, oh god, oh god."

And then she's coming, and the sensation is too much. I explode, biting the inside of my cheek to stave off the roar I want to let out. But I can't help it when I collapse on top of her and groan "Holy shit" against her skin.

With our bodies pressed together, still buried completely inside her, I know I've missed her on more than a physical level. I want so much more than sex with this woman, but I also know that this was the safest, and possibly only, way for her to allow me back in.

So after we clean up, I don't protest when she gets dressed. I don't bother, hoping it'll lure her back in, even though, deep down, I know it won't.

"I should go," she says, settling on the edge of the bed.

"Stay," I plead.

She shakes her head. "Evan, this was ... it was amazing if I'm being honest. But I can't do this." She gestures between us. "I can't let myself get attached again only to end up sitting around waiting for you to remember I exist."

Her words hit me like a punch to the gut, but I get why she feels that way. "I know it seemed like that these last couple of months, but I could never forget you exist." I sigh heavily, scrubbing my hands down my face. "I know it's not easy trying to have a relationship with me. Hell, that's where the whole playboy image came from. I didn't bother *trying* to have a relationship with anyone. I haven't even wanted to for a very long time. Not until you."

Carrie's bottom lip trembles and my heart breaks. "If this is what a relationship with you looks like, I hope you understand when I say I just can't do it. Don't get me wrong. On some level all I want is to be with you, and I waited for you far longer than I probably should have. But I can't live with waiting for you half of the time. I'm not built for that."

I nod slowly. "I know. And you deserve so much more than secret sex and broken promises." I turn my head as tears fill my eyes. "You deserve someone who is as selfless and caring as you are. Who can be here for you and give you back just as much as you have to give."

A soft, warm hand presses against my cheek, returning my gaze to hers. "You deserve that too. And I have no doubt that when you're ready to settle down, you'll have your pick of amazing women."

Now it's her turn to look away, but she's not fast enough, and I see the tears fall.

But I have nothing to say to soothe her. I can't tell her she's the only woman I want. It's unfair. Selfish. And because I care for her so deeply, I can't do that. I have to put her feelings before mine.

"I'll see you around?"

She gives me the smallest of smiles. "Yeah. Sure. See you around."

And with that, she slips out of the room and out of my life once again.

I don't sleep much despite my bone-deep exhaustion, and when I do, it's fitfully. So, I hear Mia when she comes down the stairs just after four a.m. Once she's been gone for a bit, I give up trying to sleep.

I rise and pack my bags to head back to L.A., unable to shake the feeling that I've lost something precious.

But the show must go on. In just over twenty-four hours, I'll be unveiled as the new James Bond and will have publicly achieved the dream this journey was based on.

So why doesn't that feel like enough anymore?

CHAPTER SIXTEEN

CARRIE

The crisp January air bites at my cheeks as I make my way down Main Street, my mind a whirlwind of conflicting emotions. It's been a week since Evan left, and I still can't shake the memory of his touch, his scent, the way he looked at me like I was the only person in the world.

I shake my head, trying to clear my thoughts. Just when I thought I was moving on, putting the whole affair behind me, he showed up and turned my world upside down again. His explanation for his absence made sense on some level — I can only imagine how grueling and all-consuming filming a movie must be. But at the same time, it didn't. How hard is it to send a text? To make a quick call?

I sigh, my breath forming a small cloud in the cold air. The truth is, I couldn't resist him. The moment he touched me, all my resolve crumbled. I remembered what it felt like to be in his arms, to be wanted by him, and I was powerless against it.

But now, in the harsh light of day, I'm upset with

myself for allowing it. Twice. I let myself be vulnerable and opened myself up to the possibility of more heartache. Even so, a small part of me is proud that I found the strength to close that door. To tell him that I couldn't do it anymore, couldn't live half a life waiting for him.

As I push open the door to the bakery, the warm, sweet scent of freshly baked goods envelops me, momentarily pushing my troubled thoughts aside.

"Hey, sis," Mia greets me from behind the counter, her smile not quite reaching her eyes.

I raise an eyebrow, hanging up my coat. "Hey. Everything okay?"

Mia sighs, gesturing for me to join her and Nate at one of the tables. Joanie's there, too, nursing a steaming mug of coffee.

"I just finished the financials for last year," Mia explains once I'm seated. "Business did a bit better around the incorporation approval, but now it's stalled."

My brows jump. "Well, that's no good," I murmur. "But it's winter, right? Maybe that's why?"

Mia shakes her head. "We're surrounded by ski resorts. The traffic is there. It's just not stopping in Alpine Ridge. If we can't get more people into town both permanently and as tourists, this place isn't going to last much longer."

Nate reaches out, squeezing Mia's hand. "It's not like we can force people to move or visit here, though. Maybe we can cut costs or something. We'll figure it out."

I open my mouth to suggest that with the upcoming elections, surely there's a way for us to leverage that for more traffic, but before I can speak, Joanie pipes up, a mischievous glint in her eye.

"I have an idea," she says, leaning forward. "Actually, it's something that occurred to me a while ago, but I figured I'd wait until after the elections. It could still work in our favor now, though." She pauses, presumably for dramatic effect, because Joanie is nothing if not dramatic. I smirk at the thought. "What if we get someone famous to live here? Part-time, anyway, since the ultimate plan is to make this an upscale second-home destination. It's like dominoes: get one on the hook, and other famous and rich people will want to move here. And then everyone else will want to visit to catch a glimpse of the famous people and see what all the fuss is about."

Nate's brow furrows. "Someone famous? Like who?"

Joanie gives him a disbelieving look. "Really, Nate?" She shakes her head. "I think we all know someone famous who seems to like it here."

My heart stops as I realize where she's going with this. Please, no.

"You mean Evan?" Nate asks.

"You bet your ass I do," Joanie confirms.

I wait for Nate to shoot down the idea and point out all the reasons why it wouldn't work. Surely there are reasons besides my secret desire never to be tempted by him again? But to my horror, his face lights up.

"That could actually work," he says, excitement creeping into his voice. "And it would be awesome to get to see my brother more often."

"I say go for it," Rae pipes up from behind the counter. "Old Jerry would have a heart attack if a celebrity came knocking on Alpine Ridge's door looking to stay a spell.

And if that didn't do it, the media coverage and fanfare might." She grins wickedly at the thought.

Joanie chuckles. "Is it bad that I don't even care if it pisses off some of the geriatrics in the town if it saves my bestie's business?" she adds airily.

Nate smirks. "Not in my book. We're all in at this point on breathing life into this place. There will be some people who don't like that, no matter how we go about doing it. At the end of the day, we need to do what's necessary to keep things moving in that direction, or the town won't make it."

Mia nods in agreement. "While it's good to keep in mind, I agree that we can't let the possibility that people won't like it stop us. Ultimately, though, there will be matters they have a say in and things they don't. This is definitely the latter because it's not up to them who lives here and who doesn't."

Nate nods, and I sit there, frozen, as he promises to call Evan and ask what he thinks about the idea. My mind is racing, torn between what's best for the town and what I can handle emotionally.

They're not wrong — having someone like Evan buy property here would be great for Alpine Ridge. It would put us on the map and draw attention and further investment. But can I really handle Evan having a home here? Can I handle him coming and going constantly? The many emotions I've felt from his last two visits were hard enough. The thought of experiencing that rollercoaster on a regular basis makes my stomach churn.

But as I look around at the hopeful faces of my sister, brother-in-law, and friend, I feel the familiar weight of expectation settling on my shoulders. I can't let my personal feelings wreck the town's chances of growing or deny Nate the opportunity to be closer to his brother.

So, like the people pleaser I am, I keep my mouth shut. I smile and nod as they discuss the possibilities, all while my heart aches in my chest.

As I help Mia clean up later, she bumps me with her hip, a knowing look in her eye. "You're being awfully quiet about all this," she says. "I thought you'd be excited about the prospect of Evan being around more."

I shrug, focusing intently on wiping down the counter. "It's a good idea," I say, aiming for nonchalance, as I often seem to have to do when talking about Evan. "If he goes for it, it could be really great for the town."

Mia's quiet for a moment, and I can feel her studying me. Oh no. Her Spidey senses are tingling. I can just tell. "Carrie," she says softly, "is something going on between you and Evan?"

And there it is. Curse my super perceptive big sister. For a split second, I consider telling her everything — the stolen moments, the passion, the heartache. But I can't bring myself to do it. It feels too raw, too personal, and admitting it out loud might make it all too real. Besides, it's over … right?

"No," I lie, plastering on a smile. "We're just friends. I'm worried about you and Nate, but at the same time, I'm also worried that we may pin our hopes on this only to have it not pan out. Evan's a busy guy, after all. He might not have time to deal with something like that right now."

Mia nods, seemingly satisfied with my answer. "Fair

point. And it might be too distracting to have him here while you're trying to manage the elections."

My brows jump. "I wouldn't be distracted," I protest a little too quickly. However, as soon as I say it, I realize she might not have meant me. Because it certainly could be distracting for the townsfolk, and the candidates, adding a complicating factor to a fledgling process. In any case, I can see the suspicion on Mia's face at my defensiveness.

"Mhm," she hums, clearly unconvinced. And as she turns away, I see doubt in her eyes. That makes two of us.

That night, as I lie in bed staring at the ceiling, I can't help but imagine what it would be like if Evan did have a place here. Would I be as weak as I was this last time and fall back into his arms every time he visited? Or would I have to watch him from afar, pretending that my heart doesn't skip a beat every time I see him?

I'm not sure I'd have the willpower to resist him if he's here often. And I know having to constantly deny what I feel is a recipe for heartache. Really, both scenarios are equally terrifying.

I almost wish we'd never hit it off in the first place before I admit to myself that's just not true. When we're around each other, there's something like magic between us. That's impossible to deny.

But it also feels selfish to wish he didn't have a big, shiny career that's more important than the potential between us.

Though ... maybe I should be more selfish. Or at least admit to myself that what I really wish is for it to somehow work out that Evan and I can be together while we're both able to pursue our passions in a way that doesn't interfere with that.

A girl can dream, anyway.

And as I finally drift off, I do dream of Evan. Of the tender look in his eyes when he called me "baby" while we made love. Of how it made me feel cherished and wounded in equal measure. It's, unfortunately, a feeling I'm all too familiar with. The acknowledgment causes the dream to change, and Evan's face is quickly replaced by those of my parents. In the dream, I run through darkness and rain to escape their hurled accusations and cold indifference until I'm safe, though alone. But better alone than subjecting myself to feelings of constant rejection and disappointment.

Apparently, even in my dreams, I know I need to protect myself better.

CHAPTER SEVENTEEN

EVAN

The California sun streams through my office window as I settle into my chair, ready to tackle the mountain of scripts Rick's been sending me. But before I can even open the first one, my phone buzzes. Nate's name flashes on the screen.

"Hey, bro," I answer, leaning back. "What's up?"

"Evan! Got a minute to talk?"

There's an excitement in his voice that piques my interest. "Sure, shoot."

Nate launches into an idea that has my eyebrows climbing higher with each word. A vacation home in Alpine Ridge? It's like he's read my mind. It sounds like it would help push the town in a good direction, and I've been considering a West Coast getaway, somewhere to escape the L.A. madness. This could be perfect for so many reasons.

"What do you think?" Nate asks, his enthusiasm palpable even through the phone.

I can't help but grin. "I think it's a fantastic idea. I've

been toying with the idea of a new vacation home, and having one closer would give me a solid reason to get out of L.A. more often."

As I say the words, an image of Carrie flashes through my mind. Being closer to her, having a legitimate reason to see her more often ... it's almost too good to be true. But I push the thought aside. It's not something Nate needs to know.

"Great. I was hoping you'd be into it. It'd be awesome to have you around more."

We chat for a few more minutes about development around town and all the land that's still available, and an idea forms in my mind.

"You know what? Instead of buying a place, I think I'd love to buy some land and build something custom. Maybe something like your place, but bigger."

Nate's all for it, and by the time we hang up, he's promised to send me some contacts to get started. As I set down my phone, I can't shake the feeling that this is more than a coincidence. Could this be fate nudging me in the right direction?

The next week is a whirlwind of activity. Between the Bond announcement, the many potential new opportunities it brought, and starting the process for my new home, I barely have time to breathe. But it's exhilarating. I have video conferences with an architect, a builder, and a realtor, outlining my vision for the perfect Alpine Ridge retreat.

When the property listings come in, I immediately forward them to Nate for his input. His local knowledge proves invaluable as we work together to narrow the options. Things start coalescing, and the idea takes a more definitive shape. I'm excited about that in a way I can't even explain, and I can't wait to get my feet on the ground and make this happen.

Before I know it, I'm back in Alpine Ridge, just days before the next election. I step out of my rental SUV, ready to meet with my team and make some decisions. Even if February seems to have brought even more snow than when I was here a month ago, it makes the whole town even more picturesque, if possible, and at least the 4x4 vehicle I rented can handle it.

We tour several properties before settling on the perfect site. It's one peak over from Nate's place and is secluded with stunning mountain views, yet close enough to town to not feel isolated. As the architect unfurls the preliminary sketches and walks me through the layout, I can already envision lazy mornings on the expansive deck, watching the sun rise over the peaks.

"What do you think?" the architect asks, a hint of nervousness in her voice.

I nod, impressed. "It's a great start. I love the open concept and the way you've incorporated the views. But can we make the master suite a bit larger? And maybe add a home gym?"

She jots down notes, nodding eagerly. "Absolutely. We can adjust the layout to accommodate those changes."

The builder chimes in with a ballpark cost that makes me wince internally — only because I come from a working-class family that had little to spare with three growing boys to feed — but given the millions I've made in my career, I can certainly afford it, and I have a gut feeling it'll be more than worth it.

He estimates they can break ground in late March or early April, depending on weather and permits, which, for the time being, are still being handled by the county. Apparently, that will work in our favor. I'm thrilled to hear it can start so soon, though he cautions that it'll take about six months to complete, possibly more. Though they'll definitely finish before winter sets in again.

Exhilarated by the progress, we wrap up mid-afternoon and I head to the bakery to tag up with Nate and Mia.

"Hey, you," Mia greets me with a grin. "How'd it go?"

I can't help grinning back, but I also want to wait until Nate's here to share the good news. "Oh, you know, not bad. When will Nate be done at the wellness center?"

Mia checks her watch and shrugs. "Should be any time now. Want a cup of coffee or a snack while you wait? It'll be a while before our usual Saturday night dinner party."

I raise a brow. "Dinner party?" That's got my interest. I'd been hoping to see Carrie while I was here, and that sounds like the kind of thing she'd attend.

Mia nods. "Yep. The whole gang will be there. If that's okay? You've probably had a long day."

"That's perfect," I say enthusiastically. "And you know what?" My eyes scan the glass display case, weighing the options from what's left this near to closing. "I'll take a caramel apple cupcake."

Mia gives me a mischievous grin. "Oh, I've got just the thing that'll go with that." She plates the cupcake and then goes into the back for a moment, emerging with a partially filled brandy snifter.

"Cupcakes and brandy?" I ask with a laugh.

She hands me the glass and plate. "Trust me."

I shrug and take it to the nearest table as Rae emerges from the back.

"Evan! What the hell are you doing back in this dump?" she teases.

I chuckle. "Good to see you too, Rae."

"He's here to look at properties," Mia explains.

A look of understanding passes over Rae's face. "Ah, yes, that. I didn't think he'd actually go for it, though. I'll be damned. You gonna move here, sugar?" she teases me with a wink.

"Wouldn't you like to know," I reply with a return wink. Then I bite into the cupcake … and let out an involuntary groan. The sweet, smooth caramel buttercream is balanced by a tart apple undertone, and the yellow cupcake is moist and crumbly, with more of the apple flavor — freaking perfection. "Well, if I was on the fence, I'm not anymore. I'd move here just for the cupcakes." Mia smiles knowingly and gestures at the snifter. So, I take a sip. The caramel and apple taste still on my tongue meld with the brandy to create an amazing blend of flavors that's indescribably rich, oaky, and sweet all at the same time. "Holy. Shit. I thought you were joking with this combo but *damn*."

Rae peers over the counter. "Oh yeah, that's one of my favorites of Mia's drink and cupcake pairings."

I nod as I continue to eat. "I never would've thought to put those two things together, but this is phenomenal, Mia. You could clean up in L.A. with this concept."

Mia beams under the praise. "Thanks, though I'm hoping to clean up here. It's one of my ideas to bring in more business — evening events, parties, even weddings someday."

"Bonus, it'll piss off Jerry if Mia's serving booze better than his," Rae adds.

"Jerry?" I ask, taking another bite of cupcake.

Mia shoots Rae a look. "She's kidding, I'm not trying to piss anyone off," she says, more to Rae than me. Then she turns her gaze back my way. "Jerry is … well, that's a long story. Short version, he owns the tavern and is running for mayor." Rae raises her eyebrow. "And Rae's got it out for him." Rae rolls her eyes, and Mia shrugs.

I chuckle at their antics, but Nate's arrival saves me from trying to figure out what the full deal is with this guy.

Nate slaps me on the back and takes a seat across from me. Mia scoffs. He chuckles and stands, leaning over the counter to give her a kiss. "Hey, babe."

She smiles as he pulls back. "Hey, yourself."

Nate settles back in the chair and raps his knuckles on the table. "I see Mia's converting you to her cupcake and booze ways."

I snort as I polish off the remaining brandy. "It wasn't a hard sell, that's for sure."

"So, how'd it go?" Nate asks.

I glance between him and Mia. I'm tempted to make

them wait until I can tell everyone, but I'm not that big of an asshole.

"I put in an offer on the second parcel we were talking about," I admit.

Nate lights up and holds out a fist. I bump mine against his and laugh. "That's *fantastic*," he says. "Damn. You hear that, babe? My little brother's going to have a house in Alpine Ridge." Nate runs a hand through his hair and laughs. "Man. I can't believe it."

I huff a laugh of my own. "Really? It was your idea," I point out.

He shakes his head. "Actually, it was Joanie's."

"Well, I'll have to thank her at dinner when I give her the good news."

Nate smiles. "You do that." He shakes his head again, laughing like he really can't believe it. And to be honest, I'm still a little in shock at how quickly this seems to be coming together. It just goes to show that when something is meant to be, all the doors open at the right time.

Back at Nate and Mia's that evening, I head downstairs after changing for the dinner party. I didn't know if there'd be a dress code, but I figured a fresh shirt never hurt anything. Since I only planned to be here through tomorrow morning, I didn't bring many clothes, so the navy henley I'm wearing with a nice pair of jeans will have to do.

When I get downstairs, I find Mia in the kitchen chatting with Joanie.

"Hey, Joanie," I greet her.

"Hey, stud muffin," she replies flippantly. And I'm so shocked, I don't know what to say in return.

Mia laughs and points at me. "You totally have surprised Pikachu face right now."

"I guess I just wasn't expecting that greeting," I say, a little thrown off by Joanie's forwardness.

"Oh, that's just Joanie's way of treating you like one of us," Mia explains.

"If you have another suggestion, I'm all ears," Joanie offers, batting her eyelashes.

Mia rolls her eyes. "Greg, come handle your woman. She's hitting on Nate's brother."

Joanie cackles as Greg appears from the direction of the living room. "Hey, Evan, good to see you," he says. Then, to Joanie, "Baby, we've talked about this. Ask first before assigning pet names."

Joanie pouts. "Fine," she replies with a sigh. "But I did say I was open to suggestion."

Greg smirks at her. Mia gives me a look. "Well, now that Joanie's flirted shamelessly with you, you're really part of the gang. Hope you're okay with being constantly teased and a total lack of regard for personal privacy," she says drily. "And that's just Joanie."

Greg fails to stifle his laugh and Joanie smacks him on the chest teasingly. "You know you love it."

He shakes his head, still laughing. "Not rising to that bait. Come on." He pulls her behind him toward the living room.

"Wow. So, I guess my trial period is up," I joke to Mia after they're gone. "Good to know."

Mia starts to reply, but a voice from the hall cuts over her.

"Hey, Mia, we're here."

And I'd know that voice anywhere. Carrie. I stand up taller as she walks into the kitchen. All long, wavy dark brown hair, big blue eyes, and a snug sweater that matches the pre-dawn night sky shade of her irises. And then a blond dude trails in behind her. He's about six inches shorter than me but he's broad-chested and fit, and he's standing way too close to Carrie for my liking.

I'm so distracted by him that I don't notice the silence that's fallen for a moment. I look back at Carrie to find her staring at me with wide eyes, her mouth popped open in surprise.

"Evan. What are you doing here?" I don't miss the note of panic in her voice. "I mean ... hey. Good to see you." She pauses. "What are you doing here?"

Mia and the blond guy exchange a confused look.

I extend my hand toward him, ignoring Carrie's question. "Hi, I'm Evan, Nate's brother. And you are?"

The guy gives Carrie a look before he reaches his hand out to take mine and meets my gaze for the duration of our brief handshake. "I'm Brandon, a friend of Carrie's." He studies me for a moment. "You look familiar. Have we met before?"

Carrie lets out a tinkling laugh laced with nervous energy. "Excuse us for a moment," she says, hauling Brandon behind her toward the dining room.

My heart is thudding in my chest, but I do my best to casually turn to Mia and ask, "New boyfriend?"

Mia shrugs. "Supposedly, they really are just friends.

But they were inseparable for a few summers when we were younger, and since he returned to town a couple of months back, they've been spending a lot of time together." She scrutinizes me, and I hold tight to my blank expression.

"Well, good for her either way," I respond. Joanie saunters back into the kitchen. "Hey, Legs, have you given Carrie's new boyfriend a nickname yet?"

Joanie gives me a feline grin. "Legs. I like it." I smirk back at her. She's short, but she does have shapely, long legs for her frame, and despite my initial astonishment, I'm happy to show her I'm all right with a little harmless flirting. And I'm also totally fishing for information on this dude. Joanie turns to Mia. "Carrie has a new boyfriend?"

Mia doesn't look at her, her gaze still firmly locked on me. "He means Brandon."

Joanie pulls a face. "Oh, him. Nope. Only met him a couple of times." She grabs a handful of almonds from the bowl on the counter and pops one in her mouth. "When's dinner? I'm starving."

Mia rolls her eyes. "We can eat when Rae gets here, Jo."

"Damn that woman and her fashionable lateness," Joanie grumbles, heading back toward the living room.

Mia finally breaks her gaze and steps to peek into the dining room. She turns back to me and folds her arms over her chest. "I get the sense Carrie's going to hide in there until you leave the kitchen," Mia says quietly. Pointedly.

I force my brow into a confused furrow. "Did I do something wrong?"

Mia narrows her eyes and shakes her head.

She's totally onto me.

"Oookay. If I'm not in trouble, is there anything I can do to help with dinner?" I offer.

"Thanks, but I've —"

"Helloooo," a female voice calls from the front of the house.

"Fucking finally!" I hear Joanie exclaim.

Mia and I share a look before we burst into laughter.

When we finally sit down and enjoy the amazing Beef Wellington, garlic mashed potatoes, and roasted Brussels sprouts Mia prepared, the conversation quickly turns to the upcoming election.

"So, Greg," I say, reaching for the mashed potatoes, "how are you feeling about your chances for town council?"

Greg grins, a mix of excitement and nervousness on his face. "Pretty good, I think. But ask me again after the votes are counted."

Joanie nudges him playfully. "He's being modest. He's got this in the bag."

"And Brandon, I hear you're also running for town council?" I prompt with a raised eyebrow.

Brandon nods, setting down the glass of wine he'd just sipped from. "I am. I was traveling a lot for work, but my contract was up, and I thought it would be a great opportunity to settle down a bit and get behind making this place even better."

Carrie, who is sitting beside him, pats his hand.

"Brandon is a professional photographer. He was working for an international aid organization and did relief work for them, too."

Fuck. He's talented and a do-gooder. Most women would probably go for a movie star first, but I know Carrie well enough to know that that would tug on her big, soft heart.

"How nice," I say blandly. "So, you have family here?"

"Yes, my grandfather. Who's getting on in years, too, so it'll give me the opportunity to be here when he needs me," Brandon replies.

I internalize a groan. Well, this just keeps getting better and better.

"How's John doing, by the way?" Mia asks.

"Still healthy as a horse," Brandon assures her. "He's all up in arms over the upcoming election. He has very strong opinions on how things should be run."

Carrie rolls her eyes. "Doesn't everyone?"

I chuckle and use the opportunity to speak to her. "Townsfolk giving you a hard time, Carrie?"

Her eyes flit to mine ever so briefly before she looks down to play with the food on her plate. "It's challenging, but I know what I signed up for."

"Don't let Ms. Modest over there fool you," Rae breaks in. "I've gone to a couple of the debates, and she handles it like a pro. Sweet as pie, and she's got them all wrapped around her little finger."

Carrie blushes crimson. "I'm just focused on making sure everything runs smoothly and fairly." Brandon reaches over and squeezes her hand. She smiles at him gratefully.

I nod along with everyone else, fighting the urge to round the table and haul her into my arms. To claim her, mark my territory, in case this Brandon guy thinks he has any sort of a chance with her. Being this close to her, yet having to maintain this façade of casual friendship, is harder than I expected. But I know she wants to keep things platonic, so I'll do my best to respect that. Because she's not mine, and I have only myself to blame for that.

"So, you missed out on the news earlier, Carrie," Mia says a little too casually. "Evan just put in an offer on some land in town. Operation Bring Someone Famous to Alpine Ridge is full speed ahead."

Carrie looks up in shock, first at her sister, then at me. And I can practically see the progression of emotions behind her eyes: from shock to horror, to the realization that she needs to not show how upset she is by the news, to having to put on a mask of fake enthusiasm.

And I'm pretty sure Mia sees it, too.

"That's ... wow. How fantastic for the town," Carrie says, her voice abnormally high. "And for you, Evan. I'm ... so ... happy for you." She gives me the saddest excuse for a smile.

My heart breaks a little, and suddenly, I have the urge to contact the realtor and call this whole thing off because Carrie is obviously not okay.

"Evan Edwards!" Brandon exclaims, drawing everyone's attention. "I knew I recognized you. Holy shit!"

Joanie rolls her eyes. "You're a little late to the 'Nate's

brother is a movie star' party there, Brandon." Her sarcasm is unmissable.

I'm starting to really like Joanie.

"Am I?" Brandon asks cluelessly. He turns to Carrie. "A little heads up would've been nice."

Carrie gives a feeble shrug. "Sorry? I've had a lot on my mind lately, and I didn't exactly know he'd be here tonight." Carrie shoots Mia a look.

"Well, this is awkward as ass, and I'm pretty sure everyone's done eating. How about we move on to the next portion of the evening?" Joanie suggests abruptly.

I chuckle appreciatively as everyone rises, and we all help Mia clear the table. Once that's done, we head into the living room, trying to decide on a game to play.

"Well, we have a couple of newer members to the group, so why don't we just take turns asking icebreakers?" Rae suggests.

Joanie nods. "Ooh, I like that idea."

Greg snorts. "Nothing too personal, babe."

"Spoilsport," she grumbles jokingly.

"I think that's a great idea," Mia agrees. "We each take turns asking, and everyone has to answer." There are nods and sounds of agreement all around. "All right, I'll go first. Sweet or salty? I think we all know what I'd pick."

"Ditto here, sweet all the way," Rae says.

Joanie smirks. "You bakery babes would choose sweet. Me? I pick salty."

Nate and Greg both concur.

"That's a hard one, but I'm going with salty," Brandon says thoughtfully.

"I'd pick sweet every time," I offer, my eyes flicking to Carrie. She looks up and meets my gaze.

"Me too," she says softly.

I don't miss Joanie shooting Mia a look. I break my gaze from Carrie, determined to stop giving her loaded looks before *everybody* knows there's something between us. Or there was, anyway.

"Okay, I've got one," Nate says, completely oblivious to the furtive glances happening around him. "What skill or trait do you think everyone should have? For me, it'd be critical thinking. It's fundamental to self-improvement and practically every profession there is." I smile at my serious, brainy big brother. He may not practice medicine anymore — for now anyway — but he still manages to sound like a doctor.

"Oooh, that's a good one," Greg says.

"Confidence," Joanie adds immediately. Confidently. Mia smirks at her.

"I was going to say basic first aid," Greg chuckles, "but that's better."

"Resiliency," Mia says. "You'll never achieve anything if you always give up."

Rae raises her hand. "Communication. There are eight billion people in this world. You won't get far if you don't know how to talk to them."

"And yet, without creativity, what use is communication?" I interject. "Otherwise, we'd all go around saying and doing the same things, thinking the same way."

"Good point," Rae concedes with a grin.

"Empathy," Carrie says quietly. "Because you can't have creativity or real communication without it."

Brandon looks at her with such deep admiration that it makes me grind my teeth. He then adds, "I say the ability to be grateful. I've seen a lot of the world through my work, and most people have no idea how good they have it. Life has little meaning without gratitude and understanding how blessed we are."

As one, Carrie, Mia, and Rae sigh. The expressions on their faces remind me of the heart-eyed emoji. Greg and Nate smirk at each other. For my part, I fight not to roll my eyes.

"Yeah, yeah, yeah, enough of this heavy shit," Joanie says. "I want to know everyone's hidden talent."

She doesn't add anything, and Greg gives her a look. "Aren't you going to say yours?" he prompts.

Mia pinches the bridge of her nose. "I'm sure she didn't for a reason. You did tell her not to get too personal."

Joanie grins. "My lovely bestie speaks the truth." Then she leans in and stage-whispers to Greg, "I'll show you later."

"I can't unhear that," Nate mutters, and we all laugh.

"What's yours, Mountain Man?" Joanie asks Greg.

He raises an eyebrow. "I can talk to dogs."

Joanie's brows pull together. "Like … Doctor Dolittle?"

Greg laughs. "No. They just … get me. And I get them." He shrugs.

"Oh, we're getting a dog so you can show me this trick."

Greg looks intrigued.

"I can fold napkins," Mia offers. Everyone, myself included, gives her a questioning look. She waves her hands in the air, miming folding. "Like … into pretty things. Flowers, birds, that sort of thing. I haven't done it in a long time, though. But I guess now I'm obligated to bust it out for the next dinner party."

"Man, even I didn't know that," Carrie admits. "Mine is kind of lame. I can solve Sudokus like nobody's business. I smash records on every app I've been able to find."

I can't help grinning at her cute, nerdy admission. Figures though. She's a smart woman.

"I can speed read," Nate says, though that's no surprise to me. "I learned to survive medical school."

"I'm a polyglot. I speak four languages," Brandon says. Because, of course, he does.

"Ooh, which ones?" Rae asks.

"English, of course, and Spanish, French, and Swahili."

"Impressive," Carrie says, looking at him all-too-starry-eyed. He returns her look with a gentle smile.

I'm going to need new teeth at this rate.

"Oh, I know Rae's," Joanie exclaims.

Rae waves her hand dismissively. "Everyone knows I can sing, Jo. Though unless you count being able to touch my tongue to my nose, I can't say I have any actual hidden talents."

We all chuckle, but Nate says to me, "I'm going to out you, Ev, because we're all friends here." And then to everyone else, "Evan sings, too."

I scrunch my face and drop my head in my hands, groaning. "Why you gotta sell me out like that, Nathan?" I look up and sigh dramatically.

Rae perks up. "You sing? What style?"

I shrug. "Anything? I did musicals in high school, but I'll sing ballads, classics, pop … you name it."

"Done any duets?" she asks with a mischievous grin.

I can't help but return it. "No, but I wouldn't say no to doing one." I give her an assessing look. She looks to be in her mid-to-late forties, so I know just the song to tempt her. "You look like a woman who'd appreciate An Officer and a Gentleman." Rae grins, and I know I've got her.

"What's going on here?" Joanie murmurs to Greg.

"I think they're about to —" Rae sings the opening line to "Up Where We Belong," and Mia nods. "Yep. They're going to sing."

I rise and join Rae, holding her hand while waiting for my cue. And soon, we're singing together, our voices blending beautifully, bouncing off the high ceilings of Nate and Mia's living room. It feels good to belt out a song again. I usually save it for the shower, but there's nothing like performing for a live audience.

And everyone stares at us, mouths dropped open. Carrie's most of all, and I can't help giving her a wink. What can I say? I live for the limelight. And having Carrie's eyes on me is more satisfying than anything I've experienced in a long time.

Even filming a James Bond movie.

As the song winds down, the realization hits me like a ton of bricks. And I know I can't give up on Carrie. Not yet. Even if I have to play the role of her friend for a while, the show's not over yet. Not by a long shot.

CHAPTER EIGHTEEN

CARRIE

As the last notes of "Up Where We Belong" fade away, I realize my mouth is hanging open. I quickly snap it shut, but I can't shake the awe that's coursing through me. Who knew Evan could sing like that? I certainly didn't. And when he leans in to kiss Rae on the cheek after sharing such a romantic ballad duet with her ... a surge of emotions I don't want to feel crashes over me.

Jealousy. Longing. Regret.

I push them down, reminding myself that Evan and I agreed to just be friends. But as the evening progresses, I find myself struggling more and more. It's not just his sudden reappearance or the bombshell announcement that he's buying property in Alpine Ridge. It's how impossibly hard it is to be in the same room as him and pretend we've only ever been friends.

And I know I'm doing a terrible job of it.

Every time our eyes meet, I feel a jolt of electricity. When he laughs at something Joanie says, I have to fight the urge to stare at how his eyes crinkle at the corners.

And don't even get me started on how my body reacts when he casually stretches, his shirt riding up just enough to reveal a sliver of toned abs.

I'm a bundle of nerves by the time the evening winds down. I practically jump at the chance to walk Brandon out to his car, desperate for a moment to collect myself.

The cool night air is a welcome relief as we step outside. Brandon is quiet for a moment, then turns to me with a serious expression.

"Carrie, what's going on between you and Evan?"

I freeze, my heart pounding. Am I that transparent? I consider lying, but something in Brandon's eyes tells me he'd see right through it. With a sigh, I decide to come clean.

"We had a ... thing," I admit, keeping my voice low. "But it's over now. And nobody else can know about it, okay?"

Brandon nods slowly. "Why is it over?"

I let out a humorless laugh. "Because I can't handle a movie star's lifestyle. The crazy schedule, the fans, the fact that his entire life is in L.A. ... it's just not meant to be."

He studies me for a long moment. "That's not what I saw tonight," he says gently. "Not the way he was looking at you."

My chest tightens at his words, but I shake my head. "It doesn't matter. We agreed to just be friends."

Brandon doesn't look convinced, but he doesn't push it. He hugs me before getting into his car, leaving me alone with my swirling thoughts.

Taking a deep breath, I head back inside, determined to

have a word with my sister. I find Mia cleaning up the last of the dishes in the kitchen.

"Why didn't you tell me Evan would be here?" I demand, my voice sharper than I intended.

Mia turns to face me, her expression a mix of exasperation and concern. "Carrie, I think we both know there's something going on between you two. It would have really helped to know that before I threw you together at a dinner party."

I deflate, the fight going out of me. "I'm sorry," I mumble. "You're right. I should have told you."

With a sigh, I lean against the counter and come clean ... well, mostly. I tell her about hooking up with Evan during her honeymoon, and then again when he showed up after New Year's. But I keep it vague, making it sound like it was all physical, leaving out the depth of emotions involved.

"But that was the last time," I assure her. "We agreed to just be friends going forward. It'll just be awkward for a bit while we try to forget what each other looks like naked."

Mia raises an eyebrow, clearly not buying it. "Care-bear ..."

"Please don't tell anyone else," I plead. "Not even Nate. I don't want to cause trouble, and Evan fits in well with everyone. I don't want him to feel uncomfortable when he's here, even if it probably won't be that often."

Mia sighs but nods. "Fine, I won't say anything. But Carrie, you weren't exactly subtle tonight. I'm pretty sure at least Joanie knows something's up."

I groan, covering my face with my hands. "I'll deal

with it if people figure it out. I promise I'll try to do a better job of being cool around Evan. It'll be easier going forward, I think. This was the first time I'd seen him since we agreed to be friends."

Before Mia can respond, Rae pops her head into the kitchen. "Ready to head home, Carrie?"

I nod, grateful for the interruption. "Yeah, just give me a minute."

As I gather my things, I run into Evan in the hallway. My heart flips, but I force myself to stay calm.

"Goodnight, Evan," I say, aiming for casual. "It was good to see you."

He smiles, and it's so warm and genuine that it makes my knees weak. "Goodnight, Carrie. Take care."

And that's it. He's so chill, so effortlessly casual about it all. As I follow Rae out to the car, I feel a mix of relief and ... disappointment? No, I can't let myself go there.

I climb into the passenger seat, my mind racing. I can do this. I can be Evan's friend. I can pretend I didn't get a taste of everything I ever wanted.

I have to.

Because the alternative — admitting how much I still want him, how much it hurts to see him and not be with him — is too painful to contemplate.

As Rae starts the car and pulls away from Nate and Mia's house, I close my eyes and take a deep breath. One day at a time, I tell myself. That's all I can do.

Thankfully, with the primary election on Tuesday, I have plenty to keep me busy. After that, there's round two of helping the chosen candidates, research, debates, and everything in between, and then the final election at the end of April.

I brighten at the thought. I only committed to managing the elections. So, if the situation with Evan being in and out of town becomes untenable, I only have to ride it out for a few more months. I'm not a prisoner here, after all.

Except I'm far from it. In fact, Alpine Ridge feels more like home than ever. But with so much change, who knows how I'll feel in the future?

I shake my head, refocusing on my new mantra.

One day at a time.

CHAPTER NINETEEN

EVAN

The Los Angeles sun beats down on me as I step out of my Audi, but it doesn't lift my spirits like the Alpine Ridge air. I miss the crisp mountain breeze and the scent of pine, and most of all, I miss Carrie.

I shake my head, trying to clear my thoughts as I enter my sleek, modern house. Despite the expensive furniture and state-of-the-art entertainment system, it feels empty. At least I have good news waiting for me — an email confirming that the permits for my Alpine Ridge property have gone through. Now, it's just a waiting game to see when the weather will allow construction to begin.

My phone buzzes, and I groan when I see it's Rick, my agent. "Evan, my man!" he practically shouts when I answer. "I've got great news. We're going to capitalize on this Bond buzz and set you up with a little publicity boost for your movie premiere next month."

I know that tone. He uses it when he's about to suggest something I'll hate. "What did you have in mind?" I ask warily.

"I've set up a little arrangement with Kelly Cook. You know, from that hit sitcom? She's looking for a profile boost, too. It's a win-win!"

My stomach sinks. A fake relationship. I hate this part of the business, the artifice, the manipulation. But Rick's never steered me wrong before, and he knows the industry better than anyone. "Fine," I sigh. "Set it up."

The next day, I find myself at a trendy café, waiting to meet Kelly at a semi-private booth in the back. She sweeps in, all long blond hair, perfectly round fake tits, and designer sunglasses, looking every inch the Hollywood starlet. As she air-kisses my cheek, I catch a whiff of her overpowering perfume and can't help but think of how much I prefer Carrie's subtle coconut scent.

"Evan, darling," Kelly purrs, sliding into the seat across from me. "I'm so excited about this. We're going to be the hottest couple in Hollywood!"

I force a smile, already exhausted by her enthusiasm. We chat about our careers and our "relationship" strategy, and I find myself zoning out as she rambles about her latest juice cleanse and the benefits of crystal therapy.

As our meeting winds down, Kelly leans in, her voice dropping to a sultry whisper. "We could make this arrangement even more ... mutually beneficial if you're interested." Her hand slides across the table, fingers brushing mine.

I pull back, keeping my tone light but firm. "I appreciate the offer, Kelly, but I think it's best to keep this strictly professional."

She shrugs, seemingly unbothered. "Your loss. But the offer stands if you change your mind."

Over the next two weeks, Rick and Kelly's agent, Sarah, orchestrate a series of "dates" for us. We're photographed leaving restaurants, attending gallery openings, and even taking a "romantic" stroll on the beach. Each outing feels more forced and fake than the last.

As I pose for another "candid" shot, Kelly's arm wrapped around my waist, a wave of disgust washes over me. This isn't me, and this isn't what I want my career to be about.

That night, I find myself staring at my phone, Carrie's number pulled up on the screen. I want to call her, to hear her voice, to tell her about this ridiculous charade I'm caught up in, just in case she's paying attention and is in any way hurt by it. But I don't. I can't. Because I know if I hear her voice, I might just throw it all away and run back to Alpine Ridge. Even if that's what I want, it's not what Carrie wants.

Instead, I pull up the plans for my new house, losing myself in thoughts of the life I could have there — a life with real connections and genuine relationships, a life with Carrie in it.

It's not lost on me that I've suddenly got more bandwidth to think about her and plan a new life close to her now that she no longer wants that. But if I'm persistent and demonstrate that I can show up, maybe she'll see that and change her mind.

But that's sure as hell not going to happen while I'm fake dating Sitcom Barbie. As I fall asleep, I make a silent promise to myself. This fake relationship will be over when the press tour for my upcoming movie is over, and it will be my last. From now on, I'm going to do things my way, industry expectations be damned, because life's too short for fake smiles and empty embraces.

I want the real thing and know where and with whom I can find it. It's just a matter of getting her to find her way back to it, too.

CHAPTER TWENTY

CARRIE

The crisp spring air carries the scent of blooming wildflowers. It's early April, and Alpine Ridge is finally shaking off the last vestiges of winter. The town seems to be coming alive, not just with the changing seasons but with the buzz of the upcoming election.

I can't help but smile as I pass by the numerous campaign posters plastered on storefronts and lamp posts. The race for mayor has narrowed down to two primary candidates: Jerry, the crusty tavern owner, and Arthur Burton, another of the town's older residents. Despite being a decade older than Jerry, Arthur is surprisingly sprightly and far less grumpy, though he does have a tendency towards pomposity.

I'll never admit it out loud, but I'm secretly rooting for Arthur, partly out of loyalty to Rae, who's made no secret of her dislike for Jerry. I also believe Arthur has a better vision for Alpine Ridge's future.

As for the town council, we have about twenty people

vying for the seven available spots. Greg and Brandon made it through the initial cut, which doesn't surprise me. They're both passionate about the town and have a lot to offer.

I've also been spending a lot of time with Brandon lately. Some of that is due to the election — he often seeks my advice on campaign strategies — and genuinely enjoying his company. But if I'm honest with myself, it's also because I've been avoiding everyone else. I'm afraid that if I spend too much time with them, I might let something slip about Evan.

Evan. Just thinking his name sends a pang through my chest. I've been trying not to dwell on it, but the truth is, I've been upset ever since I found out he immediately jumped into bed with one of the hottest actresses in Hollywood right after leaving Alpine Ridge. I know I was the one who ended things, but I can't help feeling hurt that I was so easy to move on from.

I shake my head, trying to clear my thoughts. I need to focus on my work and on the election. That's what's important right now.

As I reach the community center, where I've set up a makeshift election headquarters, I'm greeted by the sight of Brandon poring over some polling data.

"Morning, Carrie," he says, looking up with a warm smile. "Ready for another exciting day in the world of small-town politics?"

I laugh, feeling some of the tension ease from my shoulders. "Always. What've we got on the agenda today?"

As Brandon fills me in on the day's schedule, I can't help but feel a surge of excitement. Despite the complications in my personal life, I'm truly passionate about what I'm doing here. In fact, I've been thinking more and more about my future in Alpine Ridge.

What I really want is to work for the town as a political planner. I know I have to wait until the town government is established, but given all the work I've done and the good relationships I've built with the candidates, I'm hopeful I can convince them of my worth in helping structure the town government and planning over the next few years.

The idea is exhilarating, and the thought of a new life where I'm more independent and career-oriented is exactly what I need to stay focused on myself and my goals. And despite everything, I love Alpine Ridge. The complicating factor of Evan building a home here ... well, that's something I'll deal with if and when I have to.

"Earth to Carrie," Brandon's voice breaks through my reverie. "Are you okay? You seemed lost in thought there for a minute."

I smile, shaking off the last of my musings. "Sorry, just thinking about the future. There's so much potential here, you know?"

Brandon nods, his eyes lighting up. "I know exactly what you mean. That's why I came back. Alpine Ridge is on the cusp of something great, and I want to be part of shaping that future."

As we dive into our work for the day, I feel a renewed sense of purpose. My heart might still be healing, but my mind is clear. I have goals, dreams, and a town full of people counting on me.

Evan Edwards and his Hollywood drama can take a backseat. I have an election to run and a future to plan. And for the first time in a long time, I'm genuinely excited about what that future might hold.

CHAPTER TWENTY-ONE

EVAN

The fresh mountain air fills my lungs as I step out of my rental car, a welcome change from the smog-filled Los Angeles atmosphere I've left behind. Alpine Ridge stretches before me, the snow-capped peaks in the distance a stunning backdrop to the budding spring foliage.

I'm here for a final walk-through of my property with the architect and builder before construction begins, but my heart races with anticipation for an entirely different reason. Carrie. The thought of seeing her again, even if just for a moment, sends a thrill through me.

The walk-through goes smoothly. As I stand on what will soon be my deck, overlooking the breathtaking vista, I can almost picture a future here — a future with Carrie by my side. But first, I need to convince her to give us another chance. I know I should keep playing it cool, but something is telling me to try again one more time.

After wrapping up with the building team, I make my way into town. I spot Carrie leaving the community center, her arms full of what looks like campaign materials. Taking a deep breath, I approach her.

"Hey, Carrie," I call out, trying to keep my voice casual.

She looks up, surprise flashing across her face before she schools her features into a neutral expression. "Evan. I didn't know you were in town."

"Just got in," I explain, falling into step beside her. "Final walk-through of the property before construction starts."

She nods, not quite meeting my eyes. "That's great. I'm sure you're excited."

We walk in silence for a moment, the tension between us palpable. Finally, I can't take it anymore. "Carrie, I was hoping we could talk. About us."

She stops abruptly and turns to face me. "Evan, there is no 'us.' We agreed to be friends, remember?"

"I know, but ..." I take a deep breath, steeling myself. "I can't stop thinking about you."

Carrie's eyes flash with something — hurt? Anger? — before she shakes her head. "I'm not someone you can use for fun whenever you come to town, Evan. And I'm sure your famous actress girlfriend wouldn't appreciate that either."

My heart sinks as I realize she's seen the tabloid photos with Kelly. "It's not what you think it is," I explain quickly. "What we had though, Carrie ... what we could have ... it's real."

She laughs, but it's a hollow sound. "Real? You left town and immediately hooked up with one of the hottest actresses in Hollywood. How does that make this —" she gestures between us "— real?"

I run a hand through my hair, frustrated. "That's not ..." I step closer and drop my voice. "My relationship with her is fake, Carrie. We're not really together. It's all a publicity stunt to boost both of our careers." Carrie's mouth drops open in shock, but she still steps back. I run a hand through my hair, frustrated. "I'm trying to show you I can be more accessible and willing to make changes. But I understand if you don't want someone who can't always be here."

Carrie's expression softens slightly, but she still shakes her head. "Evan, I appreciate what you're trying to do. But it's not just that. I can't be with someone whose life is so ... public. So unpredictable. I need stability and consistency. And let's face it, you can't offer either."

As much as her words sting, I can't help but feel a surge of pride. This is the Carrie I know she wants to be — strong, assertive, not settling for less than she deserves. "I understand," I say softly. "And I'm proud of you, you know. For standing up for yourself. I know that's not always easy for you."

A flicker of surprise crosses her face, followed by a small smile. "Thanks. I'm ... working on it."

We stand there for a moment, the weight of what could have been hanging between us. Finally, I nod, taking a step back. "Well, I should let you get back to work. But I meant what I said about being friends. I hope that's still on the table."

Carrie nods, her smile a little more genuine now. "Of course. Friends."

As I watch her walk away, my heart aches with the loss of what could have been. But I remind myself that this isn't the end. I'm building a home here. There's still time to show Carrie that I can be the man she needs, the man who deserves her.

For now, though, I'll respect her wishes. I'll be her friend. And I'll keep hoping that someday, she'll decide what's between us is worth dealing with the challenges. Challenges I have no doubt we could overcome together. If she's willing.

That's the part that worries me because she's been consistently clear that my life — the crazy schedule and the unrelenting media attention — is a dealbreaker for her.

As I stand in the middle of the street alone, a thought occurs to me that I've never considered before. Asking Carrie to bend is not only unfair to her, but it's also selfish in that it means I don't have to.

So maybe the real question is: How much am *I* willing to give up to be with *her*?

My stomach sinks because I know I'm not ready to walk away from the industry. Not now that I've achieved the success I've been striving for all these years — a success I'd like to maintain for at least a few more.

Fuck.

It's not Carrie that needs to change her mind. It's me.

Maybe she was right all along, and this just wasn't meant to be. At least, not right now.

I suddenly understand the phrase "timing is everything" all too well.

And our timing, Carrie and me? Complete shit.

I trudge back to my rental car, shoulders down, heart in

my shoes. I set out to convince Carrie to give me a chance. But I realized that I'm the one keeping us from being together. And I have no fucking clue what to do with that right now.

CHAPTER TWENTY-TWO

CARRIE

As I walk away from Evan, a mix of emotions swirls inside me. His visit has left me with a lot to process, as usual. I've seen more of him lately than I expected, and I can't deny how drawn I feel to him every time he reappears.

I had convinced myself that Evan was happy with his new blonde bombshell Hollywood girlfriend and that his increased presence in Alpine Ridge had nothing to do with me. But his words today ... they've shaken up my world. The realization that Evan still thinks about me as much as I do him, that he hasn't really moved on as I thought, is both comforting and unsettling.

Still, it's also made me realize I know myself better now. I'm already prone to insecurity, and trying to be in a relationship with someone whose availability changes like the wind truly isn't going to work for me, no matter how much my heart might wish otherwise. And I refuse to let myself be a doormat for anyone ever again.

I'll happily give my heart and soul to someone when

they've shown me they'll cherish them. Unfortunately, Evan can't love me the way I deserve to be loved. And I'm not going to settle for less than I deserve. Not anymore.

So, with a deep breath, I refocus on what I need to think about right now: the elections. There's still so much work to be done. While I have my own opinions and desires regarding who runs the town, I'm determined to remain impartial until all the townspeople have had their say. It's what they deserve and what I need to do to prove myself in this role.

As April rolls on, the excitement in Alpine Ridge builds to a fever pitch. Finally, election day arrives, and the results are in: Arthur Burton is voted mayor, with Greg, Brandon, and five others elected to the town council. Rae, for one, is beyond ecstatic, though most of the town seems to be in a celebratory mood.

To that end, Greg has even thrown a post-election bash at the community center. Streamers and balloons festoon the walls, and the air is filled with laughter, the clinking of glasses, and upbeat pop music on low in the background. Everyone is congratulating the winners, and half of the town seems to have turned up to celebrate. As I survey the room, pride swells in my chest. I've been working towards this, and it's finally here.

"May I have this dance?" Brandon's voice breaks through my reverie. I turn to see him holding out his hand, a warm smile on his face.

"Absolutely," I grin, taking his hand and letting him lead me to the makeshift dance floor.

As we playfully dance to the music, I can't help but

ask, "Are you happy, Brandon? With how everything turned out?"

He nods, his eyes twinkling. "Incredibly. But what about you? Obviously, I see a future here in Alpine Ridge, but what kind of future do you see?"

I consider his question. "I see potential. For the town, for myself." And despite the truth of those words, my heart aches for more than that.

It must show on my face because he asks slyly, "And where does Evan fit in?"

I grimace. "He doesn't. I wanted him to, and you weren't wrong; he still has feelings for me. But we're living separate lives. It's just not in the cards." I sigh heavily despite the liveliness around me. "What about you? Is there anyone special you've left behind in your travels that you're pining for?"

Brandon chuckles. "Not really. My work wasn't conducive to relationships, so it's been hookups for a while. Which was fine, but it's part of why I wanted to settle down. To find someone."

I don't miss the parallels to Evan's situation. It must show on my face because Brandon raises an eyebrow.

"What?" he asks.

I shrug. "It's just ..." I trail off, deciding against discussing Evan further. "I don't know. Why settle here, then? Don't you think finding someone in Alpine Ridge might be hard? It's not exactly a bustling metropolis."

He smiles enigmatically. "You never know. The doors opened in this direction, so I walked through them. I have faith that it will lead me where I need to be. Maybe a nice guy will move into town someday, and we'll hit it off, fall in love, and build a life together."

His words strike a chord in me, and I find myself hanging on every word as he continues.

"Sometimes you have to take risks, Carrie. Pay attention to the doors that open, do a gut check whether it's what you want, and if it is, walk through with confidence. Maybe it'll be *the* door, or maybe it'll just be *a* door on the path you're supposed to walk. But you'll never know unless you try."

As the song ends, he pulls me into a quick hug, kissing the top of my head. It's reassuring, and I'm grateful for his advice and friendship.

Brandon's words echo in my mind when we take a break to grab drinks. Could it really be that simple?

It turns out he may have been on to something after all, when the following week, as I'm packing up my makeshift office in the community center, a knock on the door frame startles me. I look up to see Arthur Burton, our newly elected mayor, standing there with a smile.

"Ms. Anderson," he begins, "I was hoping we could talk about your future here in Alpine Ridge."

"Of course, come in," I offer, gesturing to a chair next to the tiny desk I've been using. "But please, call me Carrie."

"And you can call me Art," he returns as he settles in. "Now about that future …"

My heart races as he outlines the position he wants to

create: a political planner for the town. It's everything I've been working towards, everything I want.

Brandon's words come back to me as I listen to him speak. A door is opening. All I have to do is walk through it.

"So, what do you think, Carrie? Would you like to continue doing the fine work you've been doing so far? While I can't offer concrete terms until the financials are established, I plan to compensate you well. You've been invaluable throughout the election process, and I have no doubt your expertise will be crucial to establishing Alpine Ridge's government."

"I'm … flattered. Thank you so much," I reply. I take a deep breath. "I'd be honored, Mayor Burton."

The next few weeks pass in a whirlwind. With my new job secured, I take another leap: I use the money Gran left me to put a down payment on a custom townhouse in one of Sera's new developments. As I sign the papers, a sense of rightness settles over me. This is where I'm meant to be.

The first thing I do after that is head to the bakery to share the news with Mia. If she was proud when I got the job with the town, she'll be over the moon that I'm establishing firm roots in Alpine Ridge. Nothing says "I plan to be here a while" like buying property.

Walking down Main Street toward the bakery, I can't help my silly grin. I'm finally taking control of my own life, committing to this town that has come to mean so much to me. Being here reminds me of Gran, and my sister and found family are here. The history and love I have here can't be found anywhere else.

And who knows? Maybe someday, a nice guy who gives me butterflies will move into town … and stay. The thought of Evan flits through my mind, but I push it away. If it was meant to be, it would have been. And even if the nameless nice guy never finds me in this tiny town? Well, I'll just have to be awesome all on my own. Given the life I'm finally building for myself, I feel pretty good about the future either way.

CHAPTER TWENTY-THREE

EVAN

The flashing lights of the paparazzi's cameras are relentless as I attempt to drive through the crowd outside my L.A. home. I should've known better to take the convertible today. Their shouted questions blend into a cacophony of noise, but a few phrases cut through:

"Evan! Did you supply Kelly with drugs?"

"Are you going to rehab, Evan?"

"What do you have to say about Kelly's accusations?"

I grit my teeth, refusing to engage as I slowly but surely make it onto my property and into the garage. As soon as the door rolls shut behind me, I let out a long, frustrated sigh.

How did everything go so wrong so quickly?

Just a week ago, I was riding high. My latest movie had opened to rave reviews and impressive box office numbers, and the promotional tour had been exhausting but exhilarating. Then, out of nowhere, Kelly got arrested for drug possession with intent to traffic.

That alone would have been bad enough. But then she

had the audacity to claim *I* was the one who'd given her the drugs. Me. The guy who barely even drinks, let alone does anything harder.

Now, I'm caught in a maelstrom of accusations and investigations. Even though I know I'll eventually be exonerated — because they can't prove something that never happened — the damage to my reputation feels irreparable.

My phone buzzes. It's Rick.

"Evan, my man," he says, his voice tight with stress. "We've got a problem."

I laugh humorlessly. "You think? What now?"

"The studio is discussing cutting you loose from the Bond contract."

The words hit me like a physical blow. Bond. The role I've dreamed of since I was a kid. The pinnacle of my career. And now it might be snatched away because of a lie.

Part of me wants to find Kelly to force her to answer for what she's done to me, to get her to take back her story. Why would she make such a serious accusation against me? Why me at all? Is it just because I've repeatedly rejected her advances and kept our fake relationship, well, fake? It's the only thing I can come up with because surely she can't have thought it would stick enough to save her from the trouble she's in. In any case, I doubt they'd let me see her, and it probably would do more harm than good anyway. The whole situation is infuriating.

"That's not all," Rick continues, his voice grim. "Multiple other projects have retracted their scripts. They're distancing themselves until this blows over."

I close my eyes, feeling a wave of despair wash over me. "So, what do we do?"

"I'll handle it," Rick assures me, though I can hear the uncertainty in his voice. "For now, I think it's best if you get out of L.A. and go somewhere else for a while until this passes."

"Can I do that?" I ask. "I mean, legally?"

"You've already talked to the Feds, and there haven't been any formal charges. They did ask us to notify them if you were leaving town so they'd know where to find you." He pauses, heaving a sigh. "So, where you gonna go, kid?"

Finally, a question I can answer. An image flashes in my mind: mountains, fresh air, and a half-built house overlooking a stunning vista.

"Alpine Ridge."

"What? Where the hell is that?"

"Washington State. In the Cascade Mountains. I've got a house being built there. I can oversee the construction, lay low for a while."

Rick agrees, and we quickly make arrangements. Within hours, I'm on a private plane, leaving behind the chaos of Hollywood for the tranquility of the mountains.

As the plane touches down, I feel the weight of the past week settling heavily on my shoulders. The unfairness of it all burns in my chest. I've worked my ass off for years, built a career I'm proud of, only to have it threatened by a lying, drug-addled starlet.

By the time I reach the construction site of my new home, a plan is forming in my mind. Maybe I don't go back. Maybe I just ... stay here. Take a long break, or even retire altogether. The thought is tempting, almost intoxicating in its simplicity.

As I stand on what will soon be my deck, overlooking the breathtaking landscape of Alpine Ridge, I feel a sense of peace wash over me for the first time in days. With its quiet beauty and lack of prying eyes, this place feels like a sanctuary.

And it's not just the views. My brother is here. He's been there for me from the start, and I know he'll have my back no matter what. And, of course, there's Carrie. She's here, too. And while I know she's made it clear that we can't be together, the thought of being near her, even just as friends, relieves some of the tension tightening my shoulders.

I take a deep breath of the fresh mountain air, feeling better than I have since Kelly's arrest. I don't know what the future holds. But for now, I'm here. And that feels like a step in the right direction.

As I turn to head to Nate's, I make a silent promise to myself. No matter what happens with this scandal or what becomes of my career, I will use this time to figure out what I really want. Because if there's one thing this whole mess has reminded me of, it's that the glitz and glamour of Hollywood isn't all it's cracked up to be. There's good there, but there's so much more that's not worth it.

Maybe it's not where I'm meant to be anymore. Maybe real happiness is waiting for me somewhere else. Maybe even right here in Alpine Ridge.

CHAPTER TWENTY-FOUR

CARRIE

On Sunday afternoon, I'm lounging on Mia and Nate's couch, sipping tea and chatting with my sister while Nate reads in the armchair beside us, the buttery early June sunshine slanting through the windows, when the front door swings open. My heart skips a beat as Evan walks in, looking tired but relieved to be here.

"Honey, I'm home," he says jokingly, dropping a duffel bag in the hallway before kicking off his shoes.

Nate doesn't seem surprised to see him, rising to greet his brother with a warm hug. "Hey, man. Glad you made it."

Okay, I guess Nate knew Evan was coming? I shoot Mia a look, and she shrugs. But then, I shouldn't be surprised. Of course, we'd all heard the news. We even talked about it earlier today — the scandal involving drugs, Evan, and his fake actress girlfriend, Kelly Cook, that has been splashed across every tabloid and news outlet for days. If it were me, I'd get the hell out of dodge the first chance I got, too.

"Evan, I'm so sorry about what's happening," Mia says, genuine concern in her voice as Evan flops down on the other end of the couch.

"Thanks," he says with a sigh. "I'm just glad to get away from it all for a while."

"Well, you know we're always happy to have you here," Mia replies. "But I also know your name will be cleared soon. I'm surprised it hasn't been already, honestly."

Evan's shoulders relax slightly. "I love you for not asking whether I was involved."

Nate scoffs. "Anyone who knows you at all would know better than to believe those accusations," Nate reassures him.

I nod in agreement. "Absolutely. You're the least 'celebrity' celebrity I've ever met. You don't act entitled or arrogant, and you certainly don't seem to be living the crazy Hollywood lifestyle."

Evan's eyes meet mine, a ghost of a smile on his lips. "Thanks, Carrie. That means a lot."

Nate asks for an update, and Evan explains that he's talked to Federal Agents and there's an ongoing investigation, but no charges yet. "Hopefully, they'll resolve this soon," he sighs. "I'm being dropped like a hot potato and might lose my Bond contract."

Mia and I gasp in shock.

"No! That's crazy! I'm so sorry, Evan. What can we do to help?" Mia asks, ever the nurturer.

Evan shakes his head. "I don't even want to think about it. I just want to be here and have as normal a life as possible."

Nate nods. "I understand. Why don't you help me at the wellness center this week? It's physical work. Good for taking your mind off things."

"That sounds perfect," Evan agrees, looking relieved.

As they continue to chat, I can't help but feel concerned for Evan, but I'm thankful Nate will be keeping him busy. I have my own job to focus on, and while I think I can handle seeing Evan at game nights and the weekly dinner party, that's about it. I make a mental note to ensure I'm busy enough not to run into him too often.

The next week, I spend a lot of time working and hanging out with Brandon, even skipping game night. But there's little excuse to skip the weekly Saturday night dinner party since Brandon is in Seattle for the weekend, and I know I have to face the music sometime.

I arrive a little early and pull Mia aside. "Can you help run interference while I get used to having Evan around?" I ask quietly.

Mia gives me a curious look. "I mean ... I can. But — and forgive me if this is overstepping — why don't you just use this opportunity to see where things go between you two? It seems like he'll be around for a while this time."

I shake my head. "You and I both know that this will blow over, and then Evan will go back to L.A. I don't want to start something I can't maintain, and while Evan's a great guy, I'm not interested in a long-distance relationship with a famous movie star."

Mia nods thoughtfully. "Honestly? I probably wouldn't want that either if I were in your shoes. Okay. I'll do what I can."

"Thanks, sis." I give her a peck on the cheek. "Can I help with dinner?"

"You want to be in the kitchen with my bossy butt?" she teases.

I smile, knowing exactly how she can be. "There's nowhere else I'd rather be."

She rolls her eyes. "You can't avoid Evan all night, Care-bear."

I chuckle. She knows me too well.

To my surprise, the night ends up being really great. Evan is friendly but doesn't give me longing looks or try to touch me, and I find we can get along really well in the group setting with that pressure gone. We joke and laugh, and I have a genuinely good time.

Encouraged, I show up for game night and the Saturday night dinner party the following week. Things continue to go smoothly. Evan has folded seamlessly into our group, and Nate is thrilled to have his brother around, not to mention the extra help at the wellness center. Evan has even pitched in to help Greg with the increase in personal training requests on the weekends. I'm happy for him, seeing how well he's adjusting to life here.

The next week, however, throws me for a loop. I arrive for game night a little early ... and run into Evan coming downstairs in just a towel. He freezes and gives a deer-in-headlights look that I'm sure is on my face, too.

He points down the hall toward the laundry room. "Hey. I … was just going to grab a pair of pants from the dryer," he explains awkwardly.

I nod, my face burning with embarrassment. "Of course. Um … no worries." I hate that I'm this flustered. But the long expanse of his taut, golden, muscled torso throws me back into memories I wasn't prepared to relive. Sexy ones. Very, *very* sexy ones.

"It's not like it's anything you haven't seen before," he replies. And I can tell he meant it to sound casual.

Except, it doesn't. Not even a little bit. Because the husky tone of his voice tells me he remembers me seeing him naked, too. And is probably now remembering me naked as well.

For a few long moments, the air between us is thick with tension and chemistry so strong I can practically taste it. Or maybe that's just a fresh dose of Evan's ocean and evergreen scent. Either way, it's making me a little dizzy.

"Hey, Carrie, when'd you get here?" Mia asks, popping out of the kitchen.

I turn to face her, grasping for words. "I … That … Just a minute ago."

Evan takes the opportunity to continue down the hall. Mia watches him go. She turns back to me with a raised brow. "Everything okay?"

"Great. Everything's great." I smile innocently, resisting the urge to fan myself to beat back the heat on my cheeks.

She gives me a knowing look but doesn't say anything

and heads back toward the kitchen. "Good. Then get your booty in here and help me prep."

I let out a sigh of relief and follow her into the kitchen. As I help her prepare snacks for game night, I'm reminded that no matter how much I pretend, I clearly still want Evan on some level. But I'm determined to deal with that because Evan is happy, Nate is happy, Greg is happy ... everyone's fine with the situation, so I will be too.

Someday.

For now, I'll keep my distance as much as possible, continue focusing on my work, and hope these feelings fade with time. After all, I've built a life here that I love. I won't let my lingering attraction to Evan derail that.

As we rejoin the others in the living room, I paste on a smile and throw myself into the game night festivities. I can do this. I can be Evan's friend. I have to.

Because the alternative — giving in to how much I apparently still want him — is just a recipe for heartbreak.

As soon as I step into the living room, however, I'm distracted from my own troubles by a tiny creature whizzing around my ankles.

"What in the hell?" I set down the platter of chips and guac on the coffee table before I drop it.

"Oh, look, Bruiser likes you!" Joanie exclaims from her place on the loveseat next to Greg.

The small critter finally stops long enough for me to realize it's a dog. A chihuahua, to be precise. Named Bruiser. I look up at Joanie.

"You didn't."

She grins widely. "Totally did."

I look at Mia, who has her hand over her mouth to

stifle her laughter. I shake my head in disbelief. "I was about to say you're no Elle Woods, but …"

"I'm better?" Joanie teases.

I burst out laughing. "Yeah, actually." I squat down and offer a hand. Bruiser smells it with interest and then licks it. I laugh and scratch under his chin. "He looks just like his namesake, too."

"Well, duh. I knew he was it when I saw him at the shelter."

I rise, still chuckling, as Bruiser follows me to the couch. "Greg? How do you feel about this?"

Greg shrugs. "Joanie's happy, I'm happy." Bruiser runs over to Greg, hopping on his leg, his own little legs too short to make the jump to his lap. Greg reaches down and scratches the dog's head fondly. "He is pretty cute." Then to the dog, "Not now, Bruiser. Go play."

And like the damn dog understood, he runs for the corner where a knotted rope lays and starts attacking it.

"Holy crap, you *are* a dog whisperer," I say, laughing.

Greg raises his hands in a shrug. "Guess it's a hidden talent no longer," he jokes.

"Hmm. I'm still not convinced," Mia says. "Tell him to do something else."

Greg sighs heavily. "Hey, Bruiser." The dog looks up, his adorable ears perked toward Greg. "Go give Evan loves." Greg points toward where Evan is now sitting in Nate's armchair. Evan claps his hands together, encouraging Bruiser to come.

Bruiser looks between Greg and Evan for a split second before darting toward the latter. Evan scoops him up, and Bruiser proceeds to jump on his chest and lick every inch of his face. Evan laughs, petting the dog while it smothers him with doggy kisses.

Greg crosses his legs, leaning back into the cushions with a smug look on his face. "Do you believe me now?"

I look back at Mia, whose jaw is hanging open.

"I didn't believe it either at first," Joanie offers.

Mia shakes her head in disbelief. "That's ... wow."

My eyes flick to Evan, who is still soaking up the dog's affection. The silly grin he's giving the dog is adorable. And some doggie snuggles are probably just what Evan needs these days. Animals are good for the soul, after all.

As I watch Bruiser curl up on Evan's lap, I try not to notice how sweet they are together.

"Boy, he really likes you, Evan," Mia says.

"And I really like him. He's such a sweetheart," Evan says, emphasizing his words with belly rubs for Bruiser. Bruiser's little tongue lolls out as he rolls onto his back to allow Evan better access. Evan laughs. "Dogs are the best."

"You should get one," Joanie adds. "I wish we had sooner, honestly, and we've only been dog parents for three days."

Evan nods contemplatively. "I've thought about it. But I've always traveled too much to be able to commit to having a pet. Though it seems like things might be changing, so maybe I'll be able to soon," he says with a shrug, his tone equally sad and hopeful.

My heart twists in my chest as everyone else moves on like nothing just happened. But I can feel Evan's struggle from here. His despair at the sudden tumble that his career has taken warring with his hope that things might still be okay, whether that means a return to normal or an opportunity for something new. His strength and resilience in the face of adversity aren't lost on me, even if nobody else notices.

As if he hears my thoughts, his gaze lifts to meet mine. He gives me a melancholy smile, and I give him a supportive one in return. His eyes sparkle, and I know he picks up on my message: I see you.

And though it would open too much of a can of worms to voice the words, I hope he knows that no matter what we are to each other, I'm always in his corner.

CHAPTER TWENTY-FIVE

EVAN

These last couple of weeks in Alpine Ridge have been exactly what I needed. A calm environment with no pressure, no paparazzi, and no time to worry about contracts or scripts. Nate's been working me hard, but it's been good. I feel useful and clear-headed for the first time in a long time. I'd been looking for this late last year when I planned to take a break. I guess it took an *un*planned disaster to make it happen. I'm almost grateful for it. Almost.

Though as unburdened as I feel here, I still haven't been able to force myself to think about what I want for my career. I need to see how this mess with Kelly plays out first and then consider my options. Ultimately, it's hard to make a decision when you don't know what your choices will be.

In the meantime, Joanie had the brilliant idea to take a day off and go play tourist in Seattle. Nate and Mia vetoed Friday since it's one of their busiest days. And Carrie begged us to do it over the weekend so she could come too. So here we are on Sunday, the early morning sun glinting off the hood of Mia's SUV as we pull out of Alpine Ridge, headed for Seattle.

I'm in the back seat, with Nate driving and Mia in the passenger seat. Greg, Joanie, and Carrie are following in Joanie's Subaru. Despite the cloud hanging over my career, I can't help but feel a surge of excitement. It's been years since I've played tourist anywhere, so this feels like a vacation within a vacation.

I brought my hat and sunglasses, hoping they will offer some anonymity. The last thing I want is for my presence to disrupt our day.

It's nice to be a passenger as we make the two-hour drive. I've only ever been the driver on this trek, and watching the winding mountain paths transition to a sweeping descent into the Seattle area is a lot of fun. There's so much to look at between the lakes, changing cityscape, and even Mt. Rainier, clearly visible to our left. I'd seen it from the plane, but viewing it from the ground gives you a better sense of its sheer scale.

The sight of the Seattle skyline as we cross yet another lake has me itching to get there and explore. Thankfully, traveling with natives pays off, and Mia directs us seamlessly to a parking garage a stone's throw from the Space Needle.

"Hope you're not afraid of heights," Mia says with a grin as Greg, Joanie, and Carrie join us.

I grin back. "Bring it on."

As we ascend in the elevator the five hundred and twenty feet to the observation deck of the iconic structure, I feel a childlike thrill, bouncing on the balls of my feet.

Carrie laughs and shakes her head. "Trust me, it's not *that* exciting."

I bump her with my shoulder. "Says you. You've probably been up here tons of times."

"Okay, fair," she allows. "Still. I find it helps to keep your expectations low, then you're always pleasantly surprised."

I give her a look and open my mouth to say something about how that explains so much, but the doors open, and I'm so distracted by the view that all I can do is gape as we exit the elevator.

"Well, this definitely exceeds my expectations," I say, impressed. The view from the top is breathtaking — the city sprawls below us, Elliot Bay a glittering expanse in the distance. A walk around the circular deck unfurls more vistas of the city as well as lakes and distant mountains, including Rainier.

"I guess it is pretty amazing, huh?" Carrie's voice is soft beside me.

I nod, not trusting myself to speak. Our arms are almost touching on the railing, and I'm even more aware of her presence than usual. It takes me a minute to realize it might have something to do with what happened the last time we shared a beautiful view. I take a deep breath and try to brush it off.

The natives let me linger for a while, enjoying the view, though I can tell they got bored after a few minutes. Still, I snap a few selfies at various points, then insist on one of the group before we make our way back down, out of the clouds.

Next, we make our way toward the Olympic Sculpture

Park so we can walk along the waterfront. The weather is perfect as we stroll, big puffy white clouds dotting the otherwise clear blue sky. The sun shines brightly, but the morning temperatures are still comfortable.

The sculpture park turns out to be an unexpectedly wild experience. It's a blend between a showcase of seriously cool and totally out-there contemporary sculptures of all kinds and is also surrounded by beautiful backdrops with the bay and Space Needle flanking it, each on either side. But we don't linger long and are soon heading down Alaskan Way. The smell of the ocean air makes me feel at home.

As we pass the Edgewater Hotel, Carrie nudges me. "See that? That's where the Beatles were famously photographed fishing out of one of the windows."

I grin, impressed by her knowledge. "No way! That's so cool."

"Yep. They don't allow fishing anymore, though. Just in case that gave you any ideas." She winks at me, and I laugh.

"I'm not big on fishing, but thanks for clarifying."

We walk in comfortable silence for the most part, though Carrie points out the sights as we go. We pass a huge sailboat docked just off the piers, the aquarium, with tons of little kids running around outside squealing, and then another set of sculptures less ostentatious than the first ones we saw but still interesting. Finally, I spot a sign on one of the larger piers for Miner's Landing … and the Seattle Great Wheel. The childlike excitement returns as I eye the monstrosity at the end of the pier that, even from a ways away, dominates the skyline.

"Okay, studmuffin, this may not be as tall as the Space Needle, but I promise you won't be disappointed," Joanie says, gesturing to the pier just ahead of us.

"No worries on that front, Legs. It's already delivering," I say without hesitation, looking at it in awe. As we turn onto the pier and approach it, I have to crane my neck back to take it in. It may not be as tall as the Space Needle, but it's the biggest fucking Ferris wheel I've ever seen.

Since it's a Sunday, we have to wait a bit, but it's not too bad. My excitement levels as we're locked in the climate-controlled gondola are off the charts. The cabin is lined with two benches. Nate, Mia, and Carrie sit on one side, Joanie, Greg, and me on the other. But we're all turned outward toward the horizon, anticipating the coming views.

The views rise with us, the Ferris wheel halting occasionally for others to disembark and board. Within a few minutes, downtown lies sprawled out behind us, the ferry-dotted bay beneath us, and mountains in the distance still have white at their tips.

"How is there still snow on those mountains?" I ask in awe.

"They're tall," Joanie says with a shrug.

I smirk at her. "Gee, thanks."

"They're the Olympic Mountains. They're not as tall as the Cascades, but they sometimes get snow in June. Same as we do," Carrie offers.

Mia smiles and squeezes her sister against her. "You said 'we'," she points out.

Carrie blushes. "I did. Guess I've officially joined the Alpine Ridge cult."

Greg chuckles at that.

My eyes search Carrie's face. I was pretty sure she hadn't been back here since the fiasco with her parents, but based on the vibe I'm getting off of her, now I'm almost certain. "Is it weird being back in Seattle?" I ask.

She blows out a slow breath and turns back to the horizon that's slowly slipping out of view. "Super weird," she admits. "I can't believe I spent my whole life here, yet I've been away for almost a year."

I reach out and touch her on the knee, bringing her eyes to mine. "It's okay to not miss it, you know."

Her mouth drops open. "How did you …" She shakes her head. And then, hesitatingly, she asks, "Am I a bad person if I don't?"

I consider that for a moment. "I think we don't miss places so much as we do the people who made the feel like home. So no, I don't think it makes you a bad person that you don't miss a place where people didn't appreciate you the way you deserved." I remove my hand from her knee, realizing that, though I meant it as a comfort, it could be seen as pressure. And that's something Carric doesn't need more of. She's been under pressure her whole life. To meet her parents' expectations, to be something she didn't want to be, to please everyone around her. I know firsthand that even when pressure comes from within, that doesn't mean it's easy to switch off. In fact, sometimes, it's easier to cut off external pressure. That, you can walk away from. It's harder to rewire yourself after years of behaving a certain way.

Carrie is silent for a while. And so am I, as the others start to chat about where to have lunch. Because while my thoughts were directed at Carrie, I realize they are just as applicable to me. There's nobody in L.A. that makes it feel like home to me. Not a single fucking person. And yet, I've stayed for my career. I've persisted against the odds. It's just how I am. I do what needs doing. Unfortunately, I can do nothing about Kelly's accusation and the chain of events it started.

But the thing with Kelly doesn't depress me as much as realizing I don't have any true friends in Los Angeles. Even though I'm not there for friends. Still, it's odd that I can't claim a close friend in all my years there. Sure, I have tons of "friends" — in solid air quotes. They're the Hollywood kind of friends. Surface level. Fun to hang with at parties. But they're not the kind of people who are really there for you when you need them.

Not like this group, right here, plus Dylan and my parents. Oh, and Rae, who I can't leave out just because she couldn't join us today. They're my people. And maybe the fact that I'm always too far from them isn't helping my career struggles. Because how can you push through the hard stuff without a support network? One that can work out with you and lend an ear while you do. Or hand you a cupcake and a glass of brandy. Or go on a hike with you and make you feel like you're the only person in the world that matters.

My heart aches in my chest. As the revolution continues and the horizon returns, Carrie looks back at me with a smile. And I realize I've been staring at her, lost in thought, this whole time. I pull my gaze away, only to find

Mia watching me. I give her a sheepish smile and look down into my hands. But I can still feel her sharp gaze on me, seeing more than I'm ready to admit to. Thankfully, she doesn't say a word, though.

"So, what do you think, Ev? Do you want to hit someplace on the waterfront, or should we have lunch at Pike Place Market?" Nate asks.

I look up, sensing that they'd just been discussing both options. "I'm the noob here, so whatever you guys agree on is good with me," I offer, snapping back to reality with a smile.

"And the vote carries for Pike Place Market," Joanie says with a victorious wiggle.

That gets Carrie's attention, too, making it clear she also wasn't listening. "Pike Place? Really? We should've gone there first, then," Carrie groans.

Joanie gives an exaggerated shrug and grins. "Gotta earn that burger, Carrie."

I raise a brow. "What does that mean?"

Greg claps me on the shoulder. "It means … it's a good thing you're a beast on the Stairmaster, my friend."

"Noooo, not the Hillclimb," Mia protests.

Nate shakes his head and laughs. "You want me to carry you?" he offers.

She brightens at that. "You would do that for me?" He leans in and kisses her in answer.

"Great. Guess I'll be suffering by myself then," Carrie jokes. I open my mouth, but her eyes snap to me. Something in them tells me *not* to make the offer I was about to. I press my lips together to keep from laughing. Damn, she's stubborn.

I lean back and watch the views for our next two rotations as the girls bicker amongst themselves, Carrie and Mia trying to convince Joanie out of climbing what is apparently a fuck ton of stairs. But with the glacier-and-snowcapped Rainier on one side, the glittering bay filled with ferries on another, and amazing views of everything downtown from the Space Needle to the aquarium to the other iconic buildings dotted everywhere, it's hard to pay attention to anything but the peace I feel being right here, right now.

When we finally disembark, I'm disappointed. Being up in the sky felt like being apart from everything for a while. It was nice.

But I am hungry, so I'm glad when Joanie leads us off the pier across multiple converging lanes of traffic and starts up a set of zig-zagging concrete steps that seem to go on forever.

After the first set of stairs, we cross another, smaller road and wait for Carrie and Mia, who decided to hoof it on her own, I suspect to keep Carrie company.

Then we head up *another* lengthy set of stairs.

Nate and I reach the top first, followed closely by Greg, then Joanie. My leg muscles burn but I feel better for the exercise. Though we have to wait for Carrie and Mia again, this time, there's plenty to keep me busy because we've emerged smack in the middle of the famous Pike Place Market. My eyes can't take everything in fast enough, from the fishmongers to the sea of flowers in buckets to wares of every kind sprawled out across what seems like endless stalls. The street outside is crowded with pedestrians and lined with restaurants and shops.

Smells of roasting fish, pastries, coffee, flowers ... it's a feast for the senses, and the vibe is borderline overwhelming but also exhilarating.

There's so much to see that I can't possibly take it all in, and it's only whetted my appetite for more by the time Carrie and Mia appear, puffing and panting.

"No ... comments ... about ... out of ... shape," Mia pants toward Nate. He just grins and, in one swift move, loads her up onto his back, where she promptly flops her head on his shoulder like a ragdoll. It's disgustingly adorable.

As we walk out, I look back and realize the iconic Public Market Center sign was above us the whole time.

"Will you guys hate me if I take a few pictures?" I ask.

Joanie smirks. "Of course not. I think Carrie and Mia would be thrilled for the breather, honestly."

Greg snorts, and I laugh. "All right, it won't take long, though, promise."

I quickly take a few selfies with the sign in the background, then have them all join me for a group pic.

"Thanks for humoring me," I tell them as Joanie and Greg lead us into a bar and grill across from the market entrance.

Joanie shrugs. "No problem. I forget how novel this is to some people."

"I feel that. When I first moved to L.A., it was like this. Everything was new and exciting. It wears off quickly, I know."

"Ah, but some things quickly become favorites, too, and the joy goes on," Nate says, setting Mia down in the waiting area. "Speaking of which … it's Boom Boom Shrimp time, sweetheart."

Mia gives a tired smile. "Thank God."

I slip off my hat and sunglasses as we get seated. We immediately order a round of appetizers — Mia's Boom Boom Shrimp (fried shrimp with a Thai chili sauce), a smoked salmon sampler, and oysters on the half shell — plus a beer bucket, which turns out to be just as much fun as it sounds. As we eat and drink and wait for our main courses, Mia and Carrie take turns giving me Seattle history lessons in disjointed pieces — the origin of the Space Needle (built for the 1962 World's Fair), the Smith Tower (which was Seattle's first skyscraper and, at the time, the tallest building in the West). They've just started on Seattle's Underground when our food shows up.

As intriguing as a whole section of the city still existing in a spooky tomb-like underground area is, my attention is wholly occupied by the fish and chips that are put in front of me. Basic, perhaps, but simple food can sometimes be the best. And as I eat the flaky, tender battered fish dipped in tartar sauce, I don't regret it.

Though everyone ordered something different, so we all swap bites of each — best of all worlds. Carrie's seafood pasta is okay but a little all over the place for me. Mia's chicken and waffles is an unexpected menu item, and not as good as Roscoe's back in L.A., but it's still all right. Nate, who I know isn't all that into seafood, ends up with a perfectly cooked New York Steak, and Greg's Dungeness Crab is melt-in-your-mouth delicious.

I lean back in my chair, groaning after the decadent

indulgence of the meal. "Hope you guys are prepared to roll me out of here," I joke.

"You and me both," Mia agrees.

"What, no dessert?" Carrie asks Mia with a mischievous twinkle in her eye.

"Oh, oh, oh," Greg interjects excitedly. "We've got to stop by the Dahlia Bakery. My cousin Sera got me hooked on it last year. Their coconut cream pie is to die for."

Mia gives him a strange look and then bursts out laughing. "Who are you, and what have you done with the real Greg?" she asks, wiping tears of laughter from her eyes.

To everyone's surprise, Greg blushes, and now we're all laughing.

"Seriously, though, he's not wrong. It was always one of my favorites, too," Mia admits. "It's only about a ten-minute walk from here."

"Oh, but aren't we going to explore the market before we go?" I ask hopefully.

Mia hits herself on the forehead. "Duh. Yes, of course, we can totally do that. Sorry. Greg said 'coconut cream pie,' and I got distracted."

We settle up and head out, with me doing my best to tamp down my little kid level of excitement. I'm giddy today from all the normalcy and good times.

I should've known it wouldn't last. As we step back outside, I realize I left my hat and sunglasses in the restaurant. I don't even have time to vocalize that before I hear a familiar excited shriek followed by, "Oh my God, it's Evan Edwards!"

The shout comes from somewhere to my left, and

suddenly I'm surrounded. Fans push for autographs and selfies, but most hurl questions about Kelly and the scandal.

"Evan, do you really do drugs?"

"Are you and Kelly still dating?"

"Is your career over, Evan?"

The questions come rapid-fire, each one a painful reminder of why I escaped to Alpine Ridge in the first place.

"All right, that's enough!" Joanie's authoritative voice cuts through the chaos. She grabs my arm, pulling me through the crowd and around a corner to a street where a couple of cabs are dropping people off. "Evan, Carrie, Nate, get in this taxi. We'll go in that one —" she points behind us "—and meet you at the parking garage near Seattle Center."

Before I know it, I'm in the back of a cab with Carrie, with Nate riding shotgun, watching the crowd recede through the rear window.

"I'm so sorry, Evan," Carrie says softly, her hand on my arm.

I let out a frustrated sigh. "Even when I'm an outcast, I can't have a normal life."

"Hey," she says, her voice firm but gentle. "This will pass. And you're not an outcast. Not to us."

I meet her eyes, seeing nothing but sincerity there. The rest of the world fades away for a moment. It's just me and Carrie, and I'm overwhelmed by the concern in her gaze. She laces her fingers with mine, giving me a reassuring squeeze. I can't help the small smile that tugs at my lips, or tracing my thumb over her palm, or staring back at her.

She's sweet and kind and so caring, and being here with her like this …

The taxi jerking to a stop breaks the spell. I look up and realize that we're at the parking garage.

As we climb out and into our separate cars for the drive home, I'm disappointed our day was cut short. But a small part of me is grateful for the reminder. That Carrie feels for me, even if it's not how I want. That even though things fell apart, I can just be a normal guy sometimes, even if it's only for a little while. That I have a group of people who have my back, no matter what.

Even being mobbed by fans and reminded of the mess that is my life and career right now … well, it doesn't seem so bad when you don't have to face it alone.

CHAPTER TWENTY-SIX

CARRIE

The aftermath of our Seattle trip hits Alpine Ridge like a tidal wave. What started as a fun day out for our little group has morphed into a media frenzy, with paparazzi and tourists descending upon our quiet mountain town in droves. Evan's brief public appearance sent the vultures circling, desperate to uncover where he's been hiding.

For the first week, it's chaos. Evan hunkers down at Nate and Mia's while the rest of us navigate the sudden influx of outsiders. Thankfully, the paparazzi lose interest quickly when they realize Evan isn't coming out to play. The tourists, however, prove more persistent.

As I walk down Main Street, I can't help but notice the changes. There's a steady stream of unfamiliar faces, all seeming to vibrate with excitement at the mere possibility of catching a glimpse of Evan. Watching them take selfies in front of our modest storefronts as if they're posing before famous landmarks is surreal.

The town's reaction is mixed, to say the least. Mia is thrilled; the bakery is busier than ever, with lines stretching out the door most days. But for every happy business owner, there's someone like Batty Betty McDonald, who cornered me yesterday to rant about a tourist trampling her prized begonias.

As I approach the makeshift town hall — currently just a conference room in the community center — I brace myself for what's to come. Arthur asked me to prepare budget outlines and timelines for our first quarterly town hall meeting, but I have a sinking feeling those topics will be quickly overshadowed.

"Carrie," Arthur greets me as I enter, his normally cheerful face creased with worry lines. "Are you ready for the meeting?"

I nod, forcing a smile. "As ready as I'll ever be. But Arthur, I should warn you — I don't think we will get very far with the budget discussions. People are going to want to talk about the tourist situation."

He sighs, running a hand through his thinning hair. "I know, I know. But there's not much we can do except capitalize on the business and use it as a learning exercise for everything else. We'll just have to roll with the punches."

As expected, the meeting quickly derails from Arthur's planned agenda, with barely an acknowledgment that we've broken ground on the new town hall building to be finished by the end of the year and have a fiscal plan and schedule for setting up police and fire services by next year. But the room is packed with angry residents ready to explode over their tourist troubles, and it doesn't take long for the complaints to start flying.

"They're parking wherever they damn well please!" one resident shouts.

"I found three of them in my backyard yesterday, taking pictures!" another chimes in.

"The noise at night is unbearable! Don't these people sleep?"

I cringe, glad at least that they didn't bring pitchforks and torches. Thankfully, Greg, ever the voice of reason, speaks up. "Perhaps we can consider clear, designated parking areas and more signage for public versus private property?"

Brandon nods in agreement. "We could also institute local ordinances for noise and trespassing."

Janet, one of the older council members, adds, "While we haven't had any major traffic issues yet, I've noticed plenty of confused drivers. We should discuss improving our transportation infrastructure."

It seems to mollify the townspeople, for now at least. As the meeting winds down, I can't help but feel a mix of frustration and pride. Yes, we're facing challenges, but watching our fledgling town government tackle these issues head-on is oddly inspiring. In a way, this might have been a blessing in disguise.

The next evening at game night, nobody feels much like playing. Instead, we fill Evan in on what happened at the town hall meeting.

"I'm sorry I'm causing waves," Evan says, his brow

furrowed with concern. "Maybe this wasn't such a good idea after all."

Mia leans forward, her eyes sharp. "Are you going to keep going forward with building your house here?"

Evan hesitates. "I've gone too far not to finish the build, but if it comes down to it, I can always sell."

"That would be dumb," Joanie interjects, her tone matter-of-fact. "This is exactly what we hoped for when we asked you to live here — attention for the town. So what if not everybody is happy? Tough shit."

We all laugh, and I can see some of the tension leave Evan's shoulders.

"I'm with Joanie," Rae pipes up. "A good number of people in this town just like to complain. The way I see it, we gave them something juicy to bitch about." She shrugs.

"For sure," I agree. "But even beyond that, it showed us exactly the issues we will need to address if we want to manage a growing population and increased tourism over the next few years. Better to know these things now while we're still in the planning stages for the town."

"You think?" Evan asks, and the vulnerability in his voice gets me right in the chest.

"Yeah, I do," I assure him. "I know it doesn't feel like it right now, but I think this will turn out to be a good thing."

Everyone's silent as they process all that's been said.

After a minute or so, Greg clears his throat. "If we're done with the depressing stuff, I have some good news." We all turn to him expectantly. "Joanie and I have set a wedding date. December tenth, the second anniversary of when we met."

"Oh, yay!" Mia is the first to exclaim. "Congratulations, guys." She rises and pulls Joanie into a hug.

"Congrats, man," Nate says, leaning in to fist-bump Greg.

"Well, that is good news," Rae adds. "Congratulations, you two."

"That's fantastic! I can't wait to be at *that* party. I mean, if it won't mess things up," Evan says, and I feel a flutter in my chest at his certainty.

"Are you kidding? It wouldn't be a party without you, studmuffin," Joanie replies with a wink.

Despite the lightness in the room, I feel ... odd as I offer Joanie and Greg a smile and a "Congratulations." Really, though, I don't have to work hard to figure out why. It's because Evan seemed so sure that he'll be there. Which makes me wonder ... does he plan on *still* being here, or is he assuming he'll be back in L.A. at that point but is set on being here for their special day anyway? Certainly, the latter is more likely. Which makes me think that ... maybe, even once he goes back to L.A., Evan will be around more. He seems genuinely attached to this town, to all of us.

A small kernel of hope blossoms inside me, but I quickly tamp it down. Fools rush in, as they say, and I've had enough of being a fool for one lifetime. For now, I'll wait and see. After all, we've got a town to run and, apparently, a wedding to plan.

CHAPTER TWENTY-SEVEN

EVAN

The call comes on Monday afternoon, just as I'm finishing up for the day at Nate's wellness center. My phone buzzes insistently, and when I see the unfamiliar number with a D.C. area code, my heart leaps into my throat.

"Mr. Edwards?" a crisp, professional voice greets me.

"Yes?" I reply, my voice surprisingly steady.

"This is Agent Carlson from the FBI. I'm calling to inform you that our investigation has concluded, and you've been cleared of all accusations related to Ms. Cook's drug charges."

Relief washes over me like a tidal wave. "Thank you," I manage to croak out. "That's great news."

As soon as I hang up, I try to call Rick, but it goes straight to voicemail. I leave a message, my voice shaking with excitement and relief.

The next afternoon, Rick finally calls back. "Evan, my man! I heard the good news. Sorry I couldn't get back to you yesterday — it's been a madhouse here."

"What's going on?" Despite being cleared, I'm suddenly nervous that something else has happened.

Rick chuckles. "You won't believe this. Over the holiday weekend, another A-list actor got caught in a DWI scandal that outed his severe alcoholism. All eyes are off you now, kid."

I let out a low whistle. "That's ... unfortunate for him, but I can't say I'm not relieved."

"You should be," Rick says. "Because I've also been working overtime to placate the studio. They're willing to move forward with the Bond contract but want you back in L.A. ASAP. We need to do some damage control, get you back in the public eye in a positive way."

I feel a pang in my chest at the thought of leaving Alpine Ridge. But I know I can't hide away forever. "All right," I sigh. "I'll head back tomorrow."

"Why not tonight?" Rick pushes.

I snort. "I can be in your office by noon tomorrow. They'll never know the difference."

"You wanna take that risk?"

A headache starts pounding at my temple. "Fine. I'll see what I can do."

"Good. Text me your flight info when you have it." And with that, he hangs up.

Fuck. Just like that, I'm back in the fast lane.

I hang up, letting out a long breath. Nate looks up from cleaning up after a session. "Headed back to L.A.?"

I nod slowly. "Yeah. First flight I can make out,

actually." Nate grimaces. "I know. Though I should've expected that's how it would go down." I sigh heavily. "Thanks for … everything, man. This has been great, really."

Nate walks over to me and claps me on the shoulder. "It has. But don't talk like you won't be back. Don't forget, you've got a house being built."

I give him a half-hearted smile. "I haven't."

He nods. "Go say your goodbyes. I'm sure I'll talk to you soon."

A wave of emotion rolls over me, and I grab my big brother into a bear hug. "Yeah, you will." I release him quickly and turn away, blinking back tears as I grab my gear bag and head out to my rental.

I stop in the bakery on the way, the bell on the door jingling as I enter. Rae looks up from frosting a tray of cupcakes.

"Hey, sugar," she greets me.

"Hey, Rae," I respond. "Came to say goodbye. The studio wants me back ASAP, so I'm outta here."

She looks back up in surprise. "Mia!" she calls toward the back. Then she sets the frosting bag down, wipes her hands, and rounds the counter to give me a hug. She smells like vanilla and sugar, and it's kind of making me hungry. "You go back there and kick some ass."

I chuckle. "Thanks, Rae. You keep everyone in line while I'm gone, okay?"

She snorts. "I'll do my best."

"What's going on?" Mia asks, appearing behind Rae.

I pull back and give her a rueful smile. "I'm headed back to L.A."

Mia's jaw drops. "No! Really? Like, right now?"

I shrug. "They say jump, I say how high."

Mia frowns. "Well, we're sure going to miss you, Evan." She holds out her arms, and I pull her in for a hug.

"Thanks for everything, Mia. I'm going to miss you too. And your cupcakes and booze."

Mia chuckles against my shoulder. "You know you're welcome to come back for more anytime."

I pull back. "Count on it. Carrie still working out of the community center?"

Mia nods. "Yep."

"Cool. I'll say goodbye to her and Greg at the same time. Tell Joanie I'll see her and her fantastic legs later?" I say with a smile I don't feel.

"Of course," Mia returns with a similar forced smile.

I turn and walk away before I can get all emotional again. I make it out in one piece, though I know I won't be so lucky with my next stop.

To save time, I drive to the community center but sit in the SUV for a few minutes, psyching myself up. I finally take a deep breath and hop out, heading for the front door. I notice Greg on the other side of the building, hosing down the outdoor equipment.

"Hey, man," I call.

Greg looks up and grins, then turns off the hose.

"Evan, my man, what's up? Does Nate need something for the wellness center?"

I shake my head. "Nope. I'm headed back to L.A. Came to say goodbye."

Greg nods, the smile dropping off his face. "Well, glad you didn't just cut and run. We'll miss you, man." He reaches in for the hand clasp and bro hug. And I start to get teary again.

"Anyway, I'm going to go in and say goodbye to Carrie quickly, then I gotta run. I'm sure I'll see you soon. Gotta come back to check on the house and all." I say, sniffing as subtly as I can.

But I can tell Greg isn't fooled. Still, he only says, "Sounds good. Have a safe trip back."

I nod, stuffing my hands in my pockets as I head into the community center.

I find Carrie in one of the back rooms that's been turned into a small office. She's turned mostly away from me, so she doesn't notice I'm there. I take the opportunity to observe her for a minute. Her dark hair is swept up into a loose bun on her head, with a pen sticking out of the dark mass. She's chewing on her lip as she reads something, her heel-clad foot tapping on the metal leg of the chair. She's beautiful. And I'm going to miss her like crazy. A pang hits me in the chest; oddly, I already miss her. I clear my throat, partly to dislodge the thickness that's suddenly welled there, partly to announce myself.

Carrie looks up distractedly. "Evan? What are you doing here?" She turns and rises, and I notice she's wearing a tan pencil skirt and a white button-front top that shows a hint of her cleavage. My mouth dries up, and I lose my words.

"I ... I'm ..." I swallow hard. "I came to say goodbye." I lift my eyes to hers, willing myself not to continue ogling her. But Jesus, why did she have to look like hot business right now? As if leaving wasn't hard enough.

Her brows pull together, her dark blue eyes clouded with confusion until she realizes what I mean. And if it was hard before, seeing the disappointment seep into her face nearly undoes me. But she hides it quickly, so I try to do the same.

"Oh. Well … guess it had to happen sometime," she says with a resigned sigh.

My jaw tightens. She's not wrong, but it just makes me realize … Carrie's been waiting for me to leave again. I'm proving once more that even if I'm here, it's only until L.A. calls me back. This time, it just took longer.

"Guess so," I agree softly. "I'll be back, though."

"When?" she asks, looking down at her hands, fidgeting with the pen she's holding.

She cares. I shake my head, frustrated. "I wish I knew. If absolutely nothing else, I'll be back when the house is done, which is supposed to be sometime in October."

Carrie nods. "Well, that's only a few months." She looks up to meet my gaze. "We'll all miss you. You're one of us now, you know." She gives me an honest but sad smile.

"We?" I ask softly. "What about you, Carrie? Will you miss me?"

She swallows hard. "Please don't ask me that."

I nod, tears pricking at the backs of my eyes. "Sorry." I swallow back the words, "I'll miss you." I don't think she wants to hear it, either. "Well, I wish you all the best with the new job. I'll see you when I see you."

I should leave. Fuck knows I can't kiss her, no matter how badly I want to. If I do, I won't go. Or she'll hate me for it. I don't know. I just know that no good can come from pursuing her when she's not ready. If she's ever ready.

So, we simply stare at each other, the air thick with unspoken words and suppressed feelings.

At the same moment, we both seem to snap, coming together. Carrie slides into my arms and wraps hers around me. I bury my face in her hair and hold onto her like she's my lifeline. But really, she's so much more than that.

Neither of us speaks. We've said it all before. Nothing we say will undo the reality of what is.

I kiss her on the top of her head and untangle myself. "Goodbye, Carrie."

She turns back to her chair. "Bye, Evan." The emotion in her voice belies the casualness of her words.

The urge to grab her and kiss her senseless almost overwhelms me. My hands twitch at my sides. My heart aches. My body refuses to move. My frustration peaks, and rather than do something I can't take back, I walk away. I keep it together until I'm back behind the wheel. And then I let the silent tears fall.

The next few days are a whirlwind of traveling, meetings, PR appearances, script readings, and endless hoops the studio wants me to jump through. But even as I throw myself back into the Hollywood machine, I can't shake the feeling of melancholy that followed me out of Alpine Ridge.

I miss the quiet mornings there, the easy camaraderie with Nate and the others. And Carrie. Always Carrie.

But, on the bright side, the scripts coming my way aren't half bad, and I can feel my career getting back on track. It's what I wanted, isn't it? To reclaim my place in La La Land?

Yet, as I sit in my lavish home in the Hollywood Hills, looking out over the city lights, I can't help but feel a disconnect. This doesn't feel like home anymore.

An idea starts to form in my mind. If I can't be in Alpine Ridge, maybe I can bring a piece of it here. Or, more specifically, a certain political science expert.

It's crazy, but I need to do something to assuage this feeling of loss. So, I start making calls, asking around about jobs that would suit Carrie's qualifications. It's not long before I find an open assistant professorship position at UCLA's Luskin School of Public Affairs, with ties to projects for the city of Los Angeles.

I know it's a long shot. I know it won't magically win her over. But if I can get her down here, maybe it's a start. A chance to show her that I care enough that I want to find a way to keep being a part of each other's lives.

I pull some strings, calling in favors until I get them to agree to interview her. Now, there's only one thing left to do.

My hand shakes slightly as I place a call to Carrie.

"Evan? Hey. What's up?" her voice comes through, a mix of surprise and something else I can't quite place.

"Hey, Carrie," I say, trying to keep my voice casual. "I hope I'm not catching you at a bad time. I, uh, I just heard about this job opportunity that I thought might interest you ..."

As I explain the position at UCLA, she asks a few

questions, and I can hear the hesitation in her voice. But she doesn't outright refuse, so I count that as a win.

"I'll consider it," she says finally. "Thanks for thinking of me."

I resist the urge to point out that I'm always thinking of her. Instead, I give her the contact info and then we hang up. I lean back in my chair, staring at the ceiling. I know I'm walking a fine line here. I don't want to pressure her or make her feel like I'm trying to uproot her life.

But I can't just not see her for months. Not talk to her. And I can't shake the feeling that if we're ever going to have a real shot, if I'm ever going to get her to give in to how I know she feels, we need to be in the same place. And right now, that place has to be L.A.

As I return to the pile of scripts on my desk, I hope Carrie will be too tempted to pass up the opportunity. Because even as I dive back into my career, I know that success won't mean much without her.

CHAPTER TWENTY-EIGHT

CARRIE

After Evan's unexpected phone call, I sit at my desk, lost in thought. I have to admit, I'm shaken. I thought I'd be at peace when he returned to L.A., but saying goodbye this time was harder than ever before. Somehow, in the month he was in Alpine Ridge, we not only became friends, but our friendship melded with the ever-present attraction I feel toward him and became something more. And it wasn't until I heard his voice just now that I realized how much more. I miss him, plain and simple. Well, really, there's nothing simple about it because my mind hasn't changed.

Though I'm also touched that he has so much faith in my abilities and cares enough to have put me forward for such an amazing opportunity. Despite my heavily mixed feelings and having a job I love, I'm tempted because this position could open all the right doors for an amazing career.

I decide to talk to Brandon about it. I text him to stop

by when he has a few, and not even fifteen minutes later, he's poking his head into my closet-sized office.

"You rang?" he teases.

I give him a half-hearted smile. "Thanks for coming so fast because I could really use your advice."

He raises a brow and settles into the folding chair next to my small desk, crossing his legs and gesturing for me to go on. So, I launch into explaining Evan's phone call. The rest — my persistently growing feelings for Evan — he already knows.

"What do you think I should do?" I ask, fidgeting with my pen.

Brandon gives me a pointed look. "Remember what I said about walking through open doors to see where they take you? This seems like a pretty big door, Carrie."

I nod slowly, realizing he's right. "You're right. I know you're right. And I would probably hate myself if I didn't at least try."

"That's the spirit," Brandon jokes.

I huff a laugh. "Thanks," I reply drily.

"Is that all you called me over here for?" he asks with a smile. "Because that was a little too easy, and I'm pretty sure you didn't need me to confirm what you already knew."

"When it comes to Evan Edwards, I'm always second-guessing myself." I shake my head.

Brandon pats me on the knee. "Just keep making the decisions one at a time, honey."

I nod. "You're right. Again. Thank you," I reply sincerely. And while he is, it's certainly easier said than done when all my brain wants to do is constantly churn through every possibility. I sigh.

He winks at me. "I love hearing those words."

"Thank you?" I ask, confused as my mind had wandered.

He grins. "No. 'You're right.'" I chuckle, and he slaps my knee gently. "Now come on. You're going to take a break, get some fresh air, and then you're going to call about that interview."

I stand up, and he does, too. I bump my shoulder against his and smile, grateful for his reassurance.

And he's right again. After taking a breather in the sunshine, I feel much more level-headed and prepared. So, I call the number Evan gave me and schedule an interview for the following Friday. Then I make travel plans and text Evan to let him know that I'll be headed his way in one week. And then I try not to vomit from nerves. Nerves I wish were only about the interview.

After a relatively uneventful plane ride, I arrive in Los Angeles the following Thursday night, pick up my rental car, and make my way slowly through traffic to get to my West L.A. hotel. The whole time, I replay the reactions I received to this little trip. Mia's horror that I might move to Los Angeles, despite my reassurances that I had no real plans to do that, as this whole thing was a long shot. Joanie's encouragement to jump Evan's bones while I was there because my mood after Evan's departure led me to confess the situation to her, though I knew she'd suspected it anyway. Rae's support of whatever I wanted to do, even if that meant losing a friend and roommate. And, of course, Brandon's gentle encouragement to walk through the doors with faith in my heart that it's all part of my path. As if having my own jumble of mixed-up thoughts and emotions swirling around in my brain wasn't enough.

By the time I enter my hotel room, I'm mentally and physically exhausted and beyond ready for a good night's sleep. Thankfully, I'm asleep almost as soon as my head hits the pillow, only remaining lucid long enough to wonder … what if I *do* get the job? My dreams seemingly attempt to answer that question and are filled with visions of prestige, success, and … Evan. Because only in my dreams can we be everything I wish we were.

I spend the next morning going over my notes on the position, school, department, everything. I feel as prepared as possible when I head to UCLA in the afternoon for my interview. The campus is stunning — a beautifully landscaped oasis with incredible architecture amid the bustling city.

My interviewer, Stephanie, is a department chair and tenured professor about my mother's age. She's an absolute delight, and we hit it off immediately. She's had a career I can only dream of, and I know I could learn so much from her and the position. The interview is challenging but good. At the end, Stephanie leans forward, her expression kind but serious.

"Carrie, I want to be honest with you," she begins.

"While I think you're knowledgeable and have the right education, you lack sufficient experience on the teaching side to be a great fit for this particular role. But I've enjoyed talking with you today and think you'd fit in well here, so we'll keep you in mind if a more entry-level position arises."

It's a rejection but a kind one. Still, I'm not sorry I tried. Now, I don't have to wonder.

"I understand, and I appreciate your candor. I enjoyed getting to know you as well. Thank you so much for taking the time to meet with me," I reply warmly.

We rise and shake hands, and she walks me out, making small talk. In the hot July Southern California sunshine, I meander happily back to the car and realize … I'm relieved. While it was an undeniably amazing opportunity, I'm glad I get to go back to my quiet, simple, small-town life. I wonder for a moment if maybe I'm *too* happy with the status quo. But then, it's not like I've settled. I pursued the job I wanted and got it, and I'm living in a place I love. Still, I make a mental note to continue to stretch my skills purposefully as Alpine Ridge grows and beyond.

I also text Evan on the way back to my car. He replies quickly, suggesting we meet for dinner at a restaurant called Craig's in West Hollywood in a couple of hours. When I get to the car, I plug it into the GPS. Supposedly, it's less than thirty minutes away, but given it's already after four p.m. and my small amount of experience thus far with L.A. traffic, I decide to leave now.

It was a smart idea, because it takes me almost twice as long to get there and find a place to park. I decide to sit in the car and call both Brandon and Mia to let them know how the interview went.

The time-filler works a little too well, as I'm still talking to Mia when it's about to hit six, so I end the call abruptly, scrambling out of the car as I'd had to park a couple of blocks away.

Walking down Melrose Avenue, I can't help feeling like I'm a character in a TV show. The neighborhood seems unassuming, but the simple storefronts belie their luxury interiors. There's a good mix of restaurants, shops, and other buildings, and as I approach Craig's, it looks modest but classy with its logoed awning.

But a bunch of guys with cameras wait outside, looking up hopefully as I approach. They return to what they were doing once they see me, but it underscores the surreal feeling. Because I'm headed to meet a famous movie star at what is apparently one of Los Angeles's celeb hotspots, on Melrose freaking Avenue. I shake my head, chuckling to myself.

I walk in and note the modest yet classy feel continues inside. It's both modern and what I'd imagine a classic Hollywood hangout to look like. It has a relaxed vibe despite the literal white-tablecloth service in one part of the restaurant and the low, dark, decadent-looking curved booths in the other.

At one of the latter, I spot Evan all the way in the back corner, far from prying eyes but just the right distance from the kitchen. One of the perks of his status, I presume.

I smooth my hands over my lavender Ralph Lauren linen shirtdress, hoping it's not too wrinkled from my interview and being in the car.

Evan grins widely as I approach, rising to wrap me in his arms. "Hey, you," he greets me warmly. He looks fantastic in an all-charcoal suit and smells even better as he envelops me in his arms. Even in heels, my head hits under his chin. The hard warmth of his body against me is soothing in a way I don't want to think too much about.

"Well, hello," I say, surprised. "You're hugging me. In public." I keep my tone light to let him know I'm joking. Mostly, anyway.

He pulls back and gestures for me to take a seat. I slide onto the supple leather seat, unable to resist running my hands over the buttery soft material as I do. While the restaurant has an effortlessly simple look, it still has luxury touches.

"The paps aren't allowed in, and the windows are tinted," he explains, retaking a seat. "And the only thing the diners are allowed to take pictures of is their food. Why do you think it's so popular with celebrities?" He winks at me. "So, I'm dying to hear how the interview went."

I open my mouth to respond, but our waiter appears.

"Good evening, miss. May I get you something to drink?" he asks me. I glance at Evan and notice he already has what appears to be whiskey.

"Oh, um …" I pick up the menu and fumble to find the drinks section.

"Try the Gozzer Lemonade," Evan offers. "It has huckleberry syrup, and I know how you Washingtonians love your huckleberry."

I smirk and glance over the cocktail menu. The drink

also includes red berry vodka and lemonade. It sounds good to me. "I'll take that, please," I tell the waiter.

He nods. "Of course, miss, I'll be right back with that for you."

Evan grins, leaning forward on his elbows and intertwining his fingers. "I didn't mean to pounce on you. Why don't you take a minute more to look at the menu? I bet you're hungry."

The corner of my mouth tips up. He's so thoughtful, and I realize he's right — I'm ravenous, having been too on edge to eat lunch earlier today. So, I flip to the dinner portion of the menu.

"Since you're full of suggestions tonight, what entrée would you recommend?"

Evan leans back into the booth, taking a thoughtful sip of his drink. Definitely whiskey, by the smell.

"I'm partial to the Chicken Parmigiana. Though the New York Steak is damn good, too."

I drop my eyes to the menu and try not to react to the prices. They're not outrageous, but they're higher than I expected.

"My treat, of course," he says smoothly, reading my discomfort.

I look up and smile. "No, no," I object. "I wanted to treat you as a thank you for getting me the interview." I snap the menu shut and set it aside, having decided to go with his suggestion of the Chicken Parmigiana.

Evan leans forward and tucks a loose strand of hair behind my ear. His fingers linger on my cheek for what feels like a fraction of a second too long to be casual, and I feel heat creep up my neck.

"I suggested the restaurant," he counters. "And it was nothing, Carrie. I'm just so glad you're here. You don't even know."

I chew anxiously on my bottom lip. "Evan …"

"Carrie," he replies in a teasing voice. "I missed you. I miss *all* of you, so I jumped at the first opportunity to bring a piece of Alpine Ridge to L.A. to tide me over. So just let me buy you dinner, okay?" His tone is light and pleasant, but his eyes are intense. And I feel like he's trying to play off the tension I feel between us.

"Okay, fine," I agree. "Thank you."

Our waiter returns with my drink and takes our orders. Evan goes for the steak. While he orders, I take a sip of the cocktail. It's delicious.

"So," Evan says once the waiter's gone. "The interview?"

"It went great, but they were looking for someone with more teaching experience."

"Damn. I'm so sorry, Carrie."

I reach out and squeeze his hand. "Don't be. I'm not disappointed," I assure him. "It was still a great learning experience, and I'll spend some time playing tourist before heading home. This is my first time in L.A., after all."

Evan perks up at that. "I have a meeting in the morning, but if you want some company, I'd love to join you for the afternoon."

"Oh, you really don't have to do that," I assure him. "I'm sure you have more important things to do." Except, part of me yearns to spend time with him. I know it's my heart. Because my head is saying this dinner is already a little too intimate, and spending more time just me and him could lead down a path I swore I wouldn't go.

This time, Evan reaches for my hand, running his thumb over the back. "There's absolutely nothing that's more important than spending time with one of my favorite people," he murmurs, his hazel eyes roving my face.

Warmth spreads through my body, and I know it's not just the alcohol. I swallow hard. This. This is exactly why it's a bad idea. Because even a light touch on my hand makes me want more. Makes me *remember* more.

I pull back and clear my throat, then take another sip of my drink. "Well, then it's settled," I say, attempting a casual tone. "This is great, by the way."

He nods. "I know."

I laugh, shaking my head. Only Evan can still sound charming while being cocky.

Our food arrives in short order, and Evan and I take turns catching each other up. Me on what's been happening in Alpine Ridge, which is to say, not a lot he didn't already know. Him on all the hoops he's had to jump through to get back in the good graces of the studio, the fans, and the media. He also lets me have a bite of his steak, which is almost as heavenly as the perfectly cooked cheesy goodness that is my Chicken Parmigiana.

But even more amazing, no one approaches the table the whole time we're there. Sure, there are a few looks and whispers, but it's a surprisingly normal meal. Well, aside from how distracting it is to have Evan Edwards' full attention. He's intense but in a good way. A little too good.

So, after we've finished eating and paid, I'm hesitant

when Evan asks if I want to take a walk around the neighborhood.

"Won't the paparazzi follow us?" I point out. Yeah, that's why I don't want to take a romantic stroll around the block with him.

He smiles mischievously. "Not if we don't go through the front door."

I laugh. "You have an answer for everything, don't you?"

The smile slides off his face. "I wish." He huffs a laugh. "Come on." He rises and holds out his hand. "You in?"

My heart races as I look up at him. He's handsome and charming, and now that I know him better, I trust that he won't push me to do anything besides what he's offering. It's my own self-control I'm worried about, really. And I'm not ready to say goodbye to him just yet. So, I slide my hand into his and rise.

"I'm in."

Evan signals our waiter, who shows us to the staff entrance through the kitchen. Once we leave, the door closes to silence, a few parking spots, and a service alleyway behind the restaurant.

Evan takes my hand, leading me behind the row of businesses toward the main block. I contemplate extricating my hand because friends don't hold hands … but it feels so good and seems relatively harmless.

"How come there are no paparazzi back here?" I whisper.

"They're not allowed," he explains with a shrug. Then leans in and says in a mock whisper, "So you don't have to worry about them finding us." He squeezes my hand and chuckles.

I nudge him with my hip, thankful he's looking ahead so he doesn't see me blushing. Though still not convinced … surely, they're wise to celebrities pulling this kind of stunt?

But as the alleyway dumps out onto a regular city street, with cars whizzing by and people milling up and down the sidewalks, I see not a photographer in sight. Huh. It worked.

"So, what do you think of L.A. so far?" he asks nonchalantly. But despite his attempt at it, I can tell he cares about my answer. Something about the tone of his voice or the careful way he doesn't look at me when he asks … it's hard to say.

"It's busy," I reply lamely. "I don't know. The traffic is insane. But the UCLA campus was beautiful, and that was a fantastic meal. Thank you, by the way. For dinner."

We stop at a traffic light, waiting to cross. Evan strokes his thumb over my hand again. "You're welcome." His eyes sweep over me. "You look beautiful in that color."

I blush hard but can't seem to break my gaze from his. "Thank you."

We're so wrapped up staring at each other that we almost miss the light turning. We're cued only when another pedestrian passes us to cross. Evan leads us across and then across again as the light changes the other direction.

"It seems like you have a destination in mind."

The corner of Evan's lips tips up. "There's a park just down a bit. I figured we could sit and talk."

I can't help laughing. "Is that your master plan to get me to fall in love with Los Angeles? A park? Well, I hope it has swings."

Evan chuckles. "Damn, that should have been part of the plan." He gestures to the right, where a walkway branches out, and leads me down it. "But no, no swings. I figured I could show you that there are quiet places here and there despite all the hustle and bustle."

A strange sight appears on our left. "What … is that?"

Evan smirks. "Art," he says simply.

I raise a brow. A large, concrete circle like the ones that would usually hold a fountain or plants is filled with strange, elevated reflective prisms. "I … can see that," I allow.

He pulls me toward the installation, settling on the wide, circular concrete lip around it.

"What do *you* think of L.A., Evan? Do you like it here?"

Evan's brows rise. "I don't think anyone's ever asked me that." I give him an expectant look, and he pushes out a breath. "Honestly? There are things I like about it. But it also wears on me at times. After so many years, the traffic, the paparazzi, not being able to go out in public without being recognized … hell, even the fact that it's *always* sunny. That sounds insane, I know. But sometimes a guy just wants a little rain or snow, you know what I mean?"

I smile. "I do."

He chuckles. "I really enjoyed being in Alpine Ridge. It reminded me what it's like to be normal. I thought maybe if I brought a piece of that here," he nudges me playfully with his knee, "it might bring back that feeling."

"Is that all that this was all about?" I ask suspiciously.

He shrugs. "That, and I genuinely wanted to help you."

I chew at my bottom lip, trying to make sense of this. "Did you pull strings to get me that interview, Evan?"

His lips turn down ever so slightly. "Would you be upset if I did?"

A pang shoots through my chest. And I have to think about why. Am I upset that they agreed to interview me only because of his influence?

No, I realize. I'm not. Because it was obvious that I was qualified, mostly, anyway. Surely, they wouldn't have interviewed me if I weren't? I almost laugh because that was a stupid thought … I know they most certainly would've. But still, I'm not upset. Because he was trying to do something nice for me.

And beyond that … I look up at Evan in shock, realizing he was hoping I'd get the job. That I'd move here. Which means he's still struggling with this as much as I am. He still wants me in some way.

"I'm not upset. But … why me?" I ask, wanting to laugh at the absurdity of someone like him pursuing someone like me. Especially after I'd laid out my boundaries about long-distance relationships. Especially how hard I'd friend-zoned him while he was in Alpine Ridge.

God, he's trying to work *within* my boundaries, I realize. Except, part of that wasn't just distance. It was also his career and the attention that goes with it.

Evan searches my face. "Fuck, Carrie, isn't it obvious?" he murmurs, cupping my cheek and running his thumb down the line of my jaw. The touch sends tingles down my neck and arm.

I close my eyes against the wave of emotion that washes over me. I reopen them. And I pull back. A pained look flashes over his face for a fleeting moment before it's replaced by his usual casual smile.

"It isn't," I admit. I take a deep breath. "But either way, it's probably for the best this didn't pan out. I put a down payment on a townhouse in Alpine Ridge, Evan."

Evan's eyebrows shoot up. "Really? That's ... wow." He stares at his hands for a moment before looking back up at me. And if I didn't know him as well as I do, I wouldn't notice the fakeness of his smile. "It sounds like you're really making a life for yourself there. I'm happy for you, Carrie."

"Thanks," I reply softly, unsure what else to say.

He rises, this time not offering his hand. "Come on, I'll walk you to your car."

I nod and follow him. Once we're back on Melrose, I regain my bearings and lead him to my rental car.

"Thanks again for dinner." I lean against the driver's side door as he towers over me, looking up into his face. His features are pinched with an emotion I can't quite place.

"Anytime. I'll call you tomorrow when I'm done with my meeting?"

I nod, pushing off the car to a standing position. Before I can turn to get in, he pulls me into his arms and gently kisses me on the forehead.

"Drive safe," he murmurs against my skin.

And then he's walking away.

I don't watch. I can't. There's already a hole in my chest from shutting him down tonight, and if I watch, it'll just get bigger.

So, I get in the car and focus on doing exactly as he said. It's tough, as my mind is filled with conflicting thoughts.

He still wants me. But this is where his career is.

I still want him. But his best attempt to lure me close wasn't enough.

Even if it had … even if we both lived in Los Angeles … I don't fit into his world here.

The thought sets off an avalanche of yearning. Because if his month-long stint in Alpine Ridge showed me anything, he fits a little too well into my world there. Unfortunately, just as I've made it clear I can't be in a long-distance relationship, he's made it clear he has no plans to leave L.A.

Once I return to my hotel room, shower, and slide into bed, my last thought is to do my best to keep him at a distance tomorrow. I slipped tonight, letting him too close, physically and otherwise. It's not a mistake I can make again. Not if I want to keep my sanity and my heart intact.

CHAPTER TWENTY-NINE

EVAN

I'm sitting in a meeting with my PR team, but my mind keeps drifting back to my conversation with Carrie last night and the fact that she's bought a place in Alpine Ridge. The news shouldn't bother me as much as it does, but I can't shake that she's putting down roots. Roots that don't include me.

"Evan? Are you with us?"

I snap back to attention, forcing a smile. "Sorry, just thinking about the upcoming press junket. Please, continue."

As the meeting drones on, I make a concerted effort to focus, but it's a struggle. When we finally wrap up, I practically bolt from the room, pulling out my phone to text Carrie.

> Hey, you up for some company this afternoon?

Her reply comes quickly.

CARRIE

Sure! I'm at the Santa Monica Pier
right now.

Perfect. I'll meet you there for lunch.

I arrive at the pier to find Carrie waiting near the entrance, her hair windblown and cheeks flushed from the ocean breeze. Wearing a white and blue striped shirt-short combo, she looks beautiful, and I have to remind myself to keep my distance. I was a little too handsy with her last night, and I could tell it spooked her.

"Hey," I greet her with a smile. "How's your morning been?"

"It's been great. I spent some time at the theme park, which was fun. There's a restaurant down at the end of the pier that looked nice for lunch."

I know the place she's talking about — a Mexican restaurant that's decent, but there are better places in L.A. to get Mexican food. I gesture to the Bubba Gump Shrimp Co. behind us. "The food's better here, and the view is just as good. But — fair warning — we should decide quickly if you don't want to deal with paparazzi."

Carrie nods, suddenly looking a bit overwhelmed. "Bubba Gump it is, then."

We settle into a table with a view of the ocean, and I can't help but notice how Carrie's eyes keep drifting to the waves. The ocean is one of my favorite parts of living here, and I wonder if its magnetic power is working on her, too, despite what she said last night.

"So, what else did you do this morning?" I ask, trying to keep the conversation light.

She turns back to me, her expression a mix of disappointment and curiosity. "I walked down the Third Street Promenade, but it was kind of sad. So many closed shops."

I nod, remembering how vibrant it used to be. "Yeah, rising rents really killed it. It's a shame."

As our food arrives, I tell her about my meeting, but fans constantly interrupt us asking for autographs and photos. I can see Carrie growing increasingly uncomfortable, picking at her food and avoiding eye contact.

Finally, I decide enough is enough. "I'm sorry, folks, but I'm trying to have lunch with my friend. I appreciate your support, but I'd like some privacy now."

As the last fan walks away, I turn back to Carrie. "I'm so sorry about that. How about we get out of here? I have an idea for a more relaxing afternoon."

She nods, looking relieved. "That sounds great. What did you have in mind?"

"How about Griffith Park? It has an observatory and a zoo, and you can see the Hollywood sign. It'll take about an hour to get there, but I think you'll like it."

Carrie's face lights up. "That sounds perfect."

As we drive through the L.A. traffic, I can't help but steal glances at Carrie. She's looking out the window, taking in the city, and I wonder what she's thinking. Is she enjoying her trip? Or is she counting the hours until she can return to Alpine Ridge?

I'm thrilled to see Carrie's excitement when we arrive at the zoo. As we wander through the exhibits, she's like a kid, her eyes wide with wonder.

"There are so many more animals than I expected," she says, grinning. "Even more than the Woodland Park Zoo in Seattle."

We stop at the elephant exhibit, and I watch as Carrie's face softens. "The elephants were always my favorite at Woodland Park," she explains. "But they closed that exhibit years ago. This is amazing." I stand next to her, watching the gentle creatures spraying themselves and each other with water to keep cool, and I can't help but agree. They're fascinating animals.

As we continue, Carrie coos over the sloths and koalas, but it's the gorillas that truly captivate us both. I am drawn to the glass, making eye contact with one of the massive creatures on the other side. As I mimic its movements, and he does the same, I feel a connection that's hard to explain.

I turn to see Carrie watching me, her expression a mix of awe and something else I can't quite place. "That was beautiful," she says softly.

The look on her face kills me, and I want nothing more than to pull her close and kiss her. But I hold back, reminding myself of the boundaries she's set. Instead, I offer her a smile and suggest we move on to the next exhibit, all the while wondering if I'll ever be able to bridge the gap between us.

But watching Carrie stop and marvel at every animal gives me unexplainable joy. I've never seen an adult so happy at a zoo. And I only get stopped a couple of times for autographs, which Carrie seems to tolerate better here in the open, with the animals to keep her busy.

In fact, her delight is infectious, and seeing the animals through her eyes is a connection I hadn't thought to look for on this outing. She's caring and affectionate in the way some women are with babies, and it tugs at a part of my heart I didn't even know existed. I rein myself in, determined not to think about how Carrie is with babies. Because I know how much she feels and does for others.

Imagining Carrie as a mother? I can't go there, or I'll abandon L.A. without a second thought. Ironically, thinking about why I can't think about it cements my resolve. I'm so done here. Because my heart isn't in it anymore; it belongs to Carrie now.

As the sun begins its descent, I steer her toward the exit, and then we make our way to the Griffith Observatory. The twenty-minute drive is filled with comfortable silence, both of us lost in thought after our zoo experience.

We grab a quick, light dinner at the café before exploring a few exhibits. But the real excitement comes when we join the line for the Zeiss telescopes. As we wait, I can feel Carrie's anticipation building.

When it's her turn, I watch as she peers through the eyepiece. Her gasp of awe is audible, and when she turns back to me, her eyes are wide with wonder.

"It's incredible," she breathes. "I had no idea how much more you could see with one of these. How much more there even *is* out there." She shakes her head. "We're really less than ants in this universe, aren't we?" The observatory's guide smiles patiently, likely having been present for many such humbling revelations.

Having never looked through such a power telescope either, I take my turn … and I'm equally blown away. The vastness of space, the pinpricks of light representing entire worlds ... it's equal parts unbelievably stunning and a stark reminder of our place in the universe, just as Carrie said.

"And remember folks," the guide pipes up. "Many of the stars you see in the night sky will have died before their light makes it to us. So, in a way, what you'll see with the telescope is a snapshot of the past."

Carrie and I share an awed look. And it hits me that we aren't just small and insignificant in the grand scheme of things; our lives are also so fleeting. I stow the observation and its consequences in favor of paying attention to the guide as he continues to explain what we're looking at. I let Carrie take another turn before my time ends, sensing her yearning to get one more look.

After the telescopes, we find a spot on the grass in front of the observatory. As we sit side by side, watching the stars emerge in the darkening sky, I mull over the many deep thoughts the past couple of days have inspired.

Life truly is a miracle in the vastness of the universe. And our individual lives are just a blip on the cosmic radar, too short in the grand scheme to hold meaning on a universal level. All the meaning we have in this life is what we make.

Sure, I make movies that millions of people enjoy. Once that brought meaning to my life. But now? It seems like not enough.

It wasn't until I was back in Alpine Ridge, starting with my brother's wedding, surrounded by my family, that I remembered how meaningful deep connections to others are. That's how acting started for me, too. But the more successful I became, the more difficult it was to connect.

But what I feel for Carrie goes beyond anything I've

ever experienced. In the bigger picture, it's miraculous to have found someone who sees me for me, cares for me, and who I've come to crave on a level I didn't even know existed before.

Suddenly, I understand why her buying a townhouse in Alpine Ridge bothers me. It means that if I want to be with her, it needs to be there.

I need Carrie. My universe is dark without her. She's my sun, my guiding star. And I'm off kilter not having her at the center of my universe.

Something shifts inside me, and emotion floods me so fast and hard I have to close my eyes. I'm not going to let go of this connection we've found. I've had a great career, and while it doesn't have to be over for good, I'm willing to set it aside for now. I'm willing to risk it might not be there when I return. As I open my eyes and watch her profile as she stares up at the stars, I can't deny that Carrie means so much more to me. I was just too stubborn to admit it and to make the necessary sacrifices to shift what my world revolved around. I was a fool to think that once I found her, anything could have meaning without her.

I want to tell her all this, to pour my heart out right here under the stars. But I hold back. I want to put everything in place first, to show her with actions, not just words. I want her to know it's not just empty promises or an attempt to get her into bed on her last night here.

Though, God, do I want to take her to bed. It's all I can do not to run my hands over her soft skin. To not lace my fingers through the long, dark hair tumbling down her back. To not lay her back on the grass and cover her body with mine and kiss her senseless.

Instead, I sit and watch her, drinking in the sight of her profile silhouetted against the night sky. "What do you think of L.A. now?" I ask, my voice soft.

She's quiet for a moment, considering. "It's been fun exploring, and it's been good to see you," she begins. "But," she shoots me an apologetic look, "I still feel the same as I did yesterday. L.A. isn't for me. The traffic, the crowds, the noise ... it's all so much. But even if it were, my life, my family is in Alpine Ridge."

Her words both sting and soothe. They confirm what I already knew, but they also reinforce my decision. If Alpine Ridge is where her heart is, then that's where I need to be.

"I didn't ask to see if you'd changed your mind," I clarify. "Just wondering if you saw more of what I saw in it now."

She smiles, her eyes wandering over my face. "There are some wonderful things here," she says, her voice thick. And it's all I can do not to touch her. Because I'm fairly certain she's not talking about the zoo or the stars but about me.

If her seemingly conflicted responses to me this weekend have told me anything, there's a good chance she still cares for me the way I do for her. The temptation to kiss her and test the theory is strong. But I'd rather go for the grand gesture — the all-in moment. If I'm misreading her, and it doesn't work, I'll have no regrets.

We reluctantly decide it's time to leave as the night grows cooler. Like the previous night, I drive her back to her car. But this time, our goodbye feels different. Heavier. More significant.

We embrace, and neither of us seems willing to let go. I breathe in her scent, committing it to memory. When I finally pull back, I gently kiss her forehead. Same as last night, it's the most I can do without losing control.

"Have a good trip, Carrie," I murmur, my voice thick with emotion.

"Goodbye, Evan," she replies softly, her eyes shining in the streetlight. This time, I feel stronger, so I stay and wait for her to get in her rental car.

Watching her drive away, I'm filled with a sense of purpose I haven't felt in years. I know what I need to do. I turn and walk to my car, my mind racing with plans. It's time to make some changes. It won't be easy, but Carrie is worth it. She's worth everything.

CHAPTER THIRTY

CARRIE

The insistent beep of the hotel's alarm clock jolts me awake. For a moment, I'm disoriented, the unfamiliar surroundings throwing me off balance. Then reality sets in — I'm in Los Angeles, and it's time to go home.

I pack my bags methodically, my mind still fuzzy with sleep and the remnants of last night's dreams. Dreams filled with stars, gentle gorilla eyes, and Evan's warm smile. I shake my head, trying to clear the images away.

The drive to the airport is surprisingly smooth for L.A. traffic, though I suppose that's the benefit of an early Sunday morning flight. As I return the rental car, I can't help but feel a sense of relief. No more navigating unfamiliar streets or dealing with the constant traffic.

Once through security, I settle into a seat at my gate, watching as the sun rises over the airport, painting the sky in hues of pink and gold. It's beautiful, I have to admit, but it doesn't stir the same feelings in me as an Alpine Ridge sunrise.

Before I know it, I'm boarding the plane, finding my

window seat and buckling in. As we take off, I watch the sprawling metropolis of Los Angeles drop away beneath us. The city seems to stretch on forever, a concrete jungle interspersed with pockets of green and the glittering blue of the Pacific.

I reflect on my whirlwind trip. I'm glad I walked through this open door, as Brandon suggested. The interview was a great experience, even if it didn't pan out. And spending time with Evan ... well, that was both wonderful and heartbreaking in equal measure.

But as the last glimpse of the city disappears beneath the clouds, I realize I'm not sad to be leaving. With its constant noise, endless traffic, and frenetic energy, Los Angeles is truly too hectic for me. I crave the quiet of Alpine Ridge, the sense of community, and the slower pace of life.

So why does it feel like I'm leaving a piece of my heart behind?

As much as I can be in denial sometimes, I know the answer: Evan.

I close my eyes, leaning back in my seat. Despite my best efforts to maintain boundaries, keep things friendly, and nothing more, I can't deny our connection. The way my heart races when he's near, the comfort I feel in his presence, the way he looks at me like I'm the only person in the world.

But I remind myself why we can't be together. The distance, his career, the public scrutiny — nothing has changed. No matter how much my heart aches, my head knows this is for the best.

As the plane levels off and the seat belt sign dings off,

I take a deep breath. It's time to focus on the future — my future in Alpine Ridge. I have a new home being built, a job I love, and friends who have become family.

I'm blessed, and it doesn't do any good to focus on what I don't have. If I'm lucky, maybe someday I'll find love, start a family, the works. But for now, I'm going home.

And there's no place like home.

CHAPTER THIRTY-ONE

EVAN

I take a deep breath as I stand outside Rick's office, steeling myself for the conversation ahead. I'm about to tell him I'm exercising the exit clause in my Bond contract, wrapping up my other commitments, and leaving L.A. for the foreseeable future. It's a big move, but after my weekend with Carrie, I know it's right.

Before I can even open my mouth, Rick waves me. "Hey, kid, glad you're here. Sit down. I've got some news," he says flatly.

I settle into the chair across from him. My curiosity is piqued despite myself.

"Got an email from the studio over the weekend," Rick continues, leaning forward. "Looks like your tenure as Bond will conclude with just this one film. They're planning to go in a totally different direction after that. They're thinking about a female Bond if you can believe it."

I blink, taken aback. This isn't at all what I expected.

Rick barrels on, clearly trying to soften the blow. "But

don't worry, I've already got other opportunities lined up for you. There's a prime role in a rom-com with one of the hottest directors in the genre. It has a great cast and a very famous female lead. It's perfect for branching out, just like we talked about."

I can't help it. I laugh. The irony of the situation is just too much.

Rick's brow furrows. "What's so funny?"

I shake my head, still chuckling. "I'm glad they canceled my Bond contract, Rick. And I won't be auditioning for the rom-com. Or for anything else, for that matter."

"What are you talking about?"

"I came here to tell you I'm going on indefinite hiatus. I'm focusing on my personal life for a while."

Rick's face darkens. "Are you out of your mind? You can't just walk away now. If you want to stay big, you need to be here, branching out. I'm not here to wait for actors who can't make up their minds."

I lean back in my chair, suddenly feeling lighter than I have in years. "I have made up my mind, Rick. This is what I want."

"If you do this, I'll drop you as a client," he threatens.

I stand up. "No need. You're fired."

I leave the office, ignoring Rick's spluttering protests behind me. As I step into the elevator, my phone buzzes with notifications from my PR company. My stomach drops as I read the message: pictures of me getting cozy with a mysterious brunette at the zoo have been splashed all over the tabloids this morning. I click the link to see a photo of Carrie and me at the gorilla exhibit, inches apart, staring into each other's eyes.

Fury bubbles up inside me as I read through the piece. They don't know who she is yet, calling her "the Hollywood Playboy's new toy." I know there's not much I can do, but it doesn't make it any easier. All things considered, it could be a lot worse, but I know the speculation has already begun. It's only a matter of time before they figure out who she is and start digging for dirt.

I dial Carrie's number as soon as I'm in my car.

"Hey," she answers, her voice surprisingly calm.

"Carrie, I'm so sorry. I just saw the tabloids. Are you okay?"

There's a pause, and I can almost hear her shrug. "I've seen them. It's not great, but ... honestly? I'm not upset. They didn't even say anything unflattering. Just the usual general B.S."

Her reaction throws me.

"I'm glad, but you should know that it'll just get worse once they find out who you are," I warn her.

"Thanks, but what are they going to do? Report on my boring life as a political consultant? Talk to the like, half dozen people I'd consider friends who would never give them jack shit? Good luck with that."

I snort. "Fair point," I allow. I pause, briefly considering telling her what's happening with my career, but I'm not quite ready. There are still a few more things I need to do. "Let me know if anything changes, all right?"

"Of course," she agrees. "Oh, and Evan?"

"Yeah?"

"Thanks again for everything. This weekend was … well, it was great seeing you."

My chest aches, and I'm dying to hold this woman. Soon. "It was great seeing you, too, Carrie. I'll talk to you soon."

After we hang up, I respond to my PR company, instructing them not to respond for now but to keep me updated on any developments and to put out the word that I'm looking for a new agent.

I take a deep breath as I put my phone down and start the car. It's been a whirlwind of a morning, but I feel more certain than ever about my decision. The road ahead might be uncertain, but for the first time in a long time, I'm excited about where it might lead.

CHAPTER THIRTY-TWO

CARRIE

Tabloids who? If I didn't care before, I don't have time now as I'm buried in budget proposals for the new property tax levies we plan to introduce to keep funding town growth. As if that wasn't headache enough, I'm interrupted by raised voices near the community center's entrance. Curiosity piqued, I step out of my tiny office to investigate. The scene that greets me makes my blood run cold.

Greg is trying to de-escalate a shouting older couple, and with a jolt of recognition, I realize ... it's my parents. Their faces are red with anger as they rant about the changes to Alpine Ridge.

"What the hell have you done to this town?" my father bellows, waving around what appears to be the Sunday edition of the Seattle Post-Intelligencer. Oh. Shit. I'd forgotten they were printing a piece about the development of Alpine Ridge. My eyes flick back to my father's face. The fury etched there tells me they've come for blood. "Dorothy's house is a bed and breakfast now? Who the hell approved that? And what about all this new construction?"

My mother chimes in, her voice shrill, her features just as violently angry. "I've never seen so many cars in town. What exactly is going on here? We demand to know who has allowed all of this … this … *change*."

Greg attempts to explain the community center's temporary use for town offices, but they steamroll right over him. Then their eyes land on me, and all hell breaks loose.

"You!" my father snarls, getting in my face and shaking the newspaper in his fist. "You and your sister are behind this, aren't you? Ruining your grandparents' town!"

I'm frozen, old habits of shrinking away from their anger kicking in. But before I can find my voice, Joanie, Mia, and Nate burst in, followed closely by Arthur and Brandon, finally back from lunch. Thank God.

My parents turn, and their eyes widen. I can tell they're about to unleash their wrath on Mia, but Arthur steps in, his voice calm and authoritative. "Excuse me, sir, ma'am, I'm the mayor and —"

"You stay out of this," my mother snaps, not bothering to look at him. "My daughters will answer for ruining Alpine Ridge. I *know* it's their fault."

Arthur physically steps between my parents and Mia. "Now, folks, there's no need for this. The residents are thrilled with the changes coming to Alpine Ridge. It's not anyone's 'fault' — it's progress."

My mother's eyes narrow dangerously, continuing to ignore him in favor of glaring daggers at Mia. "Our family has been in this town for decades. My mother would be rolling in her grave if she saw what you've done to her home!"

Something inside me snaps. Years of pent-up anger and hurt come rushing to the surface, and suddenly, I find my voice.

"You don't know a damn thing about what Gran would have wanted," I spit out, surprising even myself with the venom in my tone. "You treated her like garbage, just like you treat everyone else. Especially us."

My parents' jaws drop, but I'm not done. "You want to know what Gran wanted? Ask Mia. She was there in Gran's final days — you know, while you were busy disowning a daughter who only wanted her own life and trying to manipulate me into taking sides. You know what? Never mind. I can tell you what she wanted since I'm finally free of your toxic bullshit and don't give a shit about your approval anymore. It was Gran's last wish that Nate and Mia start their businesses and change this town for the better."

It's the first time I've seen my parents rendered speechless, and it empowers me in a way I never could've imagined. I take a step closer, my voice low and dangerous. "So, you can take your opinions and fuck right off. You're not welcome here. You're horrible, miserable people who don't deserve to be part of this amazing community. Neither Mia nor I give a flying rat's ass what you think."

"Me neither," Joanie pipes in. Greg snorts.

"Same here," he adds, wrapping his arm around her waist in solidarity.

My parents start to bluster, but Nate, Greg, and Brandon step up and form a protective wall around me.

Nate's voice is ice cold as he says, "I think it would be best if you left without causing a further scene." He folds his massive arms over his powerful chest, and I've never seen him look so forbidding.

But my mother, ever the instigator, steps forward and points her finger a dangerous few millimeters from his chest. "This is public property and —"

Greg opens his mouth to contradict her, but a new voice beats him to it. "I believe my brother asked you to leave."

We all whirl around to see Evan standing in the doorway, his presence commanding and unmistakable. My parents' eyes widen in recognition, their protests dying on their lips. Nate smirks, and Joanie grins. Everyone else looks like they're holding their breath, waiting to see how my parents react.

"Fine. Ruin this town. Just like you two ruin everything," my mother says imperiously toward Mia and me. And then she turns and leaves, dragging my father behind her.

The sound of the door behind them makes me deflate like a balloon.

In the stunned silence that follows, Mia and Brandon envelop me in a hug. "I'm so proud of you," Mia whispers, her voice thick with emotion.

"You did good, honey," Brandon agrees, rubbing my back gently.

I'm trembling, adrenaline coursing through my veins, but beneath it all, I feel ... proud. So damn proud for standing up for myself, for this town, for the family I've chosen.

My eyes find Evan's across the room. He's looking at me with a mixture of admiration and something else I can't quite name. I offer him a shaky smile, surprised but grateful for his unexpected appearance.

As the others discuss what happened, I only have eyes for Evan. What is he doing here? I mean, I'm glad he's here since his presence clearly helped get rid of my parents. The shock of seeing an A-list celebrity standing up for their traitorous daughters was clearly more than they could handle. I don't know if I should thank him first or ask him why he's here now, less than a week after I saw him last.

One thing I do know is that in this moment of triumph, something has shifted inside of me. I've embraced the strength I never knew I had until recently. Fully and completely. I know I never have to compromise what I need for what someone else wants ever again.

Evan takes a step towards me, and for the first time, I'm not afraid. And the absence of fear ... well, it makes me realize how much I missed him. Not for being apart for only five days. But for being apart in *that* way for all these months. And as he stops in front of me, I have to work hard to remember why I've kept him at arm's length all this time. I have a feeling that also had a lot to do with fear.

CHAPTER THIRTY-THREE

EVAN

The tension in the room is palpable as Carrie's parents storm out. I can see the adrenaline still coursing through Carrie, her body trembling slightly as she's embraced by Mia and Brandon. Pride swells in my chest at her strength and her ability to stand up to people who put her through years of manipulation and abuse.

Carrie's eyes find mine as the others start to disperse, discussing what just happened in hushed tones. She offers me a shaky smile, and I feel my heart skip a beat. I move towards her, drawn by an invisible force I can no longer deny.

"Thank you," she says softly as I approach. "For backing us up."

I shake my head, unable to keep the admiration from my voice. "Carrie, I'm so proud of you. What you just did ... that was incredible."

A blush creeps up her cheeks, but there's a new confidence in her posture that wasn't there before.

"Thanks," she murmurs. Then, curiosity overtakes her features. "What are you doing here, Evan?"

I hesitate, glancing around at the others still milling about. "We don't have to talk about it right now. You've been through a lot today. It can wait."

But Carrie shakes her head, determination in her eyes. "No, I want to know. Please."

I take a deep breath, steeling myself. This is it. The moment I've been building towards since I left L.A. "I walked away from Hollywood, Carrie. I'm here to stay."

Her eyes widen in disbelief. "What? But... your career, the Bond film..."

"I'll still have to do some promotion for Bond. It's in my contract. But I'll do only what I absolutely have to, nothing more. And then I'm done. I've got a new agent who understands that's the deal."

Carrie stares at me, her brow furrowed as she processes this information. "But why? Why would you give all that up?"

I can't help but chuckle, remembering our conversation in L.A. "Fuck, Carrie, isn't it obvious?"

A small smile tugs at her lips, and there's a look of understanding in her eyes. But she doesn't let me off the hook. "I need to hear you say it."

I step closer, close enough to see the gray flecks in her blue eyes. "I'm here for *you*, Carrie. This thing between us ... it's more important than anything. More important than fame, more important than Hollywood. I want to see where it goes. If you'll have me."

I watch as a myriad of emotions flicker across her face — surprise, joy, and something that looks a lot like hope.

But there's hesitation there, too, and I understand. We've been down this road before, and I know I have a lot to prove.

"Evan, I ..." she starts, her voice barely above a whisper.

"You don't have to say anything right now. This is a lot to take in, especially after what happened with your parents. I'm not going anywhere, Carrie. We have all the time in the world to figure this out."

"I appreciate that, but it's mostly just that ... well, I'm still technically at work right now," she points out.

I shake my head, laughing at myself. "Of course you are. I'm so sorry. I forgot with all the commotion."

She smirks. "How about we meet for dinner when I'm done?"

I nod, relief coursing through me. "Deal. Tavern at six?"

Carrie smiles a real, genuine smile that lights up her entire face. "Count on it."

As I turn to leave, I feel lighter than I have in years. For the first time in a long time, I'm exactly where I'm supposed to be. And no matter what happens next, I know I've made the right choice.

Alpine Ridge is my home now. And Carrie ... well, I hope she'll be my future.

CHAPTER THIRTY-FOUR

CARRIE

I'm still in shock as I watch the clock tick slowly towards quitting time. Evan's declaration echoes in my mind, a constant loop of "I'm here for *you*." It seems too good to be true, and I can't quite shake the nervousness that's settled in my stomach.

As soon as I'm free, I rush home to freshen up before heading to the tavern. Evan's already there when I arrive, looking devastatingly handsome in a simple blue button-down and jeans that tells me he's just as nervous as I am because he freshened up too. He stands as I approach, and I feel a flutter in my chest.

We order food and drinks, then settle into a quiet corner booth. For a moment, we just look at each other, the weight of possibility hanging between us.

Finally, I take a deep breath. "Evan, I want to see where this goes too, but ... we need to take it slow. It's hard to believe you'll just walk away from your career like this."

He nods, understanding in his eyes. "I know it's a lot to take in. What do you want to know?"

"What are you planning to do while you're here?" I ask, curious about how he sees his life in Alpine Ridge.

Evan leans forward, excitement clear in his voice. "I talked to Nate about that this week. He's close to getting back his license to practice medicine. We discussed the possibility of me taking over management of the wellness side of the practice while he expands to include medical and urgent care."

I raise an eyebrow, impressed. "That sounds like a great opportunity. But are you sure it's enough for you?"

He reaches across the table, taking my hand. "I really enjoyed working with Nate when I was here before. And honestly? It feels more fulfilling than anything I've done in Hollywood lately."

I nod, still trying to wrap my head around this new reality. "Where are you going to stay until your house is finished? Surely not with Nate and Mia for months?"

Evan grins. "Actually, I talked to the builder. I'm paying for a night crew, which was an option, given how remote the building site is. We were already ahead of schedule, so the house should be done within the month."

My mind reels. He's really thought of everything. "Wow," I breathe. "You've clearly thought this through. You're serious about this."

"I have and I am," he says, his gaze intense. "I know it's a lot to absorb, but I'm all in, Carrie."

I take a deep breath, feeling something shift inside me. "I've let fear rule me for a long time. I don't want that anymore. You've taken this huge step, and … I think I can take a smaller one."

Hope blooms in Evan's eyes. "What are you saying?"

"I'm saying … let's try again. For real this time."

His smile is radiant, and I feel an answering warmth spread through me. We spend the rest of dinner talking and laughing, the tension from earlier melting away.

As Evan walks me to my car at the end of the evening, there's a new energy between us. He stops, turning to face me, his eyes searching mine. Then, slowly, just like I've wished for and feared at the same time, he leans in and kisses me.

I wrap my arms around his neck, my lips melding with his. For once, he's unhurried, and his kiss is soft and sweet and perfect. Warmth and happiness spread through me as he pulls me close, kissing me until I'm dizzy with everything he makes me feel.

It feels like coming home.

CHAPTER THIRTY-FIVE

EVAN

Being back in Alpine Ridge is everything I needed and more. Nate and I start right in on redesigning the wellness practice for the upcoming changes. Carrie and I take things slowly, which is helped by how busy we both are. Still, we see each other a few times a week, including the weekly game night and Saturday night dinner party, which are even more enjoyable as a couple. Really, just being near her takes years of stress off my shoulders.

Before I know it, the end of the month arrives, and with it, the completion of my new home in Alpine Ridge. I've done the final walkthrough and am ready to show Carrie. To prove that this is all very real. As I drive with her up the winding road to the property, I can't help but feel a mix of excitement and nervousness. This house represents so much more than just a place to live — it symbolizes my commitment to this town, Carrie, and our future together.

We pull up to the house, and I hear Carrie's sharp intake of breath. The modern structure stands proudly against the backdrop of towering pines and rugged mountains. With glass walls everywhere but the garage, it's a mirror to Nate and Mia's house, just larger. It's everything I'd hoped for and more.

"Evan, it's beautiful," Carrie says, her eyes wide with wonder.

I take her hand as we walk through the front door. The interior is even more impressive—open and airy, with floor-to-ceiling windows showcasing the breathtaking views. We move from room to room, Carrie's enthusiasm growing with each new discovery.

"It's huge," she remarks, "but it doesn't feel overwhelming. Whoever designed this really knew what they were doing."

I nod, relief washing over me. "I used Nate's architect, in case that wasn't obvious. I've never seen anything like his ability to make you feel like you're outside when you're inside. It's perfect, isn't it?"

She turns to me, her smile radiant. "It really is. Though it could use some furniture," she adds with a laugh.

I pull her close, wrapping my arms around her waist. "I was hoping you might help me with that. You've got great taste, and I want this to feel like your home, too."

Carrie's eyes soften. "I'd love to help. We can make it cozy and inviting."

As we stand there, surrounded by empty rooms full of possibility, I'm struck by how right this feels. Carrie in my arms, in our home — because that's what I want it to be, ours. But I don't voice that yet. Things have been going so well. I don't want to overwhelm her. And I know we'll get there.

"Come on, I want to show you the deck," I say, pulling her toward the back of the house. I open the glass door, letting her pass through in front of me. And get an eyeful of the view.

She gasps, hands flying to her mouth. "Oh my god," she breathes. She walks to the aluminum-framed glass barrier that serves as railings and leans against it, taking in the full view of the valley floor below us, where you can see the buildings of Alpine Ridge dotted amongst the trees. "It's *beautiful*."

I approach her from behind, wrapping my arms around her. "Not as beautiful as you," I murmur in her ear. I feel a shiver roll through her.

It sends my nervous system haywire. Because this is the first time we've been alone together, given that I've been staying with Nate and Mia, and she's still rooming with Rae while she waits for her townhouse to be finished.

I can tell Carrie is aware of it, too, as she sighs and leans back against my shoulder, her backside squirming against me.

"Careful," I murmur.

She turns in my arms and places her hands on my chest. "Or what?"

I cock an eyebrow. "I think I know what," I respond, leaning in and running my nose up her jawline. She angles her head with a breathy sigh, giving me full access to her neck. Her hand reaches for me, finding the hard length under my jeans. I suck in a sharp breath and pull back. Only to meet her eyes and see that they're filled with fire.

"I'm ready, Evan. You've been more than patient these

last few weeks. And as hard as it was to believe … this is all real, isn't it?"

I close my eyes, and my lips part in a sigh as emotion rips through me. "It's real," I confirm, reopening my eyes to gaze back into hers. "And I'm not going anywhere."

We stare at each other for a moment, soaking in this moment. It feels significant. I knew it would be, but the reality is even more intense than I anticipated. It's the culmination of everything I promised her when I came back. Of my own journey in realizing what's important in life. And for me? It's only Carrie. Always Carrie.

Then, like a tether has snapped, Carrie launches herself at me. Her arms wrap around my neck, and our lips meet, hot and hard. Her tongue sweeps into my mouth as her hands explore my chest, my arms, my back. I don't know where this confident vixen came from, but in an instant, I'm aching from her touch, her kiss.

In a flash of inspiration, I turn my back to the view, sinking down against the glass as I pull her with me. So she can fully enjoy the view while I fully enjoy her. She settles on my lap, her mouth never parting from mine. I match her energy, exploring her mouth with my tongue and running my hands under the crop top she's wearing, teasing at the clasp of her bra.

"Do it," she says against my lips, circling her hips over mine in a grind that sends sensation shooting through me.

"Fuck, Carrie," I groan. She's so sexy this way I can barely stand it. I do as she says, unclasping her bra and shoving it, along with her shirt, up over her breasts, baring them to the warm summer air. I lean in and take one of her nipples in my mouth as I pinch the other. She arches into me, causing her hot center to press harder against mine. I glance down and note that her pencil skirt is now bunched around her waist.

"Sex with a view," she muses, smirking down at me. "I could get used to this."

I lose all my words at the idea of taking each other right here. I reach up, pulling her mouth back to mine. Our lips work together with renewed enthusiasm as Carrie reaches between us, unbuttoning my jeans and freeing my cock.

"I don't have protection," I say, swearing internally. I did not expect this at all.

"We don't need it," she replies. "You know I'm on the pill."

I nod. "And there hasn't been anyone else for me since I met you, Carrie. There isn't anyone else for me but you."

She bites her lip, and her eyes take on a glassy sheen. "And there isn't anyone else for me but you," she echoes, shifting upward.

I reach between her legs, moving her panties to the side and feeling the slickness there. My cock aches, knowing how ready she is. I position her over me, and she sinks down.

We both groan as I fill her, as she stretches around me.

I take her nipple in my mouth, grasping her backside with both hands and encouraging her as she starts to move on top of me. Her eyes lock onto mine as her whimpers become more desperate, so I move my mouth to hers. Her lips are feverish, her tongue devouring. It's almost too much, and I pull back, afraid that kissing her while she fucks me will push me over the edge too soon.

Though even just watching her take her pleasure has me hanging on that edge. Normally, I like to be the one in control, but between Carrie initiating this and seeing her own her confidence, this may be the sexiest and most intimate moment of my life.

"Fuck, Carrie, you are the most beautiful thing I've ever seen," I tell her. Her lips tilt up, followed quickly by her brows bunching together. And I know she's close. I move both hands to her breasts, kneading, pinching, and pulling. "Come on, baby. Come for me."

Carrie whimpers and her hips grind against my own in a slick, hard rhythm that has her clenching around me in seconds. I drop my hands to her hips as her pace stutters, as the edges of my vision go white, rubbing her center over me until we're both crying out in orgasm.

Carrie collapses into me, her head resting on my shoulder. I run my hands up and down her back lightly as I come down from the high.

Even after the intensity of my orgasm has faded, with Carrie nestled in my arms, I feel a sense of peace and satisfaction that I've never known before.

In my sex-addled state, the truth becomes startlingly clear.

This is home.

This is where I belong.

CHAPTER THIRTY-SIX

CARRIE

The last few weeks have been some of the best of my life. Evan and I have shopped relentlessly to fill his glass mansion and promptly christened every piece of furniture delivered. Despite the constant distraction, it's coming along and starting to feel like a home.

Work has also been busy, but we're making huge leaps toward establishing town services, and it's the most satisfying feeling. I feel useful, and I can't wait to see the town become all that I know it can be.

All in all, life is good.

And It's about to get even better since I just picked up the keys to my newly finished townhouse and immediately dragged Evan with me to check it out.

I can hardly contain my excitement as I unlock the door. Evan stands beside me, his presence a comforting warmth in the cooling late September air.

As we step inside, I'm struck by the newness of it all — the fresh paint smell, the plush and freshly cleaned carpets, the blank canvas waiting for me to make it my own. Mine. The first place that's truly my own. I haven't missed Evan's hints that he'd love having me live with him, but I needed to cement my newfound confidence by living on my own for a while.

"It's *perfect*," I breathe, practically giddy.

"I'm glad you're happy with it," Evan says from the living room, where he peers out the window. "It's a great location. Your value will skyrocket as everything gets built up around you."

I huff a laugh and shake my head. He can be practical, but me? I'm daydreaming of homey touches, cozy fires, and happy nights spent cooking and making love.

As I walk through the gleaming kitchen, I run a hand lovingly over the quartz counters and glance out the big, wide window over the sink. It lets in plenty of light and has views of the tops of the trees surrounding us.

With a happy sigh, I turn to find Evan giving me a mischievous grin. I roll my eyes, instantly understanding where his head it at. "You probably associate new houses with *special* celebrations now, don't you?"

He chuckles, a warm smile spreading across his face. "That's not exactly what I had in mind, but I'm game if that's what you want."

My eyebrows rise in curiosity. Because I do want that, but the implication that he had something else in mind intrigues me. "Oh? What exactly did you have in mind, then?"

Evan takes a deep breath, his expression turning serious. "I was planning to tell you how proud I am of you, Carrie. How amazing these last few weeks have been."

My smile softens, but then I notice the hesitation in his eyes. "And?"

He sighs, approaching and pulling me into his arms, stroking a hand over my back. "And ... I just heard from my manager that the Bond press tour is starting a bit earlier than planned, and I'll be gone for an extra week."

"When do you leave?" I ask, my voice quiet as disappointment settles in my chest. Even though I knew this was coming, having it moved up means less time before I have to let him go.

"Sunday," he replies, watching my face carefully.

I nod, understanding but unable to hide my disappointment. Two days. "That's soon. But ... you've gotta do what you've gotta do." I shrug, trying to act as if I'm okay with it.

"I know, but I'm still sorry," Evan says, moving his hands to cup my face. "There's something else I wanted to tell you."

I look up at him expectantly, my heart racing, unsure whether it's a good something or a bad something. "What is it?"

Evan's eyes lock with mine. "I love you, Carrie," he says, his voice filled with emotion.

For a moment, I'm speechless. Then, joy bubbles up inside me, spreading through my body like warm sunshine. I knew he cared. And I knew long ago that I'd fallen for him despite trying to deny it. But to know he feels the same ... it takes the sting off his announcement. But mostly, it allows me not to be afraid to admit what I know I feel.

I bite my lip, looking up into his warm, hazel eyes. "I love you too, Evan."

He grins and kisses me so tenderly it makes my heart ache. The thought of Evan leaving for three weeks still stings, but now it's tempered by the knowledge that he loves me — that we love each other.

Still, I'm nervous about this separation. The anxious part of me wonders if he'll be reminded how much he left behind. How exciting it is to be in the spotlight, adored by millions. But he's given me no reason to doubt him these past couple of months and every reason to trust that what we have is more important than what he gave up.

Even so, this will be our first test as a couple. And part of me is terrified that this has all been too good to be true. But as I pull him into the brightly lit living room with soft, cushy carpets and let him make love to me in my new home — because all joking aside, I can't resist this man — it's hard to think of anything but how right I feel in his arms.

CHAPTER THIRTY-SEVEN

EVAN

The juxtaposition of centuries-old architecture and the bright lights of the Parisian red carpet is a familiar sight, but this time, it feels different. As I go through interview after interview ahead of the French release of my Bond film, I find myself genuinely enjoying the experience. Knowing it's my last major promotional tour for a while adds a bittersweet quality to each moment.

After another long day, I finally make it back to my hotel room. I pull out my phone and dial Carrie's number without even bothering to take off my suit jacket. Her voice, when she answers, instantly soothes the weariness from my bones.

"Hey, you," she says, and I can hear the smile in her voice.

"Hey yourself," I reply, sinking onto the plush hotel bed as I undo my bowtie. "God, it's good to hear your voice."

We catch up on our days, Carrie filling me in on the

latest developments in Alpine Ridge. I share some stories from the press tour, including a particularly funny moment when a French journalist's translation went hilariously wrong.

"Oh, and then a British interviewer asked me an interesting question."

"Yeah? What?"

"She asked what my favorite unscripted moment was. You know, the stuff actors ad-lib that ends up in the movie," I explain.

"I get what you mean. What did you say?"

"Something that my agent is going to kill me for," I admit. "I know the interviewer was talking about the movie, but I said that my favorite unscripted moment was when I quit Hollywood. That this would be my last movie for the foreseeable future."

Carrie gasps, "You *didn't*."

I laugh. "Totally did. And I don't regret it. But it's true, even more than I realized at the moment. I've always been fed lines. For movies, interviews, red carpets … my whole career has been scripted. But the best things in my life have been unscripted. Quitting acting. And falling in love with you. I never saw either coming."

"Oh, Evan," Carrie says, her voice thick with emotion. "You know what? I feel that way too. I mean, I'm not an actor, but I let other people tell me what to do, think, and say for so long. Living unscripted has been a gift. For us both." She pauses. "Has your agent ripped you a new one yet?"

I snort. "I wish that's all she did," I reply. "She told me I owed her for dropping that bomb when and how I did.

She also told me that I shouldn't write my career off completely and, as my penance, she wants me to agree to read scripts in the future that fit the exact roles I'd like to play. To consider coming back for the right project."

There's a pause on the other end of the line. "What did you tell her?" Carrie asks, curiosity evident in her tone, though I can hear her hesitancy, too.

I chuckle. "I told her I'd have to talk to my girlfriend about it."

Carrie's laughter fills the line, warming my heart. "I have to say," she admits, "this is all going more smoothly than I expected, so … maybe? I mean, I didn't expect you to call this much. Not that I'm complaining."

"Is it too much?" I ask, suddenly worried.

"No, not at all," she assures me quickly. "We don't talk every day, but every two or three days feels just right. Somehow, I feel closer to you for it. I guess absence really does make the heart grow fonder."

I feel a weight lift off my chest. "I'm glad to hear that. I miss you like crazy, but knowing we're making this work, even though I know you weren't thrilled ... it means everything, Carrie."

"I miss you too," she says softly. "And you know what? If you only had to do this every so often, I think that would be okay. But it's up to you if you want to stay connected to that world."

I consider her words carefully. "It's an intriguing idea," I admit. "But for right now, I'll be happy to be done with this and be with you without having to leave again for a while."

"I know, me too," Carrie says, and I can hear the understanding in her voice.

We talk for a while longer, neither of us wanting to hang up. Finally, regretfully, I glance at the clock. "I should probably get some sleep. Early call time tomorrow."

"Of course," Carrie says. "Go get some rest, superstar."

I laugh at the nickname. "I love you, Carrie. I'll be home soon."

"I can't wait," she replies softly. "I love you too. Goodnight, Evan."

As I hang up the phone, I'm struck by how different this feels from any other press tour I've done. The excitement of the Bond premiere, the thrill of the interviews — it's all there. But now, there's something more. *Someone* more, as it were.

For the first time in my career, I'm not looking forward to the next big thing. I'm looking forward to going home.

With a contented sigh, I finally shrug off my jacket and prepare for bed. Tomorrow's another day of interviews and photo shoots, but now, each day brings me one step closer to home. To Carrie. And that gives every move I make, every word I say more purpose.

I grin at the realization that I had to walk away from something I thought would give my life meaning to find what truly means something: the love of an amazing woman and the support of people who don't measure my worth by my performance at the box office — proving that sometimes the path you take isn't the path you're meant to stay on. Sometimes unscripted is the way to go in life and love. Because I know now, deep in my bones, the only path for me is the one that leads back to Carrie. To Alpine Ridge. To the life we're building together.

EPILOGUE

CARRIE

Alpine Ridge is a winter wonderland draped in a pristine layer of snow that sparkles under the mild December sun. Thanks to our resident snowplow hero, who has formalized his role, much of the town is accessible despite the heavy snowfall. It's perfect timing since today is Greg and Joanie's wedding day.

The community center, recently returned to Greg's care after completing the new town hall, buzzes with activity. Rae, as usual, takes charge of the decorations and catering, while Mia, Brandon, and I assist where we can.

"You know, Rae," I tease as we hang fairy lights, "you might have a future as the town's official wedding planner. First Mia, now Joanie ..."

Rae chuckles. "Oh, honey, I've done way more weddings than that. Back in the day, my Grams used to cater weddings at the Alpine Ridge Chapel. My momma and I would help with the decorations."

The room falls silent. "Wait," Brandon says, voicing

what we're all thinking, "You're telling me there used to be a church here?"

Rae's smile fades slightly. "Sure am. But it burned down when I was sixteen. There wasn't money to rebuild." Her tone makes it clear she doesn't want to discuss it further, so I quickly change the subject, and the conversation moves swiftly on as we finish our work.

But, as we put the final touches on the reception area, Joanie joins us, looking gorgeous in a simple white silk sheath wedding dress that clings to her every curve.

"Damn, Rae, you're good at this. Remind me why you haven't been snapped up for your own wedding yet?" she asks in classic blunt-Joanie style.

It's the first time I've seen Rae's good humor falter.

"Not everyone's cut out for marriage," she says quietly. "But I'm happy for you and Greg."

Joanie looks chagrined for the first time since I've known her. She puts a hand on Rae's arm. "I'm sorry, Rae. I didn't mean to upset you. That was tactless of me."

Mia and I exchange an incredulous look.

Rae's whole demeanor shifts. "Oh, sugar, don't you worry about me. Go on, enjoy yourself while we finish up here." And off she bustles to do … well, I'm not sure what since we're basically ready for the ceremony.

Joanie slips on a white fur stole and loops her arm in Greg's. He's wearing an all-white suit and tie that, as a pair, makes them look like the King and Queen of Winter. Surprising no one, Joanie unconventionally requested that all the guests wear white as well, which makes sense now as we make our way to the field behind the community center for the ceremony. It's where Joanie and Greg first started falling in love during the Winter Festival two years ago. And with us all matching the snow, it's a romantic ode to winter, to be sure.

Without Dylan here to officiate, this time, Nate has gotten internet ordained. He handles the ceremony, which is short, by necessity, given the temperature, and intimate, much like Nate and Mia's wedding. In addition to our core group, Joanie's parents, the town council, and some other townspeople have gathered to celebrate. It warms my heart to see how everyone has accepted Evan, treating him like any other resident, now that the shock of having a celebrity in our midst has worn off.

Though short, the ceremony is sweet, if a bit steamier than I'm used to when it comes to the kiss. But that's Joanie and Greg for you — passionate in everything they do.

Afterward, at the reception, Evan and I sway gently to the music.

"You know," he says softly, "I was wondering if you've ever thought about moving in with me?"

I smile, noting his careful phrasing. "I have," I admit. "But ... would you be upset if I said I'm not quite ready yet?"

His embrace tightens slightly. "Not at all. I don't want to pressure you. I love you, Carrie, and I see us growing old together. So, I guess it doesn't matter when you move in if we've got forever, right?"

Tears prick at my eyes. "Right," I whisper. "We've always done things on our own timeline, haven't we?"

Evan settles his forehead against mine. "We have. But you're it for me, Carrie. Always."

I close my eyes, a tear of happiness escaping down my cheek. "Promise?" I ask.

He slides a finger under my chin, forcing me to open my eyes and look at him. "With everything I am. And when you're ready, I'll say it with a ring, a wedding, kids, and whatever else makes you happy. I want it all with you, Carrie."

I bite into my bottom lip. It all still feels too good to be true. But I'd be lying to myself if I didn't admit I felt the same.

"I want all of that with you too, Evan. But don't wait forever."

He chuckles and leans in, kissing me gently. "I won't. But for now, I want to dance with you. Then take you home — yours or mine, I don't care — and make love to you." He doesn't even let me respond, his lips covering mine once more until I'm afraid we're the ones who are pushing the limits of how steamy it's okay to get at a wedding.

We break apart, breathless and happy. And as we continue to dance, surrounded by our friends and the twinkling lights, I'm filled with love and contentment. Alpine Ridge has become more than just a town — it's become a home, a community, and a future for both of us. And with Evan by my side, I know that whatever challenges come our way, we'll face them together.

In this moment, watching Greg twirl Joanie across the dance floor, seeing Mia lean her head on Nate's shoulder, feeling Evan's steady heartbeat against my cheek, I know one thing for certain: love, in all its forms, is what makes a place truly special. And Alpine Ridge? It's brimming with love.

Thank you so much for reading! Please take a minute to leave a review on any retailer, goodreads, and/or BookBub. Even if it's just a couple of sentences, your opinion is important to potential readers and to me. Thank you!

Want more Alpine Ridge? Get ready for Rae's story, coming in early 2025! In the meantime, go back to where it all started with Mia and Nate's story, *Tough Love* http://melanieasmithauthor.com/books-tough-love.html

Sign up for Melanie A. Smith's newsletter to get a FREE book plus all the latest news and more https://melanieasmithauthor.com/newsletter.html

ACKNOWLEDGMENTS

I wrote this book in a record-breaking twenty-two days. It absolutely came pouring out. And I couldn't have given it the kind of focus that took if it weren't for the support of my family. Because, really, none of this author gig is possible without them, and I'm infinitely and eternally grateful for their love and support.

As I am for my amazing book bestie, Eve Kasey, whose opinion is everything to me and without whose support I would probably have had several nervous breakdowns by now. Thank you for being the glue that keeps my author life together.

To the readers who have loved Alpine Ridge and asked for more. Thank you for living in this small-town world with me.

To the readers who are new here, thank you for taking a chance on this indie author. I hope you've enjoyed Carrie and Evan's story.

And, of course, an immense thank you to all of my readers. While I write for myself first, I publish to share the words and worlds in my head with you in hopes that it brings you joy and escape. Something we all need, and I'm honored to be part of bringing that to you.

ABOUT THE AUTHOR

Melanie A. Smith is an award-winning, international best-selling author of steamy romance with smart, self-sufficient heroines and strong, swoony book boyfriends with hearts of gold. A former engineer turned stay-at-home mom and author, when Melanie is not lost in the world of books you'll find her spending time with her husband and son, crafting, or cross-stitching.

Connect with Melanie on:

MelanieASmithAuthor.com

facebook.com/MelanieASmithAuthor

x.com/MelASmithAuthor

instagram.com/melanieasmithauthor

BOOKS BY MELANIE A. SMITH

The Safeguarded Heart Series

The Safeguarded Heart

All of Me

Never Forget

Her Dirty Secret

Recipes from the Heart: A Companion to the Safeguarded Heart Series

The Safeguarded Heart Complete Series: All Five Books and Exclusive Bonus Material

Life Lessons

Never Date a Doctor

Bad Boys Don't Make Good Boyfriends

You Can't Buy Love

The Heart of Rutherford: Life Lessons Novels 1 – 3

L.A. Rock Scene Series

Everybody Lies

Finding His Redemption

Alpine Ridge Series

Tough Love

Recklessly in Love

Unscripted Love

Elusive Love

Stand-alones

Last Kiss Under the Mistletoe

Vegas Baby

Pompous Paramedic: A Hero Club Novel

Short Stories

Cruising for Love

Hot for Santa